GYPSY EARTH

Dedicated to
Kath
for
Love, Faith and Enormous
Patience

GYPSY EARTH

GEORGE W. HARPER

DOUBLEDAY & COMPANY, INC.
GARDEN CITY, NEW YORK
1982

All of the characters in this book
are fictitious, and any resemblance
to actual persons, living or dead,
is purely coincidental.

Library of Congress Cataloging in Publication Data

Harper, George W., 1927–
Gypsy earth.
(Doubleday science fiction)

I. Title.   II. Series.
PS3558.A624777G9   813'.54
AACR2
ISBN: 0-385-17332-6
Library of Congress Catalog Card Number 81–43267

First Edition

CHAPTER 1

Landing a spaceship is tricky under any circumstances. Landing a one-man utility ship is considerably more difficult. Landing one under zero gravity on an irregularly shaped moving object only fitfully illuminated by the faint reflection of a far distant sun and a pair of arc lamps verges on the ridiculous.

" 'Twouldn't be half so bad," thought Duncan, "if only the old science fiction writers had been right. All I'd have to do," he growled to himself as he made a delicate correction on the throttle, "would be parallel the asteroid, match velocities, chop power and drift down. But wi' my luck though, I'd most like wind up wi' two thousand tons o' mass bow down against a rock wall. And then how'd I get aloft again?"

Unconsciously he made the small, deft corrections needed to center on his chosen landing site, checked his instruments to ensure zero relative velocity, then settled back to wait as the massive ship drifted slowly to the surface of the tiny asteroid whose total gravitational pull would give the vast bulk a "weight" of only 630 pounds.

" 'Tis fortunate this undersized mountain has no rotation," he considered judiciously as he waited. "What wi' everything else all I'd need would be for the damned site to rotate out from under me! No air to hold old *Sampson* in position—just enough gravity to bollix things good if she starts to land askew and not enough gravity to anchor her down or bring her in wi' any honest speed."

A final, last-minute correction in her inclination and the ship settled down onto the barren rock of EOS with a scarcely perceptible crunch echoing through her members. For a second or so she teetered in precarious slow motion on the uneven footing as Duncan fired the guy anchors. Then with a final sway as the slack was taken up she came to rest, upright and positioned for ultimate takeoff.

Swinging the external arc lamps to focus on the terrain about him, he studied it intently for several minutes before grunting in satisfaction and turning back to his transmitter. Triggering the mike he reported tersely: "UN EOS Base to UN Moon. Landing successful. Surface appears typically olivine and heavily brecciated. Grav checks at oh point oh oh three Earth norm, plus or minus oh point oh oh oh five. Site preparation to commence immediately upon your acknowledgment. Over."

Deciding he might as well enjoy the eighteen minutes it would take for the message to get to the moon and a reply received, Duncan rummaged around in his personal stores until triumphantly emerging with a plastic spacer bottle of MacCallum's Perfection Scots, then carefully squeezed a wee dram into his mouth. " 'Tis one hell o' a way to drink good Scots," he observed abstractedly as he savored the taste, ". . . out o' a damn nursing bottle!"

He was just replacing the bottle carefully into the locker when the receiver emitted a faint carrier wave hum, then came to life: "UN Moon to UN EOS," it squealed, "Roger your transmission. Permanent party personnel and ships departing Luna sixteen hundred hours this day. ETA EOS fourteen days, seven hours. Initial contact UHF channel four at minus seventy-two hours for landing instructions. Request progress reports at fifteen hundred hours daily. Good luck. Over . . . out." With a faint rush of static the receiver fell silent and Duncan was once more alone, 45 million miles from the nearest human.

"Might as well get started," he decided aloud. " 'Twon't get done if I don't." Wriggling into his spacesuit, he entered the inner airlock, waited until the air was exhausted back into the ship's cabin, then drifted into the airless hold of the ship. Grasping for hand holds, he inched himself toward the general-purpose melter-dozer. Undogging the tie-downs, he activated the fuel cells, then carefully jockeyed the bulk about until it was aligned with the cargo hatch. An electronic signal dropped the ramp and an instant later the awkward little vehicle lurched out into the maze of weirdly abstract rock pinnacles reflecting dully under the dozer's lamps.

Yawning crevasses, fifteen to twenty feet deep, meandered through the area in wild confusion, evidence of some aeons-old collision with another good-sized particle of space debris. Even using the spider-leg mode the dozer would be hard put to make its way through this, and trying to let the computer run things would be hopeless. He'd just have to do it the hard way, Duncan decided. Start his meltdown right here and go from there.

Sighting off to a spot arbitrarily selected as a corner, he indexed it into the microcomputer for permanent referencing, then eased out on the throttle. A second control brought the melter nozzle into position, then with a final touch it flamed to vivid blue light. Bucking up against the first small pinnacle, he narrowed the aperture so the rock would be vaporized with minimal melting. Luminescent, searing gasses incandesced and the rock flared into nothingness under the overwhelming radiance of the melter. Thirty seconds later a flat plate of slowly congealing lava stood where once had been a ten-foot peak.

Backing off to avoid the semimolten surface, Duncan nosed over to the next boulder and repeated the process. Then to another . . . and another . . . and yet another.

Two weeks he had to level nearly a square mile of this jumbled wasteland of rock and prepare a suitable landing field for a dozen ships and several hundred personnel. Two weeks of steady, unremitting toil and total isolation as the advance element of the whole operation.

Not all jobs in space are glamorous. Most are not. And this was one of the least glamorous. Day upon day of monotony, of isolation, of constant attention to detail . . . of muttered monologues and wild, bawdy songs. Days of semialert numbness, with half-felt noises of the melter, communicated through the dozer to his suit . . . occasional rasping lurches when the forward momentum of the dozer carried it into unyielding rock . . . the whispering noises of his suit and the dimly perceived heart and stomach sounds forming his only companionship in the solitude of space.

The landing pads were leveled, the connecting lanes cleared and the navaids jockeyed into position—all the dirty, vital preliminary work that "grounders" never associate with space. There is always one ship to go down first, one man to go out first. And until that one man has done his job there's no point in having anyone else around. Everyone simply has to wait for him.

For the EOS operation, Duncan was that man.

He was just completing his installation of the auxiliary SHF transmitter when the radio relay monitor in his helmet sprang to startling and unexpectedly clear life: "UN ship *Minotaur* to UN EOS. Do you read us? Over."

Was it that late already? Damn! Where had the time gone? Flipping his mike to transmit, he replied: "UN *Minotaur* from UN EOS. Read you loud and clear. How do you read me?"

"Loud and clear. Estimate time of arrival seventy-three hours twenty minutes. Have you any preliminary instructions?"

"Aye. Suggest you land at no less than twenty-minute intervals wi' work parties in lead craft. Site leveling complete at this time. Installation o' radio navaids will be complete afore you arrive. Preliminary tunneling will be under way wi'in twenty-four hours but 'twill be several days afore quartering will be possible so I suggest ye plan on keeping nonessential personnel aloft for a few days. No further instructions at this time. Over."

"Roger, Duncan," cut in the voice of his regimental commander, Colonel MacLeod. "You sound busy so we'll not be bothering you again till twenty-four hours before contact time. Monitor this frequency for future communications. Over and out."

The next day Duncan commenced work on the main entry tunnel, which ultimately would lead to administration and personnel quarters far beneath the surface of the asteroid. Setting the melter at its maximum intensity he sloped down at a 30-degree angle, driving the shaft nearly two hundred feet underground before leveling off to begin the main cavern.

That night and the next he slept in the dozer so he would have more time for tunneling. By the time he had to break to receive the incoming ships he had finished nearly three thousand feet of tunnel—scarcely 5 percent of the total scheduled for the completed base but well above the estimate provided for in his personal work plan.

Returning to the surface, he lit the infrared homing beacons and slipped on his IR-sensitive filters. Moments later he was rewarded by the sight of a winking lamp from a tracer missile sent out ahead of the fleet. A few minutes after this the brilliant jet trails of the seven ships swept majestically across the horizon, then began peeling off to hover over the field.

A half hour later the *Jane Grey* touched down, followed at twenty-minute intervals by the *Pipe Major*, the *Berwick*, the *Clyde* and the *Ayr*. The two fleet battle cruisers, *Ajax* and *Minotaur*, moved into station in close orbit about EOS to remain on guard until all the transport craft were secured, the airlocks installed and the primary defence computers linked to the ground weapons system. Only then would the big ships venture to the surface.

With the arrival of the main working parties, consisting of two companies of Duncan's own Argyll and Sutherland Highlanders, the work on EOS leaped ahead. Giant melters were unshipped, and by the end of the second day the main tunnel was a mile long and fifty feet wide. The first ramp leading down to the second level was started and the main airlocks installed.

With the last airlock in place and firmly sealed, atmosphere-bearing tanks were brought in and their valves cracked. Within minutes the harsh, unyielding glare of the tunnel lighting faded into subtle softness as the inrushing air gave a sense of depth and reflection to the passageways.

EOS Base was operational.

Ajax and *Minotaur* settled their massive bulks onto the landing field and except for minor odds and ends the work topside was complete.

Now it was Duncan's turn to move back into action. Returning to his ship he disengaged the guy anchors. A burst of high-pressure steam threw *Sampson* a quarter mile into space. A gentle application of lateral jets fore and aft skewed her sideways while a second application on the opposite side killed her slew-wise motion just as he passed over his assigned pad. A gentler touch on the side jets, compensated for a moment later, centred the vertical axis directly over her landing berth and she slowly settled down onto the pad.

Duncan's primary task on EOS was done. Now it was time to make his formal report and find out the next item on the agenda.

Suiting up again, he cracked the exit lock and launched himself slowly out in the direction of *Minotaur*, his few ounces of weight carrying him a good two hundred feet before he finally touched ground. Two more such bounds and he slipped into the big ship's main airlock, where he unsuited and hauled himself up to the CO's quarters.

"Well, Duncan," was MacLeod's quiet comment after he finished receiving the official report, "you've done well here. 'Twas a bit more than any of us really expected. To be honest, I'd have been happy if you'd merely completed the landing pads. This puts us three or four days ahead o' schedule."

Shrugging, Duncan countered, "The job turned out considerably easier than ye'd figured is all. If I'd come up in an area where there were major fissures or other obstacles not visible from aloft I'd have had trouble even completing the landing site."

"I have eyes, Duncan," MacLeod chided gently. "'Twas a difficult task well completed. And now I have the pleasure to announce your promotion to major, effective as of last Thursday."

"I thank ye again, sir," nodded Duncan soberly, "but how will that affect my status here? According to the organizational tables this will leave us with one major redundant in the regiment . . . and if it means transfer out o' the Argylls I'll ha' to decline it."

"Calm yourself, laddie," admonished MacLeod. "There's no need for any such heroics. I've gotten special permission for you and a new assignment that ought to keep you out o' mischief for the next few months at any rate. And after that there'll no doubt be something else."

"Aye?"

"There's a considerable amount o' space flotsam on the approaches to EOS—most of it trash in slow orbit about EOS herself, but a lot of minor odds and ends out to several thousand miles. And since traffic control will be picking up rather more business than you probably expect within the next few months 'tis needful to dispose of all such trash as quickly as possible. Tell me, Duncan," continued MacLeod, changing the subject abruptly, "when you were briefed and posted to the preliminary developmental work out here, were you also told aught o' the ultimate purpose of the EOS Base?"

"No. . . . Just offered the job and briefed when I accepted."

"I figured as much. But now that we're here there's no reason you oughtn't be told the essentials behind the EOS operation. It's really no great secret, but 'tis tied in with the world political game and therefore not to be bruited about too much."

"Aye. Ye ha' my ear."

"Some ten years ago," commenced MacLeod, feeling his way into the matter, "the major blocs entered into an informal agreement—naught on paper, mind you—but still a quiet agreement whereby the UN Bloc acquired a special role in the allocation o' space in the solar system."

"That I didn't know!" blurted Duncan in surprise. "I'd thought we were fighting it out the same as the others—and from the way our ships keep getting hit it sure doesn't sound like a very solid agreement."

" 'Tis true nonetheless. You know the situation on Earth has been unstable for decades. 'Twould've collapsed years ago had it not been for the decisions o' the major blocs to withdraw from the UN. Russia and her satellites with the United States and their client states, plus China and the European market with their satellites—all out o' the United Nations. That left the UN consisting o' a smattering of some forty small countries plus the United Kingdom."

"I know all that," argued Duncan. "I just do not ken how it applies."

"I was coming to it, laddie," continued MacLeod imperturbably, "Just let me reach it in my own way. . . . To continue, all this left the UN as a sort o' international slop jar. In effect we're the garbage can o' the big blocs.

"Perhaps 'tis no fit matter for pride, but 'tis the way of the world and we have no cause to complain at the result. Take Antarctica as a case in point. 'Twould be uneconomical and o' little purpose to occupy and fortify it. But if any o' the big blocs were to make a move in that direction the others would have to do it also. They would have no alternative, as they see it. So if any one o' the bloc countries so much as glanced in that direction all the others would have to too. . . . And then they'd all have to start putting up fortifications to defend something nobody really wants—at considerable expense to boot.

"So what did the big blocs do?" he continued rhetorically, then answered his own question: "They turned it over to the UN and forgot it. There are whole areas of the world which none o' the big blocs are interested in save as they are not committed to the other side. Privately, perhaps, they would like to see them aligned on their side, but so long as they cannot be certain which side they'll fall to they are just as happy to see them stay neutral. 'Tis for this reason only the UN nations, scattered as they be all over the world and embracing a dozen different languages, religions and technologies, have never been the target o' a concerted effort at subversion.

"Here and there, o' course, we have occasional 'people's uprisings' and 'student demonstrations,' but these are mostly insignificant and generally are no more than casual efforts on the part o' one bloc or another to pick up a piece o' cheap territory. If they succeed, fine. If not, they've lost nothing."

"I already know most o' this," shrugged Duncan. "But what has it to do wi' the present situation?"

"I'm getting to that," nodded MacLeod blandly. "What you perhaps did not know despite what I said a minute ago is that the identical situation has developed in space itself."

" 'Tis difficult to see how 'twould apply out here," replied Duncan after he had mulled the statement a moment.

"Perhaps. But it does all the same. 'Tis a recent development but 'twas utterly predictable. When the UN claimed Mercury and Pluto 'twas but the first step in an informal 'rationalization' among the blocs. 'Twas simply a case o' turning over unwanted areas to a known neutral so the rest o' the big powers don't have to worry about one of the others moving in for some unguessable—and therefore most likely dangerous—purpose.

"To make a long story short," concluded MacLeod, "we informally ceded all our claims to territory on Venus and Mars, plus all save two lunar bases, in return for sole possession o' Mercury and Pluto. The remainder o' the system—the asteroids along with the outer planets and their satellites—are still wide open to whoever wishes to stake claims."

" 'Twould seem the trade was all to their advantage," muttered Duncan doubtfully. "What wi' over two thousand automated converter stations on Venus busy breaking down the atmosphere and manufacturing water, it should be ready to take a few colonies within the century—and Mars is already being populated. In return we get two useless chunks o' rock and the privilege o' seeking out other useless chunks!"

"So 'twould seem," agreed MacLeod amiably. "But let me ask you, do ye honestly believe mankind will be confined to this one solar system forever?"

"O' course not!" snorted Duncan. "Sooner or later we'll find a way out."

"Our feelings exactly," grinned MacLeod. "But if mankind is ever going to make it out of the system he must first control it. The big blocs will spend their time fighting over the craters of Mars and the dunes o' Venus, and in the meanwhile we go quietly about the business of getting control o' the remainder of the system. . . . And EOS is the first step."

" 'Twould appear otherwise," argued Duncan. "We already ha' a Pluto base. And I recall hearing talk o' an expedition to establish a base on either Charon or Styx out beyond Pluto."

"Aye," agreed MacLeod, "and this brings us to the problem. Stop and consider the logistics of the matter. Right now Venus is nearer Pluto than Earth, Mars or Jupiter. A few years hence Mercury will actually be the closest planet to it—with all the others on the other side of the sun.

"Now I ask you, what sort of a supply line would that be? One where we ha' to dive straight at the sun to get to our base at the far edge of the system. . . . No, if we're to maintain a firm possession o' the outer planets 'twill be needful to set up a supply line which will not be subject to interruption by such routine things as differences in the various planetary years. And that's where the asteroid belt comes in. Six asteroids, spaced at sixty-degree angles around the belt and equipped as major repair and logistics depots, will guarantee that no matter what the configuration o' the outer planets with respect to one another we will always have a primary depot no farther than the belt— say within a forty-day resupply time. And that," MacLeod concluded, "is the reason for selecting EOS as the first of our bases. In another two months 'twill be in most favorable position with respect to Pluto and will remain within thirty degrees on either side o' it for the next nine months. By that time we'll have our second asteroid fitted out and be able to take over that portion o' the chores from there whilst EOS will be the staging and outfitting centre for establishing a base on Titania, around Uranus."

"Sounds ambitious," conceded Duncan, half convinced.

"Aye," nodded MacLeod comfortably. " 'Tis mighty ambitious. And that's where you come into the picture. We're going to be a staging point for vessels and expeditions o' all sorts, coming from all directions and for all purposes. Now add to that the near-certainty some o' the bloc nations will cast a few 'pirate' raids our way just to keep their teeth sharp—the same as has been going on for the past ten years."

"I'd ha' figured the agreement would cause them to leave us out o' such things," protested Duncan. "If they've agreed they want us to ha' these places, then why're they going to attack?"

"Practice, laddie, practice," chided MacLeod. "And besides, this way they figure to find out early if we've started cooking up any unpleasant surprises. 'Tis the same reason we run our own share o' 'privateers.'

With all the space in the solar system to hide in no one can chance the establishment of secret research stations which might come up with some decisive weapon. We ha' to keep probing, and so do they."

"Hell of a system!" snorted Duncan.

"I wouldn't say that," demurred MacLeod. "It's best we're still fair game to the others. Otherwise we'd be apt to grow soft. Then we would be in trouble. But to return to your part in the scheme o' things: what with so much traffic centring on EOS 'tis essential all minor space flotsam along the approaches be eliminated if the coming vessels are to avoid having to pick their way through as we did.

"Finding it out there was an unpleasant surprise anyhow, and it's giving the science types back on Earth a nasty headache. All the earlier fly-throughs had shown the belt to be mostly empty o' small chunks o' matter . . . so here we come and the first thing we find is a whole garbage can full o' boulders, all within five hundred miles o' EOS and apparently in slow orbit about it! So for the while it will be your responsibility to destroy the smaller bits entirely and nudge the larger ones out o' conflicting orbit as rapidly as possible. In addition 'twill give us a chance to train some o' the younger officers and mayhap even a few ratings in space operations.

"Ye'll take a different three-man crew wi' you on each sweep. They'll provide your work crews for use on the larger chunks o' matter and at the same time they can get in some manual gunnery on the smaller chunks. Even with our present computers and backup equipment I still mistrust the idea o' abandoning manual firing practice entirely. So long as there's a chance of malfunction in the system we'll continue to have need o' experienced gunners and loaders."

"That sounds good," admitted Duncan. Then with a quick, impish grin he added, "What would be the chances o' taking out a few o' the unmarried lassies from the women's contingent for training too? Ye never can tell when an emergency might arise and they'd ha' to replace male personnel."

Surprisingly, MacLeod nodded in agreement. "Humor aside, Duncan, 'tis no bad idea. We might do just that—but with the proper chaperonage, o' course," he added with a slightly malicious twinkle. "In the meanwhile I'll have Colonel MacGillivray set up a rotation schedule. Ye can figure to depart this next Monday morn. Make it a straight weekly schedule, returning each Friday. Pick up a new crew each time out. That should keep you out o' mischief at any rate."

"Aye, 'twill do that," replied Duncan a trifle grumpily. "And in the meanwhile the base personnel will ha' first crack at all the lassies."

"Cheer up, Duncan." MacLeod grinned. "Remember, the lassies always pine for the heroes out amongst the stars—or at least 'tis what the storytellers say."

"Mayhap," allowed Duncan dubiously, "but they date the boys at hand." Then, changing the subject abruptly, "Oh, and one other question: what do I do about quarters during ground time? Or do I remain aboard ship when berthed?"

"Ye'll have regular quarters suitable to your rank, o' course."

"I wasn't sure. The other day I couldn't even find the officers' club! They'd moved it twice during the past three days—and it hadn't even opened yet! Worse, no one even knew how to direct me to it and I had to track it down myself. If I'm to have quarters below do ye think I'll be able to find them when I get back? Or will I be a wandering Dutchman and ha' to spend my weekends rapping on doors to see whether I happen to live there?"

"Somehow I feel ye'll manage, Duncan," smiled MacLeod. "But mayhap I should assign ye quarters adjacent to the women's area. I'm certain ye'd have no trouble finding them even in the dark."

"Aye," agreed Duncan blandly as he turned toward the door. "I'll consider those your orders and direct billets accordingly, thank ye." Throwing a quick salute, Duncan glided through the door and was gone.

For a moment MacLeod eyed the door after Duncan, then grinned, shrugged his shoulders and returned to work.

CHAPTER 2

"No, no! Centre it carefully there, laddie," groaned Duncan in mock dismay. "Ye ha' your display screen wi' the blip on it. Now move your sight circle so 'tis directly atop the blip. . . . That's right. Now ye check the lateral vector readout to the side o' your screen. . . . Note 'tis reading negative, which means we're moving faster than the target so the correction has to be behind it—not ahead. . . . There, that's right. Lead to the rear. . . . Now ye're on, so fire!"

Grimly the lieutenant smashed down on the firing button as if trying to drive it through the console.

A thin, almost inaudible *whoosh, whoosh, whoosh* echoed through the *Sampson* as the 37 mm machine rocket rounds, each tipped with a tiny celaenium warhead containing a pair of 72 gram hemispheres of element 126 separated by a thin lead membrane, lanced out from the port turret. A nearly imperceptible streak of light darted briefly across the radar screen and an instant later the target vanished. A clean hit.

"I never would have believed it," exulted the lieutenant. "That rock was a scant three meters across—and at thirty miles I would never have figured on hitting her!"

"Ye probably didn't," contradicted Duncan. "Remember, we're using proximity-fused rounds wi' a two-hundred-fifty-meter sensitivity radius. Get within a quarter kilometer o' your target and she blows. Now if that had been a hostile ship out there a two-hundred-fifty-meter burst wouldn't ha' even bruised her. We'd be using a ten-meter sensitivity radius instead. But o' course the target would ha' been considerably larger so it would work about the same anyhow."

"You figure we'll ever have occasion to use manual firing in space?" queried the lieutenant conversationally.

"No way o' knowing," grunted Duncan as he deftly slewed *Sampson* on her side and commenced a long approach to a larger mass showing at the fifty-mile loop on the radar. "But the thing is, Jamie, if ye ever need to know how to do it ye can. All it would take is one hit in the wrong spot and our main battle computer goes out. A second hit on the opposite flank and our secondary is gone too. And that leaves the fighting to anyone who's left alive."

"Ye honestly think there'd be anyone left under those conditions?" doubted the other.

"Nae. Given that much, 'tis scarcely to be expected the ship would be able to do any fighting, and even less there'd be anyone left to fight her. But can ye think o' any better way to get training for the off chance?" Duncan shrugged.

"Not really," grinned Jamie. "And besides, 'tis good fun."

"Aye, that it is," agreed Duncan. "But after a while even that gets old. This is my eighth trip out here so I'm just as happy to leave the play to ye and the others."

Turning back to the screen, Duncan skillfully jockeyed *Sampson* toward the looming chunk of debris. "Fifty meters, I'd say," he frowned, studying the screen. "More than we can shoot away. Best call up Glenn and Charlie so the three o' ye can go out and attach boosters again."

"Damn!" breathed the other as he rang the alert buzzer and briefly told the off-duty pair to get suited up. "Fourth time out today. You'd think they'd rig these ships so we could attach boosters without having to go outside."

"Nobody expected anything like this out here," Duncan answered. "All the data from other fly-throughs showed the asteroid belt nearly empty o' everything save the big bodies. Based on that the astronomers figured the whole belt would be empty, so nobody ever thought o' putting on remote gear."

"Well, if it's supposed to be empty, why isn't this too?" persisted Jamie not unreasonably as he struggled into his suit.

Duncan considered for a moment. "I suspect the whole thing was mainly oversight," he mused. "Actually it should ha' been figured there'd be areas o' high concentration like this. Too many comets are known to be in orbit basically in the belt region. It stands to reason there'd be occasional trains here too. I think we just happened to pick an asteroid which has acquired its own personal comet, as it were. No doubt there are several hundred more like this in the belt, only we haven't found them yet."

"Well, 'twas our bad luck we found the first," grimaced Jamie as he inflated his suit and read the gauge for leaks before heading out the cabin lock to join the others in the aft compartment.

Flipping on the external arcs, Duncan maneuvered cautiously in toward the looming mass, checking the Doppler and transverse circle every few seconds until finally coming up zero-zero some twenty-five meters behind it. Satisfied, he flipped the rear lock switch to red, then studied the mass through the port until he saw the three suited figures swim into view, each trailing a JATO rocket on a long tether with a reel-and-line attachment.

Mere ropes would never do out there. The JATOs had to be played like a fish or they'd simply accelerate toward the men and plunge either into them or the flanks of the rock with the full kinetic energy of their three-hundred-pound mass. But with twin reels—one with a drag of some thirty pounds aboard the ship and the other to be anchored to the rock—what could have been a chancy stunt became routine even for relative grounders with only a few days of real space work behind them.

"UN EOS Base to *Sampson!*" the radio blurted with startling urgency. "UN EOS to UN *Sampson* . . . come in please."

"Damn!" muttered Duncan distractedly. This was the trickiest part of the space operation. EOS could wait. He had to keep her steady or he could kill them all.

Triggering his mike without taking his eyes from the port, he called back: "*Sampson* to EOS. Stand by. Am covering three men on a rock. Will contact you in fifteen minutes. Over."

"Negative on that," came the crisp reply. "Cut your equipment and recover your men. Contact EOS within next five minutes. Acknowledge. Over."

"Acknowledged. Out."

Something serious must be up. Fingering his ship-to-suit mike he called out, "Jamie, Glenn, Charlie. Cut your JATOs free and return to the ship immediately. Jettison any loose equipment and don't bother trying to recover anything. Just get back. . . . But be careful. I'd not want to have you make any mistakes."

"Troubles, Duncan?" queried one of the men, whose voice, he thought, belonged to Charlie.

"Never mind. Orders from EOS. Just get back fast!"

"On the way," came another voice.

Intently, Duncan watched as first one, then another and finally the last of the three space-suited figures launched back toward *Sampson*. In a moment he heard the faint *clump* as their steel-soled shoepacs slammed into the port lock. Another moment and he watched the tether lines to the JATOs slacken and the three bottles commenced a slow free rotation as they tumbled inch by inch toward the rock. He hoped they weren't armed; but even if they were he should be well out of the way before they could cut loose.

Impatiently he glared at the clock. Three minutes gone already. The outer lock was still red. Even as he watched, it flipped over to green. . . . Closed. . . . A small burst from the steam jets slewed *Sampson* sideways and the rock quickly slipped off the main port and showed up to the starboard, receding slowly as the ship drifted away.

A minute later, almost precisely five minutes after the initial call, the three slipped into the control room and began tugging at their helmets.

Waving them over to their strap couches, Duncan flipped the main mike. "UN *Sampson* to UN EOS. Standing by. Over."

"Roger, *Sampson*. Hold one." A moment's pause, then, "Major Campbell," snapped MacLeod urgently, "Stand by for a playback from Luna One. You are now tied in with my office in conference with Colonel MacGillivray, Major Logan and myself. Use scrambler code three. You have two minutes to set up. Over."

Acknowledging, Duncan indexed code three into the computer, then called for his ship's secondary converter, which, when added to the code three, would unscramble messages from the moon.

A moment later he heard the distinctive squelch over the radio and knew the tape was starting playback. A momentary gibberish as the computer strove unsuccessfully to decode the plaintext address, then clearly, "UN EOS. Pluto Base reports under heavy attack by fleet of unknown origin and composition. Preliminary account indicates a minimum of five craft, possibly more. The *Ajax* and *Minotaur* are directed to proceed immediately to Pluto for relief and rescue operations.

"If Major Campbell is available with the *Sampson* he is to embark one platoon equipped with appropriate assault and rescue gear and shall accompany the cruisers as scout.

"Colonel MacGillivray is relieved of command of *Ajax* and will assume command of EOS pending your return and is herewith directed to maintain emergency alert status pending clarification of the situation. A flotilla consisting of *Revenge, Churchill* and *Hood* departs for standby assistance your sector within twenty-four hours. Cruisers *Lincoln* and *York,* together with corvette *Davey,* will depart within forty-eight hours.

"Colonel MacLeod assigned overall command of rescue operations, seconded by Major Logan, with Major Campbell third if *Sampson* can accompany. Advise your intentions on SHF channel four, with scrambler set for emergency code 2 at 0730 hours . . . Monitor SHF channel four for further communications. Over."

A few seconds later Duncan recognized MacLeod's voice as he began talking to Logan. "I guess 'tis clear enough, Johnnie. I can ha' my crew together and lift off within ninety minutes. Think ye can raise that hulk o' yours by then?"

"Aye," replied Logan quietly. "We'll lift when ye do."

"That leaves it up to you then, Duncan," called MacLeod. "Are you coming?"

Considering carefully, Duncan replied thoughtfully. "I'm already starting vector back and will complete course alterations as soon as the conference is over. From my present position it ought not take more than three hours afore touchdown. If you can ha' things organized and ready for me below, I don't see any problem. I'll be needing two crates o' ninety-millimeter ammunition, nine crates o' thirty-seven-millimeter, to replace expended supplies. My hold oxygen has not been broached, so 'twill be simple to pressurize the cargo holds. I'll start that on the way back so 'twill be ready for the troops. But that will leave me needing new air scrubbers and replacements for thirty-six oxygen tanks. 'Twill take approximately thirty days to Pluto so I'll need ninety days' rations for the platoon plus myself and any survivors we might find. The cleanup gear for use on Pluto can be brought aboard by the infantry and they can mount their couches just before departure. If ye can arrange to ha' a section or two assigned to stowage of equipment whilst the infantry is loading I'll be ready to cast off within twenty minutes o' tie-down," he concluded. "It all depends on whether anybody in that forsaken hole knows where the supplies are."

"Then you estimate 'twill take perhaps three and a half hours from now before your departure," confirmed MacLeod. "With us lifting in an hour and a half 'twill mean you'll be some two hours behind us at the start. If you can guarantee that figure to within say a half hour we'll hold the cruisers to one point twenty-five g's acceleration till you catch up, then increase acceleration to one point five g's. That way you'll never be too far out o' detector range—not that I'd expect any ambush try this close in."

"Barring unexpected problems on EOS. I can guarantee three and a half hours," replied Duncan firmly.

"Good," grunted MacLeod. "Captain Buchan is standing by in administration. Whilst you're on your way back ye can advise him o' your needs on channel one. He'll see to all ground operations. Now—ha' ye any preference in troops, or should I just assign a platoon?"

"MacAllister if he's available. We worked together at the Farside Base and he'd be my preference."

"Very well. I'll see what can be done. I'll have a duplicate computer tape made out afore we depart. 'Twill match our trajectory for the first twenty hours so you shouldn't have any trouble catching up. If you encounter any snags advise immediately. Ye're dismissed to channel one, with standby on two and SHF four. Good luck and I expect to have you with us afore tomorrow late."

"Roger," snapped Duncan unceremoniously as he flipped over the switch and turned back to the three officers. "Ye hear the news. I want ye to get your duffle together so ye can debark immediately on landing. As soon as that's done I'll need ye to start readying the hold to receive troops. I'll crack the air and start the heaters straightaway. Ye'll be able to enter the hold comfortably wi'in twenty minutes. Think you can ha' your gear stowed by then?"

"No problem," assured Jamie. "Just let us know what's to do."

"Thank ye, laddies. Sorry to break up the party, but right now I've work to do putting this buggy on the right trajectory."

Swinging his control couch back toward the main console, Duncan activated the jets into neutral standby, cast a swift glance at the dual-reference gauges slaved to the inertial guidance system, cranked in a rough course to head him in the general direction of EOS, then fired off, starting at 0.1 g, then slowly building up to a full gravity's acceleration in order to give the three men time to accustom themselves to the idea of "down."

He was just making the final corrections in trajectory when Glenn returned with word their gear was stowed and they were ready to help. Hastily, Duncan ordered him back to the hold with directions on how to open the oxygen-storage compartments and disconnect the expended bottles. As the others turned up he sent them off with terse commands to open and ready the receiving compartments for various types of stores and to empty the JATO storage bay for off-loading as soon as they berthed. Then he turned his attention to navigation and finished indexing in the final corrections.

As they paused periodically to establish loading priorities and mass distribution over the radio with Buchan, the minutes flew by almost faster than he would have liked. Before he was really ready the flashing wink of Amber One approach beacon flared to visibility on the navigation screen. Swinging to starboard, Duncan moved *Sampson* in behind EOS with steadily braking jets. Now he was locked on, centred squarely on the approach path.

The outer marker slipped by beneath him. Eight miles to touch-down, speed 250 knots. Continue deceleration. Four miles to the DME; 140 knots speed relative to EOS. Two miles out at 90 knots. Zero-zero!

The pad lay immediately beneath him, its luminous X a scant two hundred feet beneath the hull. A gentle application of the upper steam jets, balanced an instant later by counterthrust from below, accelerated his descent and the *Sampson* settled with a scarcely audible groan, rocked slowly for an instant, then sat inert.

Swiveling back from his control couch, Duncan was immediately aware of the noise from the opening airlock to the rear of the ship. Abstractedly he waved farewell to the three men when they snatched their dunnage and slipped off into the interior airlock between cabin and hold, then turned back to the radio. No time to suit up and supervise matters in person. He'd have to take it on trust. Buchan was top-flight and so was MacAllister. Between them they could handle matters astern while he stood by the intercom.

Still it was with steadily increasing impatience he listened to the obscure clanking and shuffling sounds behind the airlocked hatchway, trying to interpret their meaning. . . . Damn it, why couldn't Buchan at least say *something* over the intercom to give him some idea how things were going! He knew that, at least in theory, it was possible for him to head back into the after hold without suiting up. He'd already released air there so he should be able to drift down. But he also knew the difference between theory and reality. Every time the outer airlock was spun there was air loss—and with so many people entering and leaving there was always the finite possibility of a malfunction and double opening—in which event anyone not fully suited was dead! Since that didn't seem particularly attractive he stayed put.

Just as the shattered fragments of his patience were about to erupt, Buchan's reassuring voice burred over the intercom. "We've got the rations and munitions stored now, Duncan. The oxygen units and regeneration cells are just coming aboard. And on the off chance ye may be needing it, we're installing a fresh celaenium fuel wire in the auxiliary storage area—section six, compartment B-five."

"Thank ye," replied Duncan. "Most likely 'twill not be needed, but I'm glad to have it. How long till we're ready for castoff?"

"Five or six more minutes, I'd guess. The infantry's boarding now and the floor sections and couches are mostly dogged already. MacAllister's aboard and heading forward. Ye can go ahead and ask clearance if ye wish. Your departure time can be set for seven minutes, barring delays from the infantry."

"Roger, I'll get clearance and call ye back." Flipping the radio switch, Duncan raised Departure Control.

"Roger, *Sampson*," came the immediate reply. "Cleared for departure. Proceed outbound on the two oh nine radial, fourteen-degree positive ascension until passing the thirty-five-mile fix. 'Twill clear you of all known debris and work parties. Good luck, *Sampson*. Over and out."

Switching off the mike, Duncan turned to MacAllister, who had arrived in the midst of the clearance proceedings. "Morning, Jamie," he grinned briefly. "Ye got the route tape wi' ye?"

"Aye," smiled the other, thrusting the cassette at him.

"Good. Ye'd best bunk to for now. We'll be off in mayhap three minutes and I'll want to see ye when things quiet down."

"Righto, Duncan," nodded MacAllister as he turned back to his assigned compartment. "Anything I can do, let me know."

" 'Tis mostly taken care of for now," replied Duncan as he surveyed the internal status board, noting with satisfaction the bank of green lights indicating the infantry were all secured for departure. That meant all the acceleration bunks were firmly mounted and slaved to the computer with the straps fastened—which in turn meant the men were bunked down.

Flipping the intercom, Duncan called Buchan for a visual check. "Infantry lights all green," he announced. "Anything left lying about loose on the decks?"

"Not so I can see," replied Buchan. "All dunnage in stowage compartments and sealed. How does your stowage board read?"

"All green," Duncan answered after a survey of the console. "The only red showing is around the aft airlock."

"Roger. Hold one," ordered Buchan. Then after a minute he came back on the intercom. "Last o' the loading personnel have departed and we're dogging the outer airlock now. I'm plugged in on the external extension. . . . All secured outside. . . . Departure area cleared. Give me sixty seconds to clear myself, then go! And good luck, Duncan. Good hunting!"

A final scan of the instrument board took more than the requested sixty seconds. All green. Then in quick order Duncan activated the steam jets. Abruptly they frothed to life and the bulky utility craft lifted a few feet. Then yards separated her from the landing pad as she struggled toward minimum departure altitude. A quick stab on the lateral jets oriented *Sampson* on the 209 radial while a slight touch on the chin jets lifted the nose 14 degrees. She was aligned, ready to go. Instantly his hand rammed forward on the thrust levers and *Sampson* surged forward with an acceleration of 1.6 g's.

Sagging back under the unaccustomed weight, Duncan struggled against the pressure and let his eyes flicker briefly along the banks of operations lights, warily watchful for the first telltale red. Still solid green.

Slipping the cassette into the computer, he turned his attention to the DME indicator and watched tensely as the miles ticked off. At thirty-five he punched the activate button. Smoothly, imperceptibly, the electronic relays slid into action as the computer took over control of *Sampson*. At last Duncan could relax. They were on their way, three hours thirty-two minutes after the conference with MacLeod and Logan and just two minutes off his original estimate.

Abruptly he was exhausted. Flipping the intercom to B compartment, where MacAllister was bunking, Duncan called out, "Jamie, ye can come up now."

"Aye," came the quick reply. "Be right there." A few moments later the hatch opened and Jamie appeared, visibly puffing under the unaccustomed acceleration.

"I'm beat," Duncan announced without preamble. "I'd like to chat wi' ye, but I've been going for nigh twenty hours now and don't think I'm up to it. We're on automatic and 'twill be near twelve hours afore we overtake the others. Ye'll be in command whilst I catch a sandwich and twenty winks. 'Twill be naught for ye to do save eye the screens and monitor the radios. We're too close in to EOS to expect any trouble, but if anything turns red on the board or we get any urgent messages wake me immediately.

"Ye'll probably want to do some sorting out in the hold, but don't go there yourself; send one o' your men up here for instructions. There'll be time for other details later."

"Aye," nodded MacAllister. "I ha' only three men who ha' worked aboard a combat ship afore this, so they'll all need training."

"We'll get to that later," agreed Duncan. "But for now I'll see ye in about eight hours," he ended as he struggled back toward his compartment, fighting the acceleration to keep from skidding as he went. A minute later he was sound asleep, an uneaten sandwich clutched in his hand.

CHAPTER 3

Ten hours later, just as *Ajax* and *Minotaur* were edging onto the extended range forward screens, Duncan and MacAllister relaxed together in the command compartment. The sorting out was done, the men in the aft section were stowed, gear had been rearranged and, most importantly, the messing facilities had been made operational for them. Now all anyone had to face were two more days at one and a half times their normal Earth weight plus the monotony of space.

"What I still don't understand," complained MacAllister hopelessly, "is why we have to rip along at one point five g's in the first place? We run this way for two and a half days, then simply coast the rest of the way out. Why not run at a single gravity or even less of acceleration for a bit longer and be more comfortable?"

"A good idea," soothed Duncan gently, "but fuel has a lot to do wi' it. The rockets are more efficient at higher accelerations and the fuel's limited. If we accelerated at one point zero g's we'd ha' to cut the wire in about three days. That would gi' us three days accelerating outbound, three days' deceleration at Pluto, three more to get away from Pluto and three to decelerate again when we get back to EOS—twelve days o' fuel in all. But we also might ha' to fight and we might ha' to stay in orbit or maneuver about for a week or more along the way, so we ha' to keep as much reserve as possible. And wi' twelve days already committed we'd be right at a minimum. But accelerating at one point five g's on each leg not only saves a couple o' days' worth o' fuel but gets us there near a week sooner. It works out to thirty-one days if we make one g, but only twenty-five days if we start at one point five g's. 'Tis just a question o' economics."

"But why hurry at all?" persisted MacAllister. "I'm reasonably certain nobody will be hanging about Pluto that long just waiting for us —at least not unless they figure they can whip anything we send out, that is."

"Right," agreed Duncan soberly, "but the most probable danger is the likelihood o' some sort of ambush being set."

"Ambush!" snorted MacAllister. "With all these miles of open space about, how'd anybody manage an ambush?"

"A lot o' ways," smiled Duncan amiably as he flipped a switch on his display console and pointed to the suddenly brilliantly speckled screen. "Each o' those blips means a chunk o' solid matter orbiting wi'in a million kilometers o' us. Unless I want a readout the computer doesn't bother showing them to me since they'd just be in the way o' what I really want to see. The computer cranks in an automatic vector around such debris so I never ha' to worry about them unless I want to—like now.

"But unless the object is radiating energy at some frequency the computer is programmed to consider significant it can't tell whether an object just drifting about is a ship or a powered mine or mayhap even a cluster o' rocket rounds set to explode in our faces if we get too close."

"Then any one of those blips could actually be a ship lurking for us!" exclaimed MacAllister in consternation.

"Aye," Duncan nodded blandly, "but 'tis not likely. And even if it were, we'd generally be safe at the speed we're making. Ye see, the computer's programmed to gi' alarm whenever the speed o' an object exceeds that proper for an orbit. That means anything going much over forty kilometers a second in this portion o' space. Since we're already tracking over six hundred kilometers per second, any ambusher would ha' to be very precisely placed to do any damage. They'd ha' to know what track we were planning to take. 'Tis one o' the reasons we're making the path we are. Pluto is actually only about five point five billion kilometers from us, but the route we're tracking will run us to nearly six point two billion. Of course, most o' that is simple vector problems, but near a hundred million kilometers is mere insurance vectoring."

"Then you don't believe we've anything to worry about from ambush?"

"Mainly on departures and approaches," Duncan shrugged. "When we were just leaving EOS or coming into the last ten million kilometers or so to Pluto. Both places our speed is low, and both places the enemy knows where we're coming from and going to. It's the routes and speeds in the middle where he has problems. Even if by sheer luck we were to run head on into each other along the way it still wouldn't be much of a problem. We'd be making good a speed o' roughly three thousand one hundred eighty kilometers per second toward Pluto and they'd most likely be making a similar speed toward the sun—say for a closing speed o' roughly sixty-five hundred kilometers per second. 'Twould mean we'd each ha' a chance to fire one broadside *en passant* and 'twould be sheer luck if either side were hurt.

"No," he concluded judiciously, "we can most likely count on two more days o' uncomfortable acceleration, about twenty days o' coasting in free fall, another two point five days o' uncomfortable deceleration and landing on Pluto, and then about two weeks o' cleaning up the mess and trying to find out who did it."

"Think we'll have any luck at it?"

"Not likely. I can think o' five or six possible blocs which might ha' done it. But why they'd do it has me puzzled. 'Twould seem most probable any bloc that would bother making an assault on Pluto would send out enough force to annihilate an unarmed station in a minimum o' time and get out long afore help could come. But somebody has to come in and clean up the mess—and we're it."

"At least it'll give me an opportunity to get my section trained in real space operations," grunted MacAllister. "You willing for me to schedule serious training operations on the way in—or should I wait until we're heading back?"

"Start 'em as soon as we're caught up and coasting. The more experienced they are the better they'll be able to function in an emergency. Besides, 'twill make the time go faster."

By evening of the twenty-third day Pluto was a vaguely discernible disk in the heavens, fitfully illuminated by a remote sun and visible only as a patch of pale grey obscuring the remoter stars. Its solitary satellite, an antique chunk of matter captured in the remote past, was near apogee in its retrograde orbit and actually more distinctly visible than the planet itself.

The small flotilla was in full deceleration and with each passing instant the chances for ambush increased. If there was anyone waiting for them, this was the time they'd be most apt to try. Not until they were nearly stationary above Pluto would the hazard again decrease.

"*Ajax* to *Sampson*," crackled the radio.

"Go ahead, *Ajax*," answered Duncan.

"We make you within orbiting distance of Pluto in twenty-seven hours, twenty-two minutes. Continue to close until able to orbit at one point oh five planetary radii in a one-hundred-minute period. Maintain search orbit until positive identification of Pluto Base is obtained. *Ajax* will maintain a two-point-four-oh-radii orbit inclined thirty degrees. *Minotaur* will maintain a two-point-forty-four-radii orbit inclined thirty degrees retrograde. *Ajax* will dispatch two all-frequency drones to pick up any radio signals, their orbits to be stabilized at one point ten and one point fifteen radii with inclinations of seventy degrees. If there's anything transmitting down there we'll be able to pinpoint it before you start down."

"Roger, *Ajax*. Will ye continue orbiting whilst *Sampson* descends after site identification?"

"Affirmative. We'll hold orbit unless there's reason to do otherwise. You should be able to handle cleanup without our help."

"Righto. I'll set a search pattern to identify the landing site. Will commence descent when positive identification made. Will contact ye as needful. *Sampson* out."

Fourteen hours to orbit. From now it was automatic. The tapes were indexed, the course set. Now even the likelihood of ambush was negligible. They were too close in and any foe would have less maneuver capability than the flotilla. Duncan flipped the intercom. "Captain MacAllister, please. Will ye kindly come forward at your convenience."

"Roger," came the quick reply. "I've maybe a quarter hour of sorting to do with the landing party. I'll be up then."

"At your convenience."

Thirteen hours thirty-five minutes to planetfall. The inner airlock door opened and MacAllister entered. "You got something, Duncan?"

"Aye, Jamie. We're less than fourteen hours till orbit about Pluto. We can't descend till we've identified the base site, and that's a mite o' a problem. Ephemeris data can let us figure the location to perhaps wi'in ten thousand square miles, or an area about a hundred miles on a side. There's no decent light to see by and a surface covered wi' nothing save a few million square miles o' craters and mountains. Wi' all the beacons out o' service 'twill be a real problem finding out where to go.

"The computer's been put to work trying to triangulate radar returns and looking for Mill Peak, Perth Peak and Burns Rift. 'Tis all automatic so there should be naught for me to do for the next eight hours or so. Spell me at the con so I can catch some sleep. Make certain I'm up and about afore orbit minus six hours. 'Tis apt to be the only sack time I'll get for a while."

Eight hours later, relaxed and refreshed, Duncan resumed station. Six hours to orbit. Pluto was now a massive ball filling a tenth of the sky beneath: a gloomy, interminable sphere of mountains and craters, stretching in jumbled array from pole to pole. Glistening coldly under the dim light of a shrunken sun, thousands of square miles of frozen gasses glittered in long ribbons, outlining the chain of the Plutonian Alps. Still the base was unidentified.

Four hours to orbit. Two. An hour to orbit, and still the frigid planet rolled unconcernedly beneath the scope with the base unidentified.

A bell! Tentative identification. A match. Three points. Let's see; with that orientation Grant's Pass should be about there. It is!

Triggering his mike, Duncan called, "Attention, *Ajax*. Site o' Pluto Base located and confirmed. Estimate touchdown in seventy-five minutes. Bypassing planned orbit. Acknowledge. Out."

A moment later *Ajax* replied, "Roger, *Sampson*. Proceed with landing per your plans. Report touchdown. Request status reports at such intervals as may be practical en route. Establish photo relay transmission on descent. Establish automatic computer slave transmission now on standby channel three. Over." There was a brief pause, then MacLeod's voice chimed in. "Good luck, Duncan. If you feel you need me I'll bring *Ajax* down. I'm a trifle envious of you setting foot on Pluto, but unless there's need 'twould be best if we stayed put up here. Over."

"Thank ye," replied Duncan simply. "I'll know better when we get down. But I'll keep your offer in mind. Over. Out."

Full deceleration. With no atmosphere a long, braking descent was unnecessary—at least not from this angle and with the fuel reserves aboard *Sampson*. Simply hit the brakes and wait for her to come to a halt a few meters above the surface.

Clang! Clang! Clang! Warning! Alarm! Combat alert!

Frantically the infantry in the aft hold dove headlong into their strap couches. As they sank back into them padded steel bands arched up, clamping them firmly into the couch and pinning them immobile. One trooper, in a toilet facility, was unexpectedly clamped and embraced, legs, knees, waist, chest and head, by padded bands which slid out from the wall and quickly tightened to hold him firmly against the coming accelerations. Jamie MacAllister, having no couch in the aft compartment, moved purposefully to a corridor wall and pressed a button. A panel slid smoothly aside to disclose a padded inner section. Stepping into it, he leaned back. Reacting to the pressure the padded arcs of steel slid out and enveloped him in their life-saving folds.

In the control room Duncan sagged back as the automatic controls in his seat reacted to the alarm and moved to encase him in rubber-cushioned bands. A forehead strap moved out to enfold him like some medieval helmet, leaving only the face exposed. Throat mikes curved upward to feed the intercom and radio systems. As his hands gripped the arms of the couch broad bands wrapped around them, gauntleting him from wrist to elbow. Beneath either hand a set of fingertip override controls glided easily from hidden recesses in the couch.

The radar repeater screens sprang to new life as the computer fed in simulated blips representing data gleaned from every available source. Simultaneously a battle screen slid down from an overhead niche. The lights blinked off so only the dull reds and greens of the instrument gauges competed with the radar data showing on the battle screen.

Duncan counted. Three, four, six . . . seven blips indicated ships rising leisurely from Pluto! Seven red blips! Ships not responding properly to the IFF code. Enemies—at least until proven otherwise.

Duncan's first, panicky impulse was to hit the override button and get out of the way. No enemy would permit himself to be caught on the ground this way. It was a trap! Unmanned drones perhaps? Torpedoes? . . . No. They weren't accelerating fast enough for those. Before anyone of them could get within fifty miles of *Sampson* it would inevitably be destroyed. But if they weren't drones or torpedoes they must be ships. And that meant . . . ?

An instant later *Sampson* lurched "over," spun "up," then arched "down" and flipped twice over to the "side" as her first evasive maneuvers carried him safely through the opening salvos of the enemy. In a remote corner of his mind Duncan wondered at the absence of the characteristic "flyspecks" on the battle screen—flyspecks which should mark the automatic detonation of rounds which missed the ship. They must be using long fuses, he thought briefly. Then his finger tightened convulsively on the firing trigger and for the merest infinitesimal fraction of a second *Sampson* stabilized its gyrations; just long enough to throw a salvo at the oncoming ships. A microinstant later it spun "down," lurched forward in a crushing, momentary 16 g acceleration, then slammed to a full deceleration at minus 9 g's at the same instant the lateral thrusters hurled him sideways at 5 g's.

Almost too rapidly to see, his battle screen showed an oncoming ship displace to the right as his salvo detonated in a series of quick flashes in a pattern surrounding the space it had just occupied. A quick repeat tap spewed out another salvo, followed immediately by yet a third.

As the second salvo rocketed out away from the *Sampson* his screen incredibly showed the enemy target ship displace *back* to its original trajectory! With ships firing salvos of from 1400 to 1700 of the 37 mm rocket-assisted rounds it was automatic for the battle computer to exclude a round from each salvo to preempt the space occupied by the hostile craft in each of its earlier maneuvers. After some 200 salvos, assuming any battle continued that long, the space-exclusion round would be dropped for the first position occupied, then for the second, and so on.

So it was not just stupid for an enemy craft to move back into a position where he must know a round was coming, it was suicidal! Everybody knew that; but apparently the enemy didn't.

Fascinated, Duncan watched the leading ship multiply in size, then vanish from the scope as it dissolved into shattered fragments of metal and flesh.

Then four times in quick succession *Sampson* lurched erratically in evasion of enemy salvos which never seemed to detonate. Briefly a pair of beams flicked across the hull before he moved out of the way. The ship stabilized momentarily as he pressed the firing stud at another of the four ships which were now in range and firing at him. The two trailing ships were still out of range, but they were closing fast and within seconds he would be facing all six.

For a full ten seconds *Sampson* gyrated wildly to the tune of the tiny Brownian particles dancing in the heart of the computer, their random walk providing the mathematical analogue for the ship's evasive pattern. In the midst of what seemed to be a looping spiral down an endless roller coaster, an extra buffet of a different character slammed his ship askew and jolted Duncan's tongue halfway down his throat. The sturdy *Sampson* spun on its axis, dipped, angled her bow up and smashed him deep into the couch with a crushing 19 g acceleration, followed by a 3 g outside loop and a 5 g deceleration.

"A hit," thought Duncan as he pressed the firing stud one more time. "That does it!" Automatically his finger curved and held down on the stud as he sought to fire off as many rounds as possible before old *Sampson* disintegrated beneath him.

Unbelieving, he eyed a second craft as it expanded, thinned, then vanished from the screen in a mist of annihilation.

Now all five remaining ships were in range and firing steadily at him. The *Sampson* was a leaping, twisting, dancing fish caught on a monster hook of explosive destruction. The battle radar was streaked as if with some dark snow as it glimpsed the hail of incoming shellfire flooding the space about the valiant little craft.

Where were *Ajax* and *Minotaur?* They should be coming up to help by now.

Duncan's finger jammed the firing stud and another salvo rocketed out. Then another and still another. *Sampson* slid off to the side, halted, then slid off one more time in the same direction. Then she blasted upward, spun to a halt, culminated with an arcing, downward-sloping dive which abruptly terminated in a jolting sidewise twist and smashing upward acceleration.

Ship number three of the enemy exploded and vanished from the screen as *Sampson* retaliated in part for the flood of shells hurtling at her. By now the foe would be in naked-eye range if only there were light to see by. The battle screen showed them all well within the fifty-mile circle. Momentarily Duncan wished he could actually *see* what was going on. The radar might be needed, but just plain seeing was better—if only it would work.

Another enormous jolt whipped *Sampson* around, throwing her upward with some unbelievable acceleration never planned by the computer. Bells commenced jangling and the air-alert monitor commenced a steady *beep-beep-beep*, indicating air loss somewhere aboard *Sampson*. They were holed!

Simultaneously ship number four of the enemy erupted and faded from the screen.

From a corner of his eye Duncan caught a glimpse of the travel scope off to the right of the battle-display screen. Possibly two dozen more red blips showed there—right off on the flank. And there among them were two green blips which represented *Ajax* and *Minotaur*. No wonder they weren't here helping!

Two more quick salvos momentarily slowed *Sampson's* insane maneuvers. Then all orientation was lost as the ship twisted in a violent, outside-sideways loop at 10 g's' deceleration followed in quick order by an abrupt forward plunge at 8 g's, another 10 g's' deceleration with a 2 g lateral component and a 10 g downward thrust all at the same instant. And always in the background was the insistent *beep-beep-beep* of the air-loss alarm.

Clearing the red haze from his eyes, Duncan sought to shake his head in order to wipe away the cobwebs, but the restraining pads held him immobile. Automatically, almost unseeingly, his finger stabbed the firing stud. A momentary fragment of vision returned just in time for him to see ship number five of the foe follow the others into oblivion.

Unexpectedly, incredibly, ships six and seven vanished! No preliminary expansion. None of the speckling to indicate detonating warheads in their vicinity. No failure of his screens to account for it. Just disappearance; total stark vanishment!

Stunned, Duncan examined the travel scopes. Save for the two green blips of *Ajax* and *Minotaur*, it was blank. No trace of an enemy. Not behind them; not over them; not streaking away for safety—just gone! For all the indications on the screens the entire battle might have been some eerie nightmare and no real combat at all. Only the persistent *beep-beep-beep* of the air-loss sensors argued that there was something wrong aboard *Sampson.*

Still disbelieving, Duncan stared at the screens, searching for some trace of the foe. Then he reached down to thumb his mike. But there was no mike stud. It too was gone!

Numbly, he felt again for the button; then looked down for it. It wasn't there. And then came awareness. . . . His straps were gone. No more bands were holding him down, no more restraints were protecting him. The computer had sounded the all-clear in the most practical possible way. It had released the straps and retracted the combat instrumentation. He was free again. The lights had come on and he hadn't even noticed them.

The battle was over.

CHAPTER 4

The intercom squawked to jarring life as MacAllister gravel-voiced over it. "Hey, Duncan. Jamie here. Are we all clear? The straps are loose."

At least someone was alive aft despite the steady beeping of the air-loss alarm. Half distracted by a lurking fear of a second attack, Duncan flipped his end of the intercom. "Campbell here," he replied tersely. "It looks like all clear right now, but I can't say for how long. 'Tis possible we'll ha' another attack any minute. Any personnel injured aft?"

"Not here. But I've two men missing and not reported yet. They were away from their couches when the alarm sounded and hopefully wound up in emergency restraints."

"Find out and let me know as soon as possible," grunted Duncan. "Use the intercom by selective sections. Don't come back at me till ye've got something certain. I'll most like be tied up here for a while."

As the intercom went silent Duncan made a hasty survey of the condition board. Ship's basic air pressure holding normal. Reserve pressure in the automatic tanks down four pounds and slipping. Stowage and dunnage compartments normal, except for C-3 winking redly. Obvious hull damage aft. Access corridor to C-3 showed green, but the red condition light intermittently flickered red. They must be losing air through the corridor. The whole section had to be sealed.

Flipping on the intercom, Duncan called aft. "Jamie, ha' ye located your missing men yet?"

"We've found one. He was in the jakes and is a little messed up, but apart from needing a good scrub-down he'll be all right. They ought to put in an automatic flush and drain in these tubs. That room is a mess! Private Gillie's still missing, though. If he didn't get to an emergency couch I'm afraid he's in trouble."

"We're losing air in C-three. Apparently the automatic interior lock is sprung, too, since there's escapement down the access corridor. We'll have to establish a manual seal to close the whole section temporarily until we can get a better patch on. Take a quick personal look through the C section. Don't bother wi' C-three. If Gillie was in there he's had it anyhow. As soon as ye're satisfied the section is clear drop the manual seals. 'Twill hold for the while. Come forward after ye've completed the preliminary seal. In the meanwhile dispatch Sergeant Beeson wi' a reliable party to check the remainder o' the ship for signs o' damage. We took two near-hits. C-three got one but I don't know where the other made it and 'tis just possible some o' our sensor equipment was knocked out and we've damage I don't see from here. . . . No more calls for a while. I've got to contact *Ajax*."

"Roger," answered MacAllister as the intercom fell silent.

Flipping the transmitter to emergency hailing frequency, Duncan beamed a query to the other ships. "*Sampson* to *Ajax* . . . *Sampson* to *Ajax*. Do ye read?"

"We read you, *Sampson*. We're tied up assessing damage. Call back in ten minutes if we don't contact you first. Over."

"Roger. Out."

Turning back to the ship's console, Duncan commenced a general instrumentation cross-check. Hold section A checked out. Every backup system agreed with the primary display. Not much likelihood of both systems being damaged in precisely the same way, so he could assume the A section was intact. B section the same. C section he already knew about. D section showed an air loss of slightly less than a pound of pressure, but both systems agreed there was no other evidence of damage. For the time being he would assume it was caused by cross-leakage into the C section. E section was good. F section.

At G section he ran into trouble. The main display showed normal but the backup system showed a pure random pattern of reds and greens. Clearly it was damaged. And if it was giving bad readings there was a distinct possibility the primary system was out but locked in the green mode. H, I and J sections checked clear.

He was just finishing his console check when the radio belched back to life. "*Ajax* to *Sampson*. Come in, *Sampson*."

"Roger, *Ajax*. I'm showing all clear in my sector but maintaining full alert until advised otherwsie. *Sampson* sustained two near-hits. C section being closed off due to air leak. G section fails display cross-checks. Private Gillie o' the infantry not accounted for as of last report. Must be considered probable casualty. We engaged seven hostile ships, destroying five. The two remaining ships vanished. No explanation. Present status: ready for combat but damaged. Munitions status at approximately one third full and approaching critical if new combat action necessary. Over."

"Aye. We read you, *Sampson*," came the informal reply. "We had sixteen ships out against us. Eight destroyed, eight vanished. No damage to either *Ajax* or *Minotaur*. We have ample munitions reserves for transfer to you before making any further moves. Continue your repairs and as soon as you have a final report available let us know. Till then, we'll leave you alone. Over."

"Thank ye kindly," acknowledged Duncan. "Over and out."

Ten minutes later MacAllister came forward, grim-faced and distinctly green about the gills. Gillie's dead," he announced without preamble. "He was in C-five storage and had a couple of cases of equipment dismounted in anticipation of touchdown. He never made it to a couch and the cases smeared him about the compartment pretty badly."

"Sorry about that," nodded Duncan. "He was a likely soldier. What ha' ye done wi' him?"

"We've shoveled what we could into the torpedo tube betwixt the C-two, D-two sectors. I've detailed two of our stronger-stomached men to clean up the mess with a vacuum hose."

"Then the C section is still open?"

"Aye. The inner lock was warped at the frame. We threw on a plastic patch, which is holding for now. As soon as we've transferred the gear from the C-section dunnage compartments we'll finish sealing her off."

"Be sure to gi' me a mass-transfer estimate for each compartment," ordered Duncan. "Ordinarily the ship's internal sensors gi' automatic compensation for mass imbalances, but we've sustained some electronic damage so I'm not as confident as I'd like to be. If we start acting up when we head down to the surface I'd like as good an estimate as ye can manage."

"Will do."

"Ha' ye checked out the G section yet?"

"Aye. Beeson went through every compartment. G-twelve registers an automatic seal and only twelve pounds of pressure. Evidently a slow leak on the other side but the lock is holding. The inner door to the compartment is bulged so 'tis likely something slapped into us and cracked the skin. G-eleven, B-eleven and B-twelve above both show evidence of denting and interior buckling, but the air pressure is holding up so the skin is still tight. No other signs of damage we could find."

Glancing over at the manifest readout Duncan decided quickly. "'Tis little o' immediate value in any o' those lockers. Throw on a plastic seal and slap it over each o' them. Continue spraying till the coat is at least a half inch thick. If we ha' the time and are not interrupted we'll set about repairing the outer hull after we land. Also, make damn sure the C section is fully sealed afore we start down. I'd hate to ha' us land and crack open a whole side o' the ship."

"Will do," agreed MacAllister, then changed the subject abruptly. "You know, what these buckets need are some view screens in the passenger holds and corridors. For a while there I figured that ship really had us. At least it would have been nice to have a view of him on the way out."

"I scarce think ye would ha' cared for your peek," Duncan replied drily. "For one thing, 'twas not just one ship. 'Twas seven."

"Seven!" MacAllister exclaimed incredulously. "Against the three of us?"

"Seven," was Duncan's carefully casual reply, "against the one o' us. *Ajax* and *Minotaur* had sixteen against them."

"You're joshing!"

"Not a bit. Ye can play back the battle on the reserve screens if ye've a mind to. I'll pull the tapes as soon as we've the leisure. *Sampson* destroyed five o' them and *Ajax* and *Minotaur* took eight betwixt them."

"What happened to the others? Did they run?"

"I wish I knew, Jamie," Duncan shrugged nervously. "I just wish I knew. They simply vanished, that's all. Just vanished!"

"Whoosh! I think you're right. I wouldn't have wanted to see that on my screen. 'Twould be hard on the nerves."

"Aye. Now hop to in getting things sorted out aft. We've got some work ahead."

As MacAllister drifted out the lock, Duncan turned back to the radio. Raising *Ajax* he finished his report.

"Roger," cut in MacLeod's voice when he had finished. "Now for instructions. I'm going to want both you and Logan aboard for a personal conference afore you set about landing. You'll also have three men detailed to come aboard with you to complete transfer of additional munitions whilst we're talking. We'll provide you with enough to bring you to two-thirds supply. Your immediate orders are to take search orbits about Pluto to make as sure as we can no more of those laddies are about. When complete we'll assume stationary track at twelve thousand miles on the opposite side of the Pluto Base. You're to complete such emergency repairs as may be needful, then take up search orbit number two. *Ajax* will take number one orbit and *Minotaur* number three. Orbital altitude will be programmed for four hundred fifty miles. Start point will be directly over the station. *Ajax* and *Minotaur* will release all four automatic drones each. They'll take up composite patterns at two hundred miles above the surface and programmed to attack anything taking off the planet or in power above it, so keep your IFF on the air or you're apt to be shot up by our own equipment. Any questions?"

"Just one. Stand by to monitor my IFF signal on both regular and standby radios. I've sustained some electronics damage and would hate to think the IFF wasn't working proper. Apart from that I'll be moving directly to search orbit two. Emergency repairs are nearing completion and there's not much more we can do until we get to proper repair facilities."

A moment later a second voice cut in. "*Sampson*, *Ajax* radio monitor. I've checked you on both primary and secondary frequencies. Your IFF is loud and clear and shows no sign of drifting off band. I see no problems. Over."

"Thank ye kindly," acknowledged Duncan. "Moving to take up search orbit now. Over and out."

Turning back to the control console, Duncan pulled a prepared chip from the storage rack and added it to the already compiled data concerning Pluto. Punching in the desired altitude, he pressed the execute button.

With a smooth, sweeping curve, *Sampson* moved downward into her assigned orbit and proceeded into the programmed search pattern. In mere seconds the record tapes began spitting out data. Every peculiarity of the Plutonian surface had been recorded on the original survey tape. Any peculiarities or unexplained surface features not matching these survey tapes would be spotted by the computer and recorded as anomalies. If there were any more ships on the surface—even any new craters from random chunks of space debris—this would pick them up. With the readings from the three ships and eight drones all being cross-fed into the computers, it was highly unlikely any significant objects would escape attention.

Only the Pluto Base site showed anomalies. There was unmistakable evidence of bombardment. Discouragingly, though not unexpectedly, there was no indication of any infrared heat radiation to suggest life there.

Two days were spent pursuing the search pattern. Two days at full alert, with Duncan napping fitfully in his command couch and eating catch as catch can, making quick excursions to the head only when MacAllister was there to spell him.

At last they were satisfied. No more enemy were in the vicinity—or if they were they were undetectable.

The drones were recalled. Slowly the ships climbed to the rendezvous point, finally coming to rest a scant hundred yards apart, drifting idly in space. Leaving MacAllister at the controls, Duncan suited up, then with the three men detailed to munitions transfer pushed off in the direction of *Ajax*.

"Well, Duncan, I'm right glad to see ye," grinned MacLeod as Duncan entered the cramped captain's quarters. "'Tis no small feat for a utility craft in combat against battle craft to survive a pitched battle against seven ships of any class. And ye killed off five at that."

"Thank ye, Gregory, but I'd rather know what happened to the other two ships."

"Aye. And Logan and I'd like to know that too. I take it you've already guessed 'twas what I called this meeting about."

"I assumed it."

"'Tis absolutely certain we didn't destroy them," muttered Logan positively. "They were there!" he added unnecessarily. "And then they vanished—spoof!—right off the screen before my eyes!"

"The same wi' me," agreed Duncan. "But to my thinking there's more to it than just that. We've got good ships and I don't doubt we're the best fighting men anywhere. But I can't accept that we're *that* good. Those people put up no proper fight or they'd ha' had us for sure. Coming up off the ground the way the seven against me did would ha' given us a definite winning margin in an even fight and may ha' kept things about equal in a five-against-three battle . . . mayhap even six to three. But against twenty-three ships we had no reasonable chance! You think they may ha' been unmanned drones perhaps?"

"Not likely," judged MacLeod. "Had they been drones their computers would have been able to outperform anything we could hope to do."

"Aye," emphasized Logan. "With no crews aboard the g-force limits would have been the structural limits of the ships rather than accommodated to human bodies. They'd have walked rings about us."

"But then again," considered MacLeod, "had they been busy taking aboard cargo they might not have had a chance to tie down properly. That would've imposed additional g limits. They might have figured we'd come tooling in after a one point zero-g acceleration and wouldn't be due for nearly another week. When we hove into their screen-detection limits sixteen of them made it off the ground and moved around to the far side of the planet whilst the remaining seven loaded as fast as possible and got off only when we were coming in. If they were mainly cargo ships 'twould account for their relatively weak showing."

"But they weren't weak," objected Logan firmly. "They were throwing out a god-awful amount of shells. No cargo ships should be able to do that."

"Besides," butted in Duncan, "their tactics were flat-out wrong."

"Then we all agree on that point," nodded MacLeod. "They fought a poor fight and their computers were distinctly second rate. Yet at the same time they seem to have some sort of device which permits them to vanish from the scopes when they found the three of us were whipping them."

"Another point too," added Duncan. "It may ha' been accidental, but I didn't notice any detonation from the rounds they fired. That means there's apt to be all sorts o' explosive warheads wandering about the system from now to doomsday, just waiting for some ship to show up. All our shells are designed to detonate wi'in a few seconds o' passing beyond the programmed distance, and then the plastic fragments outgas and disassociate in the vacuum. My aft screens showed no evidence o' this."

"That's right," agreed Logan. "And besides, even those which detonated when they closed on us were either faulty and exploded too soon or the Cn-three-oh-nine load was inadequate."

"Then I'd suggest either the fuses were faulty or the pellets designed for use against craft with less defensive armor," opined MacLeod. "Do you think that an accurate assessment, gentlemen?"

"Very possibly," conceded Duncan thoughtfully. " 'Twould tie in a bit wi' something I think I spotted in the opening phases o' the battle. . . . I may be wrong but I recall having the distinct feeling the enemy threw a couple o' laser beams our way at the start. Mayhap I was wrong, and just as possibly they were using them all along if I'm right. But either way, if they're using lasers against combat craft they must certainly be under some fundamental misapprehension. Trying to keep one o' their beams locked on a ship equipped wi' a reflective surface and a computer-driven evasive system would be an exercise in futility."

Pausing for a moment, Logan waved the others to silence, then commented, "You know, I think it may just be possible we might actually have engaged some genuine pirates and not merely some other government's ships out playing games!"

"No way," snapped Duncan. "Ye cannot manufacture spaceships wi'out government knowledge. And as for capture, there's no' been enough ships o' all the blocs put together disappear to make a flotilla half so large as the one we just fought. For my part, I wonder if mayhap some small, unaligned nation might ha' commenced a fleet buildup in secret? Look at the evidence. They ha' a gadget which takes them off our detectors. That's a plus for them. But at the same time their computers don't measure up against ours or any other bloc presently in space. Additionally, they ha' not installed self-destructs on their warheads, their fusing is inadequate and they possibly are still trying to make effective use of lasing weapons. So far as I can see this adds up to a new entry into space."

"I doubt that," objected MacLeod. " 'Twould be extremely improbable any nation could set up a program of that sort without having the espionage services of every major bloc aware of it long before they ever launched their first ship—let alone a fleet."

"Then ye don't think it could be kept secret," queried Duncan.

"Exactly," replied MacLeod. "If 'twere something like making swords or pistols, or even machine guns, it could certainly be done. But consider all the specialties involved in constructing a spaceship. First you have the technology to manufacture the celaenium. That means the ability to machine the magnets down to tolerances of within a hundred thousandth of an inch. Then you need the half ton or so of liquid helium for a bath, electricity to build up nearly a million gauss per head on each of more than a hundred magnets. . . . And that's just for starters. After that it gets difficult. The electronics gear, the chrome and titanium and other elements, are too scarce to be collected in secret. Then by the time you put together perhaps twenty thousand highly trained men to construct the ships and the engineering personnel to do it right you can forget about keeping it secret."

"Then what do you suggest?" demanded Logan grumpily. "It seems to me we're simply arguing about in circles; making suggestions only to kick them apart."

"Suppose," considered MacLeod carefully, " 'tis not another nation but another race?"

"Bosh!" snorted Logan incredulously. "There's no other race in the solar system. Nothing like that could have remained unknown this long. And there certainly isn't anything lurking inside Pluto."

"Perhaps," agreed MacLeod imperturbably. "But let's do some extra thinking. Just suppose there's another race gallivanting about in space somewhere. Some while ago it was able to start building elements up to one hundred twenty-six and developed celaenium. Then later they developed some gadget which permits faster-than-light travel. Now they're booming about in the space between suns the same way we gad about the solar system.

"Now also figure these people don't relish the idea of some other race maybe finding the same thing and becoming competition, so when they run across our base and realize we're getting out into space they shoot on sight. . . . Either that or they just got scared when they found we were there, albeit without their hyperdrive gadget."

"Then why didn't they make a better fight of it?" challenged Logan. "If they have gadgetry like that 'twould be logical to expect they'd be considerably ahead of us in other ways too."

"Not necessarily," interposed Duncan, warming to MacLeod's idea. "That might make very good sense. Say they aren't organized the way we are on Earth—wi' a half dozen little space wars going on continually. We're constantly developing new weapons and counter-weapons. But if these aliens never had any o' their own around to gi' them a real fight then they probably would never ha' developed very highly advanced computers and battle techniques. Look at our own history in that area. Our original computerized combat techniques were no better than theirs. And we'd still be using them if it hadn't been for other blocs punching holes in the system. After all, 'tis not like buying a new copter model every year. In something like this if there's nobody to look for weaknesses in the system ye figure there's none there and keep on using the old one.

"Even their failure to do noteworthy damage wi' their artillery would be in line wi' the hypothesis. Evidently they figured laser technology would be enough and they use a minimum hull thickness and expect anyone else to do the same. But we've beefed ours up to the maximum possible as a defensive measure, so 'twould perhaps take a direct hit by one o' their projectiles to punch a hole in our armor."

"Aye," agreed MacLeod enthusiastically. "And possibly their faster-than-light drive isn't very maneuverable. Say they're either headed for the next sun or in ordinary celaenium drive. In that event their hypervelocity capability wouldn't be of any use to them in combat save to get them out of the way when they find they're overmatched."

"Fine in theory," grumped Logan doubtfully, "but we'll need proof when we get home—and a lot of proof at that," he added unnecessarily.

"I may ha' an idea on that if our theory's right," put in Duncan. "When we break up here both *Ajax* and *Minotaur* are going to stay in orbit anyhow. My infantry's all we need below. So whilst I'm down cleaning up the mess on Pluto the two o' ye can scout about wi' detectors wide open to pick up debris left over from the combat. There ought to be some remains to be analyzed when we get home."

"Another thought too," added Logan. "Mind you, I'm not saying I agree with all this, but if 'tis true we may find something of use by playing back the battle tapes till we reach the instant the ships vanished. There must have been at least a fraction of a second of acceleration afore their ships reached light speed. If they had their celaenium drives in operation when they cut in the other drive we ought to be able to spot a Doppler shift toward infinity. If so 'twould be proof absolute."

"I'll buy that," nodded MacLeod. "that should be proof enough for anyone. And you, Duncan—when you land your infantry have them conduct a careful search of the area and keep a wary eye out for artifacts the invaders may have left behind. Most likely there'll be nothing, but the possibility should be kept in mind. They may have thrown out some garbage. If so I want it packaged and brought back."

"Even if I have to leave some of our equipment behind?"

"Even if you have to leave it behind. Just don't leave any of our living personnel. Everything else would be secondary."

"I'll see to it. And whilst we're thinking about it, if those were alien ships there's at least a possibility their air was different from ours. When their ships were destroyed the gasses would be ejected. If ye could get the primary destruction site between ye and the sun the absorption bands in the spectrum might gi' a readable atmospheric analysis."

"It's probably a little late for that, but the idea's good, so we'll try it. And now I have some positive instructions for all of us."

"Aye?" grunted Logan.

"Suppose we're right and 'twas a genuine alien attack. 'Twill be no easy task convincing anyone on Earth of that fact—particularly the politicians. After all, they're mainly solicitors, with the mentality of lawyers and preachers. If we present them with an unpleasant fact the first thing they'll do is try to find a loophole. They'll ask if the evidence *could* have been tampered with or altered. And if they can find even the remotest possibility where tampering could have occurred they'll immediately conclude it *did* occur. They'll set about arguing away the existence of aliens by playing games with their words, and I'd hate to think we might doom mankind simply because we failed to satisfy some lawyer or preacher. I therefore expect each of us to withdraw the tapes of the battle, and in the presence of at least two witnesses seal them under lock and key behind a plastic patching sheath. That will be your first order of business after this conference is broken up. . . . And now—is there anything else to consider?"

"I think we've pretty nigh talked ourselves out," Logan shrugged. " 'Tis my present opinion there's some simple, rational explanation for all this. But damn it, I have to agree the idea of aliens seems most apt. The trouble is, I don't believe we'll be able to convince anybody back on Earth. The scientists will say there's no theoretical basis for a faster-than-light drive, therefore none exists. The politicians will listen to the scientists. Preachers only believe in themselves so it won't matter what sort of proof we might offer. The yellow-sheet newspapers will cry wolf until nobody knows what to believe. And that will be the end of it till the aliens come back in *real* strength!"

"In the meanwhile," noted Duncan, "I think we ought to get to work. I don't feel comfortable wi' all o' us bunched up like this and ten enemy ships out there that might pop up at any time."

"I agree with that too," nodded MacLeod. "Very well, gentlemen; you'll return to your ships and proceed according to the plans outlined here. Working on the premise no one is alive below, we should be able to complete work within forty-eight hours. I propose we schedule our departure from Pluto orbit for fifty-two hours from now, barring unforeseen circumstances, of course. Good day, gentlemen."

CHAPTER 5

Cheng Yi-kai, the Chinese foreign minister and second-ranked member of the Chinese Presidium, was openly contemptuous of his surroundings. It had long been a matter of principle for the Chinese to pretend lack of knowledge of any barbarian languages. Even their interpreters were barbarian hirelings, usually Malay or Indonesians of at least partially Chinese descent. And for a Chinese diplomat to answer a summons from the UN was almost unheard of since China's withdrawal from that body nearly a half century before. But this summons had been so peremptory and incisive a decision to attend had been made.

If Cheng was contemptuous, the Soviet foreign minister, Dmitri Yankovich, was simply unhappy. The message from the UN Security Council had employed the phrase "extraordinary emergency" in requesting the conference. And to be perfectly blunt, nowhere had Soviet intelligence sources indicated any developments which might conceivably justify such a phrase. The implications of an intelligence lapse were singularly unpleasant. Somebody might have to answer for it.

Josiah Hamilton, current head of the American Birch Bark Society, and as such *de facto* head of the State Department, the FBI and the CIA—and incidentally the almost certain nominee of the ruling America First Party for President in the upcoming election—was relaxed and nonchalant. He *knew* the reason for the summons. Obviously it was some sort of trick to reentrap the United States in the toils of international communism. Ever since the United States had withdrawn from the UN, a little more than a century ago, it had been all the foreigners had thought of—getting the United States back into the UN so the rest of the world could get back onto the gravy train and live off the American taxpayers. Knowing this truth to begin with, it was merely a matter of discovering the specific techniques to be used by the UN on this occasion.

Frankly, it amused him to attend such conferences. He could never be trapped. That he knew for certain. And to be perfectly honest with himself, it tickled his vanity to be so easily able to penetrate the devious deceptions employed by the other nations in their futile efforts to obtain concessions and dollars from his country.

The European Union minister, Heinrich Frankl, was moderately curious. Possibly the British Government was planning to employ this as a dramatic means of proclaiming a return to solidarity with the civilized nations of Europe. Nothing else could remotely justify the unusual wording of the message. "Extraordinary emergency" indeed! If the British were that desperate for reunion with Europe a few added concessions could no doubt be extracted in advance.

Carefully, Hamilton consulted his watch. The meeting was scheduled for 9 A.M., and punctuality was a uniquely American virtue. It was up to him to set an example before the rest of the world. Not one second before; not a second after. Arriving at 9 A.M. on the dot, he marched through the ancient doors of London's Parliament building with head erect and eyes straight forward, looking neither right nor left. Inwardly he appreciated the figure he knew he cut. Leonine white hair wreathing a strong, rugged face. And if you ignored the very slight evidence of a paunch there could be no denying the powerfully developed body. The day would surely come, he acknowledged with complacent pride, when generations of the future would look back on him and his generation as he looked back on Washington, Jackson and to a certain extent Lincoln.

At nine-fifteen Yankovich arrived at the head of a delegation consisting of five heavily laden automobiles carrying an entourage of assorted clerks, stenographers, interpreters and an unknown number of secret police.

At nine-twenty Frankl leisurely strolled in, examined the row of paintings lining the walls with a connoisseur's critical eye, grimaced in mild distaste at the gaucheries of English artistry, then took a seat off to the side of the room.

At nine-thirty Cheng made a languid appearance, escorted only by his interpreter, cast a supercilious glance about him, then waited patiently while the interpreter carefully wiped the seat clean of all noxious western dust. Then with elaborate indifference he took his seat, cast a single negligent glance at the empty podium, folded his hands across his lap and sat patiently, waiting for the proceedings to commence.

Hamilton, observing the spectacle, burst out with a loud guffaw while Frankl curled his lips in an imperceptible manner which included both barbarians impartially.

The seating of Cheng was the signal for the start of the meeting. Alpin Grant, Prime Minister of the UN nations, paced briskly from a side door and took his position at the podium without further ado.

"Gentlemen," he commenced without preamble, "in the messages sent to your respective governments the phrase 'extraordinary emergency' was employed. I wish all of you to understand that if anything this was an understatement!

"As all of you are undoubtedly aware, the UN Pluto Base was attacked and destroyed by an unknown force some weeks ago. What you do not know is the fact that these forces consisted of aliens originating outside the solar system."

"Nonsense!" exploded Hamilton, interrupting angrily. "I came here to hear what you had to say, not to listen to some silly twaddle! If you have an emergency let's hear about it. If not, I have better things to do with my time."

"If you will wait, Mr. Hamilton," Grant replied amiably, "I can prove my statement."

"Mr. Grant," replied Hamilton viciously, "I wouldn't believe you if you *showed* me an alien!"

"Then I apologize for summoning you here. You may leave at your convenience. The door is by no means barred."

Grumbling, Hamilton subsided momentarily. It was crude and an obvious trap for the United States, but he was interested in seeing this alleged proof. He'd wager Hollywood produced better monsters six days a week than these foreigners could muster in a dozen years.

Frankl was thinking rapidly. "Ingenious," he muttered to himself. "A few odds and ends of 'proof' and the British will be able to claim the emergency requires their withdrawal from the UN and allegiance with a power possessing a strong space fleet already in existence. Clever tactics. These British are shrewd. They can claim their withdrawal from the UN is for the good of all mankind and possibly even expect to obtain a concession or two from us. If Grant thought this up he's far cleverer than I imagined. He might even be a bit of a menace if the opposition party gets to him before I do."

Cheng sat with studied impassiveness. "Truly," he thought, "the ways of the barbarians are devious. Could this be a maneuver set up by an alliance against the People's Celestial Republic? This Grant (what ridiculous names they have) obviously knows we cannot associate on terms of equality with barbarians so he conjures up a threat from outer space—celestial space—and attempts to unite all the powers against it. Then in the course of affairs, when we refuse to ally ourselves with these real barbarians against those imaginary barbarians, they can use our 'noncooperation' as proof of league with the 'celestial aliens' and attack us."

Yankovich was numb with despair. Prior to leaving Moscow he had been exhaustively briefed on every potential subject and the official party line toward it. But there was no party line yet established for invaders from outer space! Despite himself, he felt a reluctant admiration for the UN minister. "He must have known we would not be prepared for a discussion of this topic and hopes to catch us off balance. The question is, what do I do now? I can always walk out, claiming the whole affair is a capitalist hoax, but then if this Grant continues the meeting without the Soviet delegation and can succeed in lining up the other nations behind him we could face serious difficulties. I wish I knew what that oriental devil, Cheng, is thinking. This must be a perfect opportunity for him to embarrass the Soviet Union. . . . No, the best approach would be to stall the meeting until I can obtain instructions from the Kremlin."

Suiting action to the thought, Yankovich rose abruptly to his feet and shouted angrily, "Mr. Grant, I must protest this statement! Prior to my arrival here I understood this was to be a foreign ministers' meeting to discuss matters of—as you put it—'extraordinary emergency.' If this be the case then obviously it is necessary to establish a procedural committee to begin with. Any emergency of the sort you have suggested patently requires an agenda."

"Just how do you arrive at that conclusion, Mr. Yankovich?" inquired Grant softly. "At this particular moment I propose to show you the proof we currently have in hand and advise you of our intended actions. If after that you are still of the opinion an agenda and full-dress foreign ministers' debate is required then one of my assistants will collaborate in preparing an agenda. I am certain that should prove entirely satisfactory. After all, I suspect your government would look with some disapproval on your requirement for the preparation of an agenda prior to any knowledge of the general subject to be discussed."

"Not at . . . ," started Yankovich bitterly, then thought of the possible indiscretion and ended with a lame " . . . all. . . . No, not at all. By all means show me your alleged evidence first, then we will commence on the agenda." This was even better than he had hoped. The evidence would occupy at least one full session of the conference, which would give him an extra day not counted on. His momentary admiration turned to inner contempt. "Just like the capitalists," he gloated inwardly. "They obtain an advantage then throw it away. It proves the decadence of nonsocialist thinking!"

Frankl's admiration, on the other hand, went up a few more notches. "He's certainly faked that Russian out cleverly," he conceded. "Now the British can present their 'proof' and make the switch to us before the Russians can even get a debate going."

Cheng was getting more disturbed by the moment. The Russians had given in far too quickly. Was there already a secret entente worked out between the UN and the Soviet Union? If so he would have to win that Yankee ape away from collaboration with the UN–Russian bloc. The very thought was distasteful, but sometimes politics forced unpalatable manipulations—"made strange bedfellows," was the term westerners sometimes employed—felicitous even if it did come from barbarians.

Hamilton was simply tickled. He enjoyed sitting on his Olympian height watching the playacting put on by the rest of the world in their futile efforts to enmesh his country in their affairs. And this was turning out even better than most of their farces. Now the British could make a pitch for mutual cooperation, and when that failed they would make a big show of alignment with either Russia or China in the expectation the United States would then align itself with Europe and start pumping in aid which would then be split up among all the nations. That way they would be back living off the American taxpayer. What they did not really appreciate, however, was his personal acumen. *He* would not be trapped. Josiah Hamilton—plain, ordinary American—was so far ahead of these foreigners he could simply sit back and enjoy himself for the rest of the play, now that he knew the plot.

"I take it then we're all agreed," observed Grant from the podium.

"You will see the proofs first, then discuss the matter afterwards." Hearing no immediate further objections, he continued: "As all of you know, our service vessels carry monitor tapes which automatically record all data during a period of combat. I believe each of your spacecraft carry similar equipment, so there is no need to elaborate on the techniques employed. Duplicates of these monitor tapes for the three of our craft engaged in the Pluto combat—the cruisers *Ajax* and *Minotaur* and the utility craft *Sampson*—will be made available to you prior to your departure this afternoon.

"To be brief, these tapes record a combat by these three vessels against a force of twenty-three hostile ships of unknown but provably alien origin. During the combat thirteen of the alien ships were destroyed while our craft suffered minimal damage. While this might seem cause for elation, the fact remains, the hostile craft possessed a hyperdrive of unknown characteristics—a fact which will give them a virtually insuperable advantage in the event of future combat. They will be able to strike at us at their leisure while we have no means of striking back. As for the superiority of our force in this one battle, it can be traced directly to weaknesses in their computer and armaments systems. These are currently markedly inferior to our own, but I feel it is safe to assume both will be improved prior to any further attacks on this system. Such an improvement is clearly within their power and we feel any race capable of developing a hypervelocity drive has already amply demonstrated its potential to refine existing equipment and bring it to a par with anything we have. We may therefore anticipate that future developments will bring them more nearly equal to us in direct combat capabilities.

"Analysis of the metals recovered from hull fragments of the destroyed ships indicates more extensive use of lithium compounds and less use of beryllium alloys than is normal on Earth ships. In addition, a few fragments of wire recovered suggests the widespread use of gold rather than silver in their electronics and electrical systems. Other than that, little of significance was learned from the ships' debris left over after the battle.

"There were, however, three small fragments of flesh recovered during the search of the battle area. A report of the analysis of these fragments is appended, together with duplicates of the other data. While we lack proof that these flesh fragments came from bodies of crewmen, it is considered unlikely they represent remnants from food lockers or pets or zoological specimens, but none of these alternatives can wholly be ruled out.

"Analysis of the cells shows certain characteristics unique to our experience. The skin surfaces, while superficially quite similar to our own, show a distinctive pattern of microscopic scales, each with an almost invisible feather embedded in a manner similar to human body hair. The chromosomal structure has two sets of fifty-two, rather than the normal forty-eight in man.

, "From one portion of flesh, tentatively believed to originate in an area we identify as corresponding to the human thigh, we obtained a small group of still viable cells which we are presently attempting to culture, though with indifferent success to date.

"Spectroscopic analysis of the gasses released from the alien ships was inconclusive since it began more than forty-eight hours after the battle, but it suggests the atmosphere is essentially the same as ours except for a somewhat higher percentage of oxygen and a correspondingly low nitrogen. We were unable to obtain reliable readings for inert gasses and carbon dioxide but we believe the values of these cannot exceed five percent.

"Preliminary conclusions indicate the possibility that the species may be oviparous, or egg-laying. This is based on the scaly skin structure plus certain features of the chromosome system. Some of our scientists, however, have suggested the aliens may be marsupials or even viviparous, so the matter is by no means definite and the margin for error is large.

"No artifacts of any sort which could be related to the aliens were found on the surface of Pluto. As the bodies of several of our base personnel were not accounted for, we conclude they were removed for study by the aliens.

"As a final item of proof, spectral studies of the tape monitors aboard our ships reveal that at the instant the enemy craft vanished from the battle screens there was a violent Doppler shift toward infinity; an observation which confirms the assumption that the aliens switched to some sort of faster-than-light drive system.

"In the opinion of the UN governments there is a distinctly high possibility we may at any time be subject to a full-scale assault by these aliens. Their attack on the Pluto Base was totally unprovoked since the base itself was unarmed. No effort was made at friendly contact—no attempt to open communications at any level—a simple, all-out surprise attack.

"It must therefore be assumed the aliens are, for whatever reason, determinedly hostile to our existence and may attack at any time. Consequently the matter does not admit of lengthy debate and windy resolutions. Accordingly, the UN governments have unilaterally ordered a maximum increase in the production of spacecraft of all varieties, but most particularly of battlecraft. Every facility at our command will be devoted to the construction of ships and the training of personnel. And as a patent of our good faith in this matter, all nations of the world are invited to join with us.

"As a further patent of our good faith, immediately prior to this meeting an exact summary of our findings, including photomicrographs and details of the combat, were released to news media throughout the world along with our decision to commence a concentrated shipbuilding program.

"I realize this matter requires extensive study by your respective governments and your scientists must be given time to examine the data. Consequently none of you can be expected to reply at this time. You are, however, acquainted with our data, our conclusions and our intentions. More than this you cannot expect of any power. What actions your respective governments may wish to take are, of course, up to you and them.

"I see no reason to detain you longer. As you depart from this room you will be provided with a packet containing the complete details of our evidence. In addition, you are severally invited to send bacteriologists and biologists to work with us in an effort to discover more about the alien cells we are attempting to culture. I thank each of you for your attendance here today and now bid you adieu for the time being. Good day, gentlemen."

Turning abruptly at the end of this announcement, Grant strode off the podium and out the side door before any of the stunned delegates could phrase an objection.

After a moment Cheng rose languidly to his feet and started for the door, preceded by his servant-interpreter. Airily he brushed aside the proffered package containing the promised information. So the fools actually thought he would be interested in their child's games! The significant item in the whole charade was the UN shipbuilding program. Obviously they were in secret alliance with the Russians! And that meant the Russians would now use the UN announcement as their excuse for stepping up their own construction of spaceships.

With two states collaborating in the construction of spacecraft this would mean China must tread warily for the next few years. Of course, an all-out program of space construction was also a must if his nation was to survive. And China must also watch the United States and Europe to see what they would do.

For the briefest of moments a shadow of doubt flickered across the studied, oriental impassivity of Cheng's face. Possibly the Celestial Empire might even be overrun by the barbarians—provided the whole remainder of the world united against her. . . . But no! It simply could not be permitted to happen. He and his people had thousands of years' experience playing one barbarian off against another. Nothing could defeat the Celestial Empire! Nothing!

Josiah Hamilton was almost jubilant as he departed. Gravely he accepted the package at the door and thanked the usher for it. It would make a pleasant souvenir for his home. Upon his death, he acknowledged with complacent pride, his residence would no doubt be converted into a national shrine. This packet would certainly be one of the prize items since it represented a noteworthy intelligence triumph scored singlehandedly against the forces of international communism! They had unwittingly tipped their hand. The only point of real significance behind the charade was the revelation by that Grant fellow—strange how they seem to keep coming up copying good, historic American names—that they were going to start building spaceships. Using this as an excuse, all the other nations would no doubt follow suit. Then when they felt certain of their power they would descend on American bases and seek to force the United States completely out of space. Clearly this left him with no alternative. He must immediately engage the nation in a massive shipbuilding campaign.

Frankl was lost in admiration for Grant. The man was far cleverer than he had ever imagined possible. A true political genius! In one deft move he had put the entire European Federation in a position where it might have to come begging to Britain. Obviously they would have to start building spaceships to counter the inevitable reaction of the other nations. In a few years the British, with their overall greater access to natural resources, would have a far greater fleet than the federation. And by that time both the Russian and the American fleets would be substantially greater also. That meant his European Federation would be forced to make some outside alliance or face being submerged without a trace. China was a hopeless anachronism despite her powerful fleet. Russia was unthinkable and the United States was downright barbaric. Clearly the federation would be forced to ally itself with the UN and Britain. Clever—extremely clever—of Grant. At one stroke he had changed the whole complexion of bloc politics. That man would bear watching.

Yankovich was worried—very worried. Somehow the conference had gotten away from him. And that could easily mean a trip to Siberia. But what did the conference itself mean? Surely not even the capitalists would go to so much trouble merely to eliminate a single Soviet diplomat. . . . Or would they? No. He dismissed the thought. The shipbuilding was the clue. If the UN had simply begun building their ships without making an issue of it there wouldn't have been more than a few weeks before the whole rest of the world caught on to the expanded construction program. The Soviet Union could then have claimed it was an act of aggression and have taken steps accordingly. Now it might even be difficult to justify the sabotaging of the shipbuilding facilities.

The more he thought about it the more he acknowledged the unpalatable truth: he'd made a terrible mistake in not insisting on a preliminary meeting to work out an agenda. That devil Grant had completely outmaneuvered him! He could see that now. He might have been able to stall things in committee if only he had insisted on arguing the evidence point by point. Now everything was lost!

Hopelessly he considered the ramifications. Some word of the British propaganda would inevitably filter into Russia herself. And no matter how hard they pushed their counterpropaganda there would still be that nagging element of worry. Worse yet, there would always be the few people with improper orientation who might actually believe there *was* an alien invasion threat! No, his country's only recourse would be to pretend to accept the UN evidence and use it as a basis for building up her own fleet as rapidly as possible. And the havoc that would wreak on an already overstrained budget! In shocked dismay, he realized he would be lucky if he were merely sent to Siberia! That would be the best he could hope for now. To repeat, Yankovich was worried —very worried.

After the last of the dignitaries were well departed from the ancient halls of London's Parliament building, Alpin Grant sat sipping a whisky with Gordon MacLintock, the UN minister of defence. "Well, Gordie," he mused, slipping unconsciously into the informal dialect of the hills, "what do ye think?"

"No doubt of it, Alpin; 'twas the only effective way. If every man on Earth knew beyond a doubt the Judgment Day was tomorrow ye'd still not be able to get the big nations to agree to greet the sunrise together. This way, whether they realize it or not, they're all dancing to your tune and building ships for war."

"Aye," Alpin nodded forlornly. "But God help us if the aliens never return. Because if they don't those ships will for certain be turned against Earth!"

CHAPTER 6

The shrill skirl of the massed pipes keened through the heavy-laden skies. Gusty winds whipped up a froth of salt spray and mingled it with the chill drizzle of the sodden clouds. The water-soaked wool of the regimental dress tartans steamed under the pelting rain as the colorful files passed in review beneath the wintry skies of Scapa Flow.

To Duncan, now brevetted Colonel in the steadily expanding forces of the UN Bloc, the months had passed far too fleetingly. His own Argylls had been transformed out of all recognition. Where before there had been a single fleet battle group and a solitary infantry battalion, now there were three infantry battalions and two fleet battle groups—and each of the battle groups contained four times as many ships and eight times the striking power of the original group. Where scarcely a year ago the entire UN combat fleet mustered fourteen widely scattered cruisers and an irregular number of armed utility ships, now his battalion alone counted three cruisers, a dozen of the new type of battle scouts and six auxiliary utility craft.

Colonel Logan, standing erectly alongside Duncan and to his right, commanded a like number of craft. Brevet Brigadier MacLeod, at attention to the far right, thus commanded a force equal in power to virtually the entire UN strength a scant year earlier.

Now the Earthside Support and Replacement Battalion of the Argylls was coming out of the turn and passing before the immobile First Infantry Battalion, which was posted as base-level support for their new assignment. The pipers swung into the familiar "Earl of Sutherland's March" as their flags dipped in salute to their starbound brethren.

Hard on the heels of the Argylls came the conflicting strains of "Heilan Laddie" as the sombre tartans of the Black Watch heeled round the turn and commenced their march-past; rank upon rank aligned in perfect precision as the proud regiment honored its cousins.

Now the banners of the Argylls were abreast the reviewing stand as the three commanders stiffened to return the salute. As the head of the marching column swung past the reviewing stand and began to pass before the men of the fleet units themselves, the leading elements of the Camerons spun on the pivot and the "Pibroch of Donald Dubh" added to the swelling torrent of sound.

Two months before not a one of the ships now afloat behind them in the waters of Scapa Flow had even slipped down the ways at Falkirk. Duncan called back anguished memories of those days when he and Logan and MacLeod fretted impatiently at the old shipyards wondering if the new, prefabricated battlecraft being constructed at obsolete shipyards could ever be as effective as the older, handcrafted types.

As the last of the Argylls passed and he received the salute of the Black Watch, Duncan could look back shudderingly on the thousands of headaches of those hectic months. New troops to replace the cadres moved out to form new battalions and regiments. Transfers from infantry to space units. Inadequate housing. Insufficient uniforms and equipment. Occasionally even shortages of food. And worst of all, not enough qualified instructors to do the job properly. Commercial computers substituting for genuine battle gear as men were trained in the elements of space navigation and programming. Dummy guns and torpedoes substituted for working models. Dummy mines were armed and disarmed a thousand times as raw recruits labored sixteen hours a day learning not only their specialties but the basic fundamentals of soldiering at the same time.

And besides all this, there were the details of ship construction to be attended to. Harried engineers argued desperately in futile efforts to stabilize construction against changes being incorporated daily. MacLeod, Logan and Duncan had pushed for the maximum amount of weaponry. The logistics people had argued for a maximum of supplies and fuel capacity. The xenologists had added a supplementary computer and sensing system designed to afford insight into the aliens' purposes. Theoretical physicists—those who were prepared to accept the reality of a faster-than-light drive—had placed aboard their own computer and specialized communications relay systems in hopes of learning something of the characteristics of a hyperdrive.

Bureaucrats wanted to incorporate a number of "lifeboats" as a sop to worried constituents who lacked the least idea of the fundamentals of space war. Someone in the Admiralty office, no doubt left over from the Napoleonic Wars who had somehow been overlooked by Father Time, had tired to persuade the War Office to install plastic sails capable of catching the solar wind and sailing home if the conventional fuel gave out! It was with some difficulty that MacLeod had been able to convince the Admiralty that while the idea might conceivably be technically feasible it could only work if the men aboard carried a thirty-year supply of food!

Then there had been more subtle problems. How much should be included aboard each ship in the way of PX supplies? What number of men would be a minimum for round-the-clock operation of the fleet over an extended period of time? How many microfilmed books and how many cassette projectors? Assume a crew of six for one of the new scouts; how long could those six be expected to remain in isolation before relief became necessary? How many tours could a single crew be expected to make before rotation back to Earth became necessary? And these were only a few of the problems.

MacLeod, Logan and Duncan had won most of their arguments so far as armament was concerned. The cruisers had a double pair of torpedo launchers added to their "chin blisters" to allow for lengthy stern chases. Two additional mine-laying ports graced each flank. Six additional 37 mm and two more 90 mm machine rockets had been placed in the bow turrets.

A new note jarred Duncan back to the present as the Seaforths rounded the pivot and their pipers struck up "Caber Feidh." The wind was picking up by the moment and fine droplets were beginning to lash across the open field. A trace of sleet stung the faces of the regiments and commenced freezing against the woolens. Still the marchers kept their even pace and still the reviewers stood immobile in defiance of the elements.

Casting a covert eye at the men of his First Fleet Battle Group, Duncan felt a surge of pride. Not a man had moved. Not an arm or a face had flinched before the blowing sleet and rain. A year ago these men had been civilians, untutored in the rites of war, but withal Scotsmen. Today they were still inexperienced; but they were soldiers!

The Camerons were passing before him now, their regimental colors dipping in salute, the distinctive Erracht plaid glittering beneath a thin sheen of ice crystals which was thickening by the minute.

Returning the salute automatically, Duncan debated the merits of the battle scout in his mind. Admittedly they were only a modification of the old utility craft and were capable of being operated by a single man, but he still felt a crew of four was inadequate. There should be at least five, preferably six. Of course there was the ever-present problem of logistics, and the problem of training new personnel was a real headache. Is it better to train six men, put them into one ship and get optimal efficiency, or to put them into two ships and get 50 percent efficiency for twice the length of time until their on-ship food supplies are exhausted? The compromise took twelve men and put them into three ships. Right or wrong, they had to live with it now.

But if the personnel problem was a source of worry the armament was a thing of joy. Forty 37 mm guns and four 90s gave the battle scouts a firepower not significantly inferior to that of the cruisers. The addition of two mine-laying ports and a magazine of some sixty mines and thirty special detector devices placed in mine casings made them true scouting vessels. They would be effective fighting craft, no doubt of that.

Now the Cameronians swung about and their pipes struck up "MacLeod's Praise" in honor of Duncan's commander. The leading files of the Seaforths were coming up on the stand, their uniforms aglitter under an increasing burden of frosted sleet. The dun-grey sky was perceptibly darkening and the rising wind lent an eerie echo to the keening of the pipes. Still the marching files continued relentlessly on their way, and still the departing troops stood motionless at attention, damning the elements to do their worst.

The trial runs had given Duncan a few precious days to work with each of his crews and he had made the most of it. These ships were made for space, and once departed from Earth's atmosphere it was unlikely they would ever return. They'd never get much closer than the moon and special shuttles would carry crews and equipment back and forth. But it was still possible to complete many of the initial trial runs right here on Earth. After all, as one imaginative engineer had pointed out, spaceships are supposed to be airtight—and that also means watertight.

Launched into the water like some old-style submarine, his ships opened their water intakes and maneuvered out to blue water on their steam jets. Speed runs, deep dives to five hundred feet and erratic simulated evasive maneuvers proved the hulls and guidance mechanisms fully as well as any deep-space test runs. Preprogrammed tapes checked out the computers for magnetic bias or malfunctioning while mock battles, employing special frangible ammunition against towed targets, tested combat capabilities.

A month of such operations completed the trial runs and gave Duncan at least a limited ability to weld his fleet into the semblance of a fighting unit. Much was left to be done, but at least a start had been made.

With an inward sigh of relief Duncan heard the strains of "The Gordons' March" keening shrilly above the steadily mounting gale. The Gordons were the last of the regiments stationed at Scapa Flow. All other units were either at Clydebank or Perth. The driving sleet had peeled his face raw and he knew the others in his command were in no better shape. Another half hour and it would be over.

The snow was beginning to drift up against the feet and exposed legs of the motionless troops by now. Dimly Duncan was aware of a numbness in his own feet and realized the same must be happening to him. Stolidly he resisted the temptation to shift stance and try to brush the snow away. He was glad there was nothing in the ceremony to require a smile. He was certain his face would split wide open if he tried. This was one time he almost wished he were in the American Army. Their commanders stood in glass-encased, specially heated reviewing stands for such purposes. Their troops might freeze, but *they* would be comfortable! No, he really didn't wish it; but it was something to laugh about, a momentary way of forgetting his own misery.

Surprisingly, he felt the ice on his sleeve cracking as he raised his hand for the final salute. It must have crusted a quarter inch between the time he returned the Cameronian salute and now. That meant it would be perhaps a half-inch thick on the motionless troops to either side.

The final element of the Gordons passed and now the infantry battalion to his left shuddered into frosty life as the field commander wheeled them around behind the receding Gordons. It was almost over.

The First Battalion passed, and now the fleet units slid in behind with practiced precision. A distant pipe band took up "The Thistle" and suddenly Duncan, Logan and MacLeod were alone on the empty field. The review was over. The departing troops were on their way either to embarcation or to their barracks.

"Foosh! One more review like that and I'll apply for permanent duty on Pluto, where I can at least be warm!" exploded Logan decisively as the three lurched, half frozen, toward the administration building for their final briefing before leaving Earth.

"Aye," agreed MacLeod fervently as he gingerly rubbed at his frostbitten face. "'Tis my opinion we could have done without so much review. But at least the following units won't have it so bad. When the Black Watch goes out next month they'll have only a single battalion of the Argylls to pipe them off. The Camerons will have it easier yet."

"Mayhap," countered Duncan pessimistically, "but 'twill be later in the winter."

"Ah well, 'twill soon be over with at any rate," sighed MacLeod philosophically. "We should be able to relax for a few hours after lift-off."

"We'll be lucky if we get that much all the way out to wherever we're bound," rejoined Logan. "We've got work to do getting the command in some sort of order. My men are so raw 'tis pitiful."

"Aye," agreed MacLeod, "but neither of ye have half the troubles I do. Ye've got all the combat ships whilst I get an odd assortment of cargo craft, utility ships, transports for the infantry and base personnel, basing equipage fitted with jury rockets to be hauled out pickaback on utility ships plus a four-hundred-woman contingent of auxiliaries. Many of those ships I've never even seen yet. Getting them to work together will be no lark for sure."

Seating themselves in the auditorium, the three gratefully accepted the proffered dollop and waited in company with a dozen or more senior officers from the other regiments.

Evidently they were the last arrivals, for as soon as they were seated the curtains parted and Gordon MacLintock strode to the lectern.

"Gentlemen," he announced after the group had come to order, "over these past several months there has been scant time for small talk or reflection. We've all been too busy with immediate problems to deal in conferences and such like. But now that the first elements of you are about to depart it's fitting you know as much about the overall situation as I have to tell.

"Whilst you've been working to build ships and organize your units, other agencies have been working in other areas." Turning directly to MacLeod, MacLintock hesitated momentarily, then continued. "General MacLeod, your force of Argylls is to be designated Task Force Lupus and will be based directly on the planet Pluto. Details of your orders will be released to you as you leave here.

"And now, for the benefit of all present, I must point out that we expect Task Force Lupus to bear the brunt of the anticipated alien assault. The High Command feels the original assault on Pluto was largely accidental. An enemy approaching from the opposite quadrant would never even notice Pluto since it would be some six thousand million miles distant and on the opposite side of the sun. And even had they broken out of their space drive just thirty or forty degrees on either side of her 'twould be highly unlikely they would have altered course simply to investigate a frozen ball of ice and metal far off on their flank. To the High Command's way of thinking this indicates the enemy must have broken out of their hyperdrive somewhere in the immediate vicinity of Pluto, detected the base on their electromagnetic devices and attacked.

" 'Tis this assumption which governs our present actions. Since we lack the power to be strong at all points about the periphery of the solar system we must either elect to be weak at all points or try to be strong where we think we are most vulnerable. We have chosen the latter."

"May I ask a question?" interrupted one of the officers from the Black Watch.

"Of course, General. I expect all of you to feel free to interrupt at any time. I'm here to clear up any questions I can."

"I accept what you say concerning the origins of the aliens," noted the other, "but wouldn't that make it more likely they will elect to attack from some other point—say at ninety degrees' difference? And wouldn't that make it advisable for us to concentrate our forces closer in?"

"A good point, sir. To answer your second question first, the High Command had initially planned to hold the fleet in close, based on precisely that line of reasoning. But this was a bit of a dilemma. We are convinced the defence of Earth must be based as far from Earth as possible, but until our xenologists were able to agree on the direction of the assault we had no choice but close-in defence.

"The danger of close defence, of course, is the almost certain probability of individual enemy ships slipping through to bombard Earth with celaenium warheads. When you consider that two dozen of the twenty kilomegaton torpedoes would obliterate an entire continent and two hundred would wipe out Earth, this would mean that if only four ships slipped through during a general battle Earth would be so crippled it would take a half century to recover—a half century we obviously lack.

"The solution, then, becomes obvious. Keep the foe as far from Earth as possible. Break up his formations at a distance and then destroy any individual ships which might slip through the main line of resistance.

"But to do this we first had to have a clear line of probability concerning the enemy intentions. And 'tis here the xenologists have come to our aid. To recapitulate their thinking, they concede they may be wrong, but as a whole they are confident the aliens have received a terrific psychological shock. The analysis of the movements of the alien fleet during the battle of Pluto suggests the aliens began with a pattern of downright contempt for anything Earth might be able to do.

"Their fleet of twenty-three ships lazed about until the last moment before blasting off to destroy MacLeod's three ships. When they attacked it was headlong and arrogant. But instead of an easy victory they suffered a humiliating defeat. In a trifle over four minutes their proud fleet was a broken shambles running for deep space with its tail atwixt its legs and the Earth flotilla was untouched.

"Looking at it from their standpoint, at least one of the Earth ships should have been destroyed. Colonel Campbell's ship took two hits but went right on fighting without even a pause. At odds of close to eight to one in their favor, and with the added advantage of surprise working for them, they were not even able to damage the enemy!

"When the xenologists coupled this with the aliens' headlong attack on the Pluto Base without even attempting to establish peaceful communications they arrived at a disturbing picture. As they see it, the alien must be assumed to be a strongly aggressive, arrogant and militant race. Without such a personality it is not likely any species will ever push far enough even to get into space to begin with. Lacking aggression a species is foredoomed to a stone-age technology. In short, the alien is assumed to be psychologically similar to humans, but with the probable difference that he has evidently had a single unified government for perhaps many centuries and has gotten out of the habit of fighting amongst himself and has forgotten how to tolerate difference. We are not like him; therefore we must be destroyed! That is how he sees us—or any other race for that matter.

"Given this sort of psychological profile, which may not be correct but is the best we can do with the data at hand, it then becomes overwhelmingly probable the alien will analyze the battle of Pluto in order to learn as much from it as possible. Presumably he will increase the burst power of his missiles—a factor which may be giving mankind an additional time margin, since it would mean they must redesign their warheads and scrap their existing munitions. We can also be reasonably certain they will either scrap or drastically modify their existing computer systems. Most likely they will come up with some sort of monte-carlo randomized battle computer of the sort we discarded a generation ago for the Brownian model. He will probably assume the monte-carlo is what we use since the two approaches have a number of superficial elements in common.

"He will not, however, scrap his existing fleet and construct new models with improved hull design and thickness. This will be a definite advantage for us. In analyzing proved hull fragments we have concluded that the proximity burst radius for our missiles can be increased by some twelve percent and still guarantee a kill. If the alien returns within the next ten years we will use the greater setting. After that we will presume he has had time to construct a new fleet to higher specifications. In either event your battle computers will be programmed to take this into account. If a longer burst radius proves ineffective the computer will automatically adjust all subsequent rounds to progressively shorter radii and broadcast the new data to all other ships.

"You gentlemen can easily visualize the results," MacLintock continued with a smile. "With anything less than five-to-one odds in his favor the next battle will be a disaster for the aliens! He should suffer severe loss and retire to lick his wounds and prepare for the next round.

"But this brings us to the crux of the matter. We are already looking ahead to the third battle! And here we have a problem which cannot be solved so easily. The aliens can choose their own time and place for an assault. They can be defeated a hundred times without suffering more than the loss of a number of machines and crews. A solitary defeat by humankind means our extermination—to the last man, woman and child! And, gentlemen," he added solemnly, "it's our responsibility to do everything within our power to prevent such a catastrophe if there is any way it can be done.

"So to finish the question, the xenologists agree the alien will probably go out of his way to attempt a fairly even crossing of swords in the next battle. He will deliberately seek battle and force it upon us as a proving ground to test his advances in weaponry and computers. Only when this fails will he set about using the advantage of his hypervelocity drive to force a victory. But that will be the third battle, not the one to come.

"In the third battle we see only defeat. He will most likely put his ships in one sector and start driving in. When we go to meet him he'll slip into his hyperdrive and come about to the other side of the system, leaving us six or seven weeks behind him. Two or three such feints and all of Earth's fleets will either be driven into the vicinity of Earth itself or be so scattered as to offer no effective resistance.

"But I do have one small point of good news for us, however. I'm certain you've all worried about the possibility of the enemy ships moving past you in hyperdrive and showing up betwixt you and the Earth. If so then I have a ray of hope from a couple of our theory types. Professors Limnovski and Hodges have recently come up with a few observations. They cannot give a rational means of creating a hyperdrive but they are reasonably certain 'tis based on gravitational principles. While I cannot hope to explain it myself, the gist is they have made a few studies of the Jovian gravity sink and some of their experiments suggest that aspects of gravity operate at velocities far in excess of light. From this they have concluded the use of a hyperdrive in the midst of a solar system or in close proximity to a sun—say much within the orbit of Pluto—would be highly dangerous. Gravitational stresses would throw any calculated trajectory off, and if the maneuver started within too close a range the ship would be caught in something the physicists choose to call an 'Einsteinian whirlpool,' whatever that might be, and be drawn into the sun.

"Of course, this is all speculation, but 'tis the best we have to go on. Until we have reason to modify these hypotheses, we will continue to assume they are accurate. Any questions?"

"Yes, sir," called an officer Duncan recognized as one of the newly attached technical physicists assigned to his command. "Isn't this Hodges the American who defected into Canada a few months ago?"

"I believe so. Why?"

"Well, perhaps he could give us some insight into the American thinking on the matter. Is this a general consensus among their physicists?"

"Regretfully, no. That was a primary factor behind his defection. The American Physical Society officially denies the possibility of a faster-than-light drive and claims either the whole attack was faked or we misinterpreted the evidence. Based on this supposition they have officially discouraged any sort of research or experimentation in the field, claiming it is merely a trick on our part to push them into diverting some of their best researchers off onto a wild-goose chase. About a dozen of their research physicists have left the country, but so far as the States themselves are concerned I fear we can anticipate no help there. Even if one of their people actually developed a complete theory for a hyperdrive he would be unable to get anyone to look at it and no one to publish it. Any further questions?"

"Aye, sir," called MacLeod, rising to his feet. "I realize we are the first to go out and so will necessarily be alone for a while. But what are the future plans concerning support and flanking forces? Are we simply to flit about Pluto by ourselves with no support nearer than the asteroids? Secondly, have the xenologists any idea of the strength with which the aliens will be apt to return? Finally, have they any idea *when* they will return?"

"Answering your last question first, General, no, we have no idea when they will return. We have no idea of the velocity of their hyperdrive and we lack any data telling us how far his base is from Earth. Finally, as if that weren't enough, we don't know his reaction time. So that portion of your question must be left unanswered.

"Your second question, regarding the strength of the aliens, is susceptible of a lower limit. The nature of the alien attack on Pluto suggests they may have had earlier experience in obliterating ground-based targets. The fact they popped out and attacked our base without warning argues that they have a planetary culture and government. Had the situation been reversed, for example, and any of our blocs come across an alien installation of that type, some attempt at peaceful contact would be made—if only because of the possibility the aliens might have some weapons capable of being turned against the other blocs.

"From these facts the xenologists conclude, first, that the alien probably possesses a number of star systems; second, that they have encountered and obliterated other intelligent races; and third, that with this sort of development behind them they probably would not commit more than a relatively small fraction of their total forces against a neighboring star system. Consequently, the twenty-three ships off Pluto most likely represented no more than five percent of their total military strength and most probably represents about one percent. And if this estimate is correct they will be able to throw between five hundred and twenty-five hundred ships against us in the next battle. 'Tis speculative but not unreasonable. That's all I can say for it.

"And now to answer your final question," continued MacLintock. "As soon as it's ready Task Force Corvus will be dispatched to your left flank. It's already organizing at Clydebank and should depart Earth within two months. 'Twill consist of the Caledonians and will be based on the outermost moon of Uranus. Your right flank will be secured by some old friends of ours, the Poona Highlanders of India. The first elements have already moved out and are designated Task Force Aquila. They're to be based on Titan, off Saturn.

"If Lupus is broken the remaining units are to retire and fall back to the vicinity of the orbit of Jupiter and make a stand there while additional forces are mustered. If given time we expect to have nine regiments posted to the general area, with six others forming an inner-defence core around the asteroid belt. The total strength will approximate four hundred fifty combat craft of all types.

"For the moment, however, we are not contemplating the establishment of a ready reserve force. For one thing, we lack the ships if we're also going to man our forward lines. For another, we're using the fleets of America, Russia, Europe and China for the purpose. Whether they know it or not they're dancing to the UN tune and we're making full use of them for our backup reserves. As soon as you move out each of these blocs will feel itself compelled to move out strong observation forces disguised as 'training operations' or whatever. Since each group suspects the others as well as the UN they'll all be unwilling to launch exploratory attacks and can be counted on to stay within mutual detection range.

"Considering you'll have three regiments out in the general Lupus sector within the next three to four months, your combined forces should be fairly close to a hundred and twenty warcraft of all types. Add three hundred and sixty more from the other blocs as an estimate and we arrive at a total of four hundred eighty available combat vessels to withstand an attack coming from the direction of Pluto—a respectable combat force.

"Given an additional six months' preparation, the combined Earth fleets will total more than eight hundred, and if a year after that is allowed it ought to run to nearly thirteen hundred cruisers and over five thousand scouts, or nearly sixty-three hundred fighting ships. Provided the quality of the men and training can match the quantity of ships, the aggregate force should be more than adequate for a pitched battle in any sector—always providing one or another of the blocs doesn't get tired of waiting and decide to start its own war with us. Now . . . does that answer your question, sir?"

"Aye. Very adequately," nodded MacLeod.

"Good. Then if there are no further questions I shall adjourn the conference and say my personal adieus to the men of Task Force Lupus. They have a lonely job afore them. A wee deoch an' doris would be quite in order afore they gang awa'."

CHAPTER 7

The outbound journey was almost casual. No effort was made to build up to speed. Instead, each ship was put through its paces with maximum-effort battle-evasion maneuvers. Welded seams popped, bulbs and gauges shattered. Aboard *Gules* a man was killed when his strap couch tore loose from its moorings. A subattachment computer wrenched loose in one of the scout ships and half demolished the main computer before shattering against a bulkhead. Electricians and repair crews kept busy tinkering with miscellaneous bugs and weaknesses which kept cropping up. But eventually the wrinkles were ironed out and the bugs eliminated. Crew efficiency grew apace as the men came to know their ships and gained confidence in their ability to handle problems.

Within weeks the alert-response time was cut from the original forty-five seconds down to a scant ten seconds as the crews learned to hit their restraint couches and emergency wall safety hatches the instant an alarm sounded. There were occasional sprains and bruises, and even a couple of broken bones, but they learned.

Passing Neptune's orbit, Task Force Lupus began its deployment to full combat dispersion. A section of scouts was detached from each battle group and assigned to MacLeod as a special reserve. From now on each battle group would consist of three cruisers and nine scouts, with the Pluto main base commanding a force of six scouts plus whatever utility ships happened to be in the vicinity. Duncan's flotilla moved wide to the left and high while Logan's force moved low and right.

The utility ships, together with the tankers and supply craft, remained at fleet center with MacLeod.

More days passed as the ships closed leisurely on Pluto. No attempt at speed here; there simply wasn't time for it. More urgent was the task of welding the by now reasonably efficient individual crews into an effective combat group. By the time the central support group commenced its intensive deceleration for landing on Pluto, Duncan's command was at least beginning to approach the desired level of efficiency. What remained to be done could be accomplished during the next few weeks while the two combat groups cruised to cover the construction crews at work on the planet.

A week passed. Two. By the end of the third week the primary defence installations on Pluto were far enough advanced for the two groups to depart for their respective duty stations. A final conference was called and within hours Logan's flagship, *Vert*, and Duncan's *Argent* commenced their descent onto the jagged surface of Pluto.

To Duncan the contrast was striking. Scarcely eighteen months ago, as a freshman major commanding a utility ship, he had made the same approach to a desolate planet drifting in lonely orbit along the fringes of the solar system. Today he approached it as a colonel commanding a powerful fleet. The planet was no longer desolate. Radio beacons provided invisible guidance. Infrared orbiting buoys channeled traffic in two separate spirals in order to expedite arriving and departing traffic. A broad plain had been created for the moorage of dozens of ships. Pinpoints of light speckled the forbidding surface as they delineated areas of work in progress. And finally, over three thousand of his fellow humans were busy converting the barren cinder into human habitation.

A brief, last-minute discussion of plans, an informal dinner, a final toast, then departure. First Logan, then Duncan lifted skyward on blazes of fiery light. For a few seconds the flaming luminescence of the jets cast eerie shadows across the tumbled landscape of ever-dark Pluto. Then they were gone.

Duncan, aboard *Argent*, remained in the center of his flotilla with *Azure* and *Gules* to either flank. Three scouts were detached on wide-ranging detector-laying operations which would take a full month to complete. They would cover the whole of his sector high, low and wide at a distance more than twice the normal detection range. A fourth scout was sent straight out in the direction of Lupus, almost a third of the way out to the planet Styx. It was to make an even wider sweep of his front and drop off special detectors dreamed up by some of the physics people back on Earth. The line would have more holes than a Swiss cheese, but if time permitted the holes would be plugged, one by one. But in the meanwhile they might with luck give a crucial few minutes' warning.

The remaining five scouts were moved out, one on either flank and two between the cruisers, with the fifth deployed somewhat farther out than the rest of the flotilla. And now came the hard part: waiting. Just waiting.

First the flotilla would form a line moving slowly to the right of center and moving away from Pluto. After four or five days the ships would end over and cruise slowly back toward Pluto. Always they maintained a constant 0.4-g acceleration to preserve a sense of weight.

Three weeks. A utility ship caught up with the flotilla bringing replacement fuel reels and mail from home. Three more weeks. A second utility ship brought in more fuel and more mail. By the end of the seventh week the air regenerator aboard *Gules* started to go bad and she had to be pulled off the line and sent back to Pluto. The advance scout was moved back into her slot. When the three long-range scouts returned from their detector-laying mission, one was sent to Pluto for a week's rest and refitting while the other two relieved scouts on the line for their turn on Pluto.

Of his fifteen ships only seven were available for immediate combat operations. Three were permanently detached to MacLeod; the remainder were either in ordinary for repairs or on relief at Pluto. There was no other choice. For all anyone really knew the aliens might never return. Or they might return tomorrow. Or it might just as easily be ten years. Some system of regular relief was essential if the crews were not to go mad waiting.

Two weeks later *Gules* returned to station with the three scouts as escort. The long-range scout was due back within the next two days, so rotation was postponed until it returned. When the flotilla was reunited one of the newly returned scouts was posted for a second long-range detector-laying hyperbola and the returned scout rotated back to Pluto along with two other scouts.

By the end of the fourth month every ship of the line save Duncan's own *Argent* had been relieved at least once. The long-range detector system was essentially complete. There were still gaps for ships to slip through, provided they knew the system. But for a fleet not in hyperdrive to succeed would be difficult if not impossible. Of course, no one even knew if the detectors would work on ships in hyperdrive, so there was a large element of uncertainty. But it was the only game in town, so they played.

Duncan had planned to transfer his pennant to *Azure* and send *Ar-*

gent back for relief when the order came from MacLeod for him to return in person. Leaving Major Grierson of *Azure* as second, *Argent* pulled out of line and began the week-long trip to Pluto.

The planet was a surprise. Tunneling had progressed nearly thirty miles into the interior. The main administration building and complex were absolutely spacious. Located eight miles underground, it was nearly a quarter mile in diameter and arched upward over seven hundred feet. Fluorescent lighting cleverly concealed in the peak of the dome gave a realistic illusion of daylight, and in the evening, as "sunlight" faded, smaller lights resembling stars speckled the ceiling. All offices were built into the walls of the cavern, so to all intents and purposes the dome resembled a vast office building with a spacious outdoor mall in the middle. To someone who had lived cramped in a single ship for four months it was the next best thing to being back on Earth.

The population on Pluto had passed seven thousand and was steadily climbing as manufacturing equipment and berthing facilities and general repair shops were added, and every arriving ship brought in its quota of maintenance and support personnel. Even food was being taken care of locally. In other tunnels, working under artificial light and using minerals and water extracted from the surrounding rock, a hydroponics plant was turning out fresh vegetables in quantities adequate for a population twice as great. A future ship from Earth was scheduled to bring in a small stock of cattle and sheep in an effort to build up a regular meat and dairy supply. Plans were even afoot to bring in a few swarms of bees and ants to help in fertilization and mulching of soil. Earthworms had already been introduced and self-taught ecologists were busy debating the types and varieties of flora and fauna needed to complete the self-sustaining cycle.

Wonderingly, Duncan shook his head. All this in only six months—and most of it in the mere four months since he had departed to station.

MacLeod greeted him personally as he entered the administration building. "Duncan, lad," he exclaimed, "how does it feel to be back in civilization again?"

Grinning, Duncan pumped the proffered hand then gazed about bemused. "Gregory, I ha' to admit ye've done a job on Pluto. I'd never ha' believed it possible, especially after the way she looked when I first landed on her."

"Come on to my office and we'll bend an elbow while you give me a report on operations. I suspect I already know what you'll be saying, but I want to hear it from you anyhow."

"Well, Gregory," Duncan started as he closed the door behind him and accepted the proffered dollop, "I don't rightly know how to start so

I'll just bull my way into it. 'Tis a boring job—no mistake about it. As I see it, one more tour around the relief roster and morale and efficiency will start down. Mind ye, I've got good men—damn good men—the very best mayhap; but neither they nor anyone else can take too much o' dreary patrol out at the edge o' nowhere wi'out losing their edge. And as I see it, 'tis perhaps four months away. But 'tis there; no doubt about it."

"As I figured," nodded MacLeod soberly. "I had Logan in last week and he said much the same. So now the question is, what can we do? Ye, Logan and I well know there's a war on. But how our lads on patrol feel about it is another matter. They've no personal experience with the war. To them 'tis only an abstract thing without any reality to back it up."

"Right!" chimed in Duncan. "I've already heard grumbling that the aliens will never dare come back after the trouncing they got the last time. The men feel 'tis a waste of time. And if enough o' them come to feel that we'll be forced to pull in our horns and mayhap even see Earth destroyed simply because nobody chooses to perceive the truth."

"I fear you're right, Duncan," MacLeod frowned, eyeing his drink moodily. "But there's one ray of hope anyhow. I've heard rumor there may be a task-force relief in maybe a year. But we can't hope for it afore that—if even then. You think you can hold morale in your group steady that long?"

"Frankly, I doubt it. If I could return to station and say, 'I promise ye relief and rotation home in twelve months,' then I think I could. But if I go and say ' 'Tis a rumor, but ye may be relieved in a year or so,' 'twould actually make matters worse."

Sipping carefully of his drink, MacLeod considered the answer, then ventured, "If we could redeploy your patrols closer in we might allow more frequent relief on station, which would be a help. But unfortunately we cannot do that either. We need you as far out on screen as possible if we're to have time to muster strength when the aliens return. So as matters stand we'll have to continue as is and hope morale doesn't sink too low. But damn it, lad, there must be a solution somewhere!"

"Well, I ha' one idea for an alternative," suggested Duncan. "I scarce think it has much chance o' approval, but looking at what ye've done here and thinking back to what we did on EOS, it seems to me we ought to be able to make better use o' the asteroid belt. After all, there's a good many chunks o' rock out there. Some o' them are the size of EOS or larger, but most o' them are about the same size or smaller. Now if we take a piece—say, ten or twelve miles in diameter—and tunnel it out like Pluto here, we could easily make a population of several thousand entirely self-supporting. Each would ha' its own manufacturing capability and food supply. We've done it here, so why not there? Then if we also tunneled and sleeved it wi' rocket tubes we could make the whole damned asteroid a spaceship."

" 'Twouldn't be very maneuverable, now would it. And it'd have to have some hemongous big rockets or we'd spend centuries just getting it into position."

"Not necessary," Duncan considered. "The rockets would ha' to be large; no doubt o' that. But 'twould be technically possible. In addition, if we installed a celaenium-manufacturing operation aboard we could use the magnetic flux eddies to work on the general galactic magnetic field. Betwixt the two we ought to be able to generate a pretty respectable acceleration and maintain it wi' a minimum o' effort. She'd be slow in starting and slow in stopping, but wi' mayhap five miles o' rock overhead in the bow section, so to speak, she'd plow right through any small space debris and still ha' enough maneuverability to miss the major chunks.

"Now if we just put it out on station supporting our flotillas we could solve a raft o' problems. For instance, we're only averaging three-quarter strength on station, not counting the ships ye took for central support. In effect, we've nine ships instead o' twelve or fifteen. Wi' an asteroid immediately behind us we'd ha' the full force ready for action wi'in minutes—wi' the asteroid being a stationary fortress for support. Then if we put the families o' the men aboard to handle much o' the routine work we'd just about crack the whole morale problem. The families would be 'home' out here and probably safer than they'd be on Earth."

" 'Tis a first-rate idea," MacLeod nodded. "I can kick myself for not having thought of it myself." Then, changing the subject abruptly, "Have you stopped to consider the consequences if the aliens breach our defences?"

"Not strongly," Duncan conceded. "I've thought of it, but apart from being here there's naught I can do about it, so I've put it out o' mind."

"Then think now. To date we've made no real effort to make Pluto self-supporting. There are no plans for developing a celaenium-manufacturing capability, no plans for being able to construct our own spacecraft or munitions and only limited projections for growing our own food. These are poor tactics. From a purely military standpoint it means we're tying up vessels which could otherwise be used for combat and employing them to maintain a three-billion-mile-long supply line.

Elimination or reduction of that would increase our combat capabilities by fifty percent and mayhap even double it.

"And besides that," he continued didactically, "suppose the aliens break through and blanket Earth with radioactivity. We'd be gone. Our military might would probaby be almost the same out here but the human race would be dead. 'Twould just take longer to finish off. We'd be gradually growing older and none coming up to replace us. But bringing up the families and converting the asteroids to make them self-sufficient would force the alien to settle down and root us out one by one—and I don't think he can manage that."

"I hear you," nodded Duncan. "But now that we've got the idea what do we do wi' it? Nobody will listen anyhow. The UN bureaucracy may not be as mindless as some o' the others but 'tis still a bureaucracy. Besides, they're probably too busy recruiting manpower and building conventional ships to gi' much thought to this proposal."

"Mayhap not," grunted MacLeod. "If 'twere put in the right way I think they'd go for it. . . . Say you were simply suggesting the idea of converting a small asteroid to be used as base-level support. The logistics angle, for instance, would be a good point. The present system is already intolerable, and the UN Command knows it.

"This means if the matter is presented in a strictly military context as a way to provide close-in support for individual battle groups they'll be apt to buy it. Then afore the asteroids are pulled out of orbit we could point out that complete self-sufficiency would release cargo vessels for conversion to military operations. That would appeal to any high command, no matter how blind. Then when we suggest 'twould ease the personnel rotation problem if the families of the men were brought out and stationed with them we'd have a bunch of happy bureaucrats and a satisfied High Command."

"Ye really think they'd buy it?" snorted Duncan doubtfully.

"They might. Afore you return to station I want you to write the whole thing up as an official recommendation. I'll affix my comments and add a first endorsement together with an urgent recommendation the matter be expedited and then forward it on to Menzies. I know he'll approve it. After that 'tis in the laps of the gods."

"Which means they'll get around to thinking about it in mayhap ten years," added Duncan skeptically.

"Not this time, lad. What the bureaucrats do is out of our hands, but the High Command is definitely worried. They had a near-mutiny in Task Force Phoenix last month. Of course, that's an Irish outfit so we can't expect much of it, but to be blunt not even the clans can hold up indefinitely. Ultimately we'll need either a battle or a radical solution—and the faster a solution can be put out to the men the better the effect on morale. You get to work on your idea and I'll see to it they go out on the next ship back."

"I'll see to it," replied Duncan, rising.

"Good. I'll expect it afore you leave. In the meanwhile have whatever fun you can. As you go, ask my secretary for a chart of the underground installations. We've a lot of tunnels down here and we've not even been trying very hard. Some of them may surprise you."

"Thanks much, Gregory. But if your secretary's the bonnie lass I saw on the way in here, I might just ask her for a guided tour."

"Find your own secretary, Duncan. I saw mine first."

"Now don't ye go pulling rank," grinned Duncan as he felt for the door. "Wi' the lassies it doesn't work—and ye're a married man to boot. Besides, I don't ha' to wear my kilt long to cover a pair o' knobby knees."

Throwing a mock salute at the grinning MacLeod, Duncan slipped out to track down the secretary.

He enjoyed his week on Pluto.

CHAPTER 8

Deep in the reaches of space, a billion miles beyond Pluto, a solitary metal cannister drifted idly in slow orbit about the sun. Inside the cannister was a maze of printed circuitry: detection devices the theoreticians hoped would be able to record the passage of vessels in hyperdrive—devices which might or might not work.

Somewhere in the space around the cannister there was a momentary straining, a brief breeze of nothingness, a disturbance. The cryogenic magnet inside stirred, then relaxed. A microscopic iron filing embedded in liquid helium sluggishly tried to realign itself with the breeze. The perpetually constant eddy current within the toroidal magnetic field flickered, momentarily inconstant. A relay flipped an explosive charge which ruptured a vial of special acid contained inside a specially insulated section of the cannister. Draining onto a zinc plate, it generated an electric current to a transmitter. The SHF transmitter responded nobly, sending its message winging back to Pluto at the speed of light.

It was never noticed.

To span a billion miles at the speed of light takes about eighty-five minutes. To a ship traveling in hyperdrive the same distance can be covered in something like two and a half minutes.

Aboard every ship in Duncan's flotilla alarm klaxons blared. Men on bunk duty barely had time to gasp as the restraining bands caught them tightly in their embrace. Willy-nilly they were carried into the battle but were never part of it. Their more fortunate companions who happened to be on duty when the alarms went off leaped for their couches and stations.

Aboard *Argent* a toggle switch was flipped and a carrier wave set out on a twofold journey back to Earth and Pluto. It was simple and straightforward; "Q-Q-Q," "Q-Q-Q." That was all. Translated, it said "Battle joined."

Aboard the scouts and other cruisers only a single alarm sounded. Aboard *Argent* a dozen alarms were sounding, each representing the tripping of a specific detector in the inner ring, the one a scant twelve light minutes beyond them.

Inside Duncan's cabin, repeater screens on the ceiling sprang to life. Lights dimmed and were replaced by a red glow from the various controls as they slid out of their recesses. His strap bunk slid automatically to the center of his cabin as emergency override controls slipped from concealed niches inside. A pair of microphones extended from the headrest to nestle by his mouth and a compound computer instructor moved out from the other side of the bunk and fitted itself deftly under his fingers.

Now the central screens came to life as the first of the approaching fleet swam into detector range. Dozens of tiny red fireflies danced onto the outer ring. The dozens multiplied themselves into a hundred, and the hundred into more and more hundreds.

"Damn it anyhow," Duncan muttered to no one in particular, "We always seem to forget something. . . . There should be an automatic counter here so I can tell how many there really are. . . . No matter, though; there's enough."

Looking over at his own small fleet showing green on the screens Duncan laughed hopelessly. It was silly. The last time he was one against seven. After more than two years of preparation it was now nine against perhaps a thousand or more.

No matter if there were hundreds of ships behind him—ships which would ultimately be brought into action. The simple, obvious fact remained that he was worse off now than he was the first time.

Fingering his computer input console, he relayed his orders directly into the battle computers aboard the various ships. The crews would never have time to handle their own data input during the battle, but the computers could be given orders to make good a relative position even while engaged in full combat maneuvers.

Thinking rapidly, Duncan first contemplated setting up an orthodox defensive formation with the six scouts to the van and the three cruisers lagging behind in support. "Hell no," he grunted. " 'Twouldn't even delay matters. We might take out a few dozen, but wi' their relative velocity toward us it's a drop in the bucket. . . . At least mayhap I can gi' them something to worry about—three cruisers to the van and six scouts to the rear. Their screens won't tell them which is what so they may be just a mite surprised at the amount o' lead we throw out. . . . Better yet—cruisers to the attack. Scouts to defend whilst falling back on Pluto."

With a barely felt ancestral thrill of battle joined against overwhelming odds, Duncan stabbed instructions into the computer. The last time it was three ships against twenty-three. Now it was going to be three against a thousand. But at least it might confuse the enemy a bit.

If he attacked with his entire flotilla the aliens might feel the Earth squadron was stupid, suicidal or just plain desperate—possibly a combination of all three. But to have only three ships move in to the attack while the others stood back might just strike the enemy commander as a gesture of supreme contempt. Conceivably it might provoke him into an error of judgment later, when he came up against Earth's main fleet.

Triggering his microphone as *Argent* commenced her wild plunge toward the enemy, he called back to the scouts. "Wallace is assigned command o' the scout element wi' instructions to maintain resistance whilst falling back upon Pluto to support them there. Under no circumstances attempt to support our present assault with the cruiser contingent. Good luck and good hunting, gentlemen."

By now *Argent* and the other two cruisers were picking up momentum. With each passing second under their crushing 6 g acceleration they added more miles per second to their already considerable speed. In from two to three minutes the two fleets, if by any stretch of imagination his three ships could be called a fleet, would be closing to within firing range.

Stabbing at his console, he coded additional instructions into the cruisers. Aboard all three vessels mine-laying ports opened and dozens of mines were squirted out atop small rockets. Automatically arming themselves after five seconds, they carried heavy JATO units capable of hurtling them into a screaming 35 g acceleration into any ship passing within 750 miles. One or two might succeed in picking off enemy ships.

Another set of instructions sent out their full complement of on-line torpedoes, each carrying precoded instructions to track down and destroy any massive flying object not responding properly to its automatic interrogation signal.

A few seconds later the first of the enemy ships swam over the combat range marker on the screens. Instantly *Argent* danced off to one side, gyrated downward, then spun upward and over to the other side. Now it was slammed up at 10 g's, leveled, stopped, spun up, then down, and down and down some more. Bottoming, it rocketed up, halted abruptly, slipped off into a spiraling corkscrew and recovered just in time to commence an end-over at maximum acceleration. A faint popping noise was the solitary indication *Argent*'s own guns were firing.

Faint blips of speckled light zipped across the battle screen. The enemy fleet had begun to break formation as a few of their ships commenced evasive maneuvers of their own. The computer analyzers aboard his ship commenced a steady clicking as they studied their data and broadcast it back to Pluto and Earth. No matter what happened to his three ships a full record would be available back home. Possibly it would help the remainder of the fleet plan more effectively.

Now the alien fleet was within easy range and the dance of *Argent* became even more frantic. It was a calypso-jitterbug-tarantella aboard a three-dimensional roller coaster with a crack-the-whip thrown in for good measure. Small blips on the screen suddenly enlarged and vanished. *Argent* was spinning like a top. There was neither up nor down nor sideways. There was no way to get set and brace against the overwhelming accelerations—nothing but the continuing, incessant jolting as the ship lurched through its evasive maneuvers. There was only the wrenching agony of accelerations in a dozen different directions.

A speck of green to the side of the screen flared and vanished. *Gules* was gone. Only two of them left now. A slam richocheted *Argent* up against nothing as she spun back with a long, continuous salvo.

More red blips expanded and vanished from the screens as the mines, torpedoes and guns of the cruisers took their toll of the aliens. But to Duncan it was all the same. Too numerous to count, the loss of one, a dozen or a hundred could make no impression on that fleet. What was important was the effect his unexpected charge was having on the enemy. Their flanks still swam serenely toward the sun, but the centre was a boiling mass of confusion. Some of the hostile ships were possibly even being destroyed by their own fire as numbers of the enemy seemed to be shooting at anything in sight; but it was still a drop in the bucket.

Two red blips vanished into destruction, then another. Then *Argent* spun wildly only to reel drunkenly a fraction of a second later from another near-miss. Duncan became vaguely aware of the air-loss alarm ringing wildly throughout the ship. Another slamming blow and more alarms sounded.

"Not long now," he muttered as he watched yet another enemy ship vanish. "Not long now."

Abruptly, virtually without warning, the screen was empty. No, not quite empty. There were still a few red dots showing along the periphery of the screen, and there was the green dot representing *Azure*. As Duncan watched numbly the remaining red blips slipped smoothly off the screen leaving only *Argent* and *Azure* in possession.

Momentarily Duncan thought they had fled back into hyperdrive. Then a glance at the aft screen told the reason. They had passed completely through the enemy forces. Going at full tilt the two fleets had no room for fundamental maneuvers except along a straight line. All the halts, pauses and other gyrations experienced during the combat were merely relative to his overall forward velocity. Now with each passing second the foe was falling further behind.

Even as he ordered *Argent* and *Azure* to reverse course and set about overtaking the enemy he saw several of their ships vanish from the screen as they were destroyed by the scouts, the mines and the torpedoes.

Keying the intercom, he raised damage control. "Campbell here," he ordered briskly, "What's our status?"

"Roger, Colonel," came the prompt reply. "Food lockers and galley broached with loss of four men. Aft control and computer room opened with one man lost. We'll have to use the battle computer for routine navigation till we can get things back together. Apart from that we have parties out assessing the extent of other damage now. Barring more enemies coming up, we should have a pretty good estimate of damage within the hour." There was a barely perceptible pause, then, "If I may say so sir, 'twas one hell of a fight."

"That it was, soldier," agreed Duncan wholeheartedly. "But I'd as lief not ha' too many more like it. The odds tend to get a wee bit short. . . . There's been good work aboard ship. I'm proud o' all o' ye."

Switching to radio, he beamed a message to MacLean. "*Argent* to *Azure*. . . . A good hunt. What is your present status?"

"Negative damage," replied MacLean casually. "How about you?"

"Holed twice and short five men. We've also lost some o' our kitchen facilities and the main navigational computer. I don't yet know how much o' this can be made good and we may ha' to call on ye for the transfer o' one or two men plus supplies and spare parts. We'll let ye know on that, but for now we ha' a job ahead o' us. I want a three g deceleration commencing in five minutes. 'Twill take at least a week to kill off our own speed and match that o' the enemy and about another week after that to catch up. If we can manage it we might be able to pull wi'in range o' the tailing elements o' their fleet about the time they're being intercepted by Aquila and Corvus. If so we may still be able to do considerable execution."

"Roger, Duncan," replied MacLean, "And by the by, I'd like to tender personal congratulations. The way you charged us straight through them was superb. I didn't think we had a chance at breaking through."

"I didn't either," Duncan answered. "'Twas no tactics at all—purely strategy. I figured to shake their commander loose a bit and mayhap disrupt their formation and take as many o' them wi' us as possible. But I didn't expect to break through to their rear. Break now whilst I raise Pluto and Earth. They'll be wanting to know what happened."

Switching over to SHF frequency, Duncan hailed Pluto. "UN *Argent* to UN Pluto. Stand by to receive transmission direct to General MacLeod. . . . Attacked by enemy fleet estimated in the vicinity o' one thousand craft. Velocity unknown. Should pass abeam Pluto at range of fifteen to twenty million miles. *Argent, Azure* and *Gules* attacked centre o' opposing fleet in effort to force them to break formation. *Argent* and *Azure* succeeded in breaking through to rear o' enemy fleet. *Gules* lost. *Argent* severely damaged but still combat operational at estimated ninety percent efficiency. *Argent* and *Azure* now killing velocity at three g's preparatory to overtaking enemy from rear. Estimated time to contact wi' trailing elements o' aliens approximately two weeks.

"Part two o' report: Scout force attached to group has been detached from my control and placed under command o' Captain Wallace with instructions to execute fighting retreat while falling back upon Pluto and to place themselves under your immediate command upon arriving at a mutual support point.

"Part three o' report: Impossible to assess damage to hostile fleet at this time. Mines, torpedoes and enemy cross fire probably inflicted some damage. Successes, if any, o' *Gules* unknown. Successes o' scouts unknown. From personal observation would suggest from twenty-five to thirty enemy vessels destroyed.

"Part four o' report: I should like to commend officially the personnel o' my command for the character shown in the recent battle. End o' report. Standing by for instructions. *Argent* out."

Fifty minutes later the radio crackled to life and Duncan heard MacLeod's voice. "Congratulations, *Argent*. Wallace had already informed me of your decision to attack. 'Twas brilliant. From his estimate the total number of kills attributable to your attack exceeds sixty. More important, the enemy still has not been able to regroup his centre and his ships appear to be jockeying about trying to get back into formation. 'Twill probably delay him twenty-four to forty-eight hours en route to Neptune's orbit. Now for your orders. Your pursuit plan approved. Three scouts from Corvus were engaged in long-range detector-laying work in your general direction. They've been given orders to overtake you and place themselves under your command. Instructions call for them to make good an acceleration at three point five g's and to contact you on channel nine to arrange rendezvous.

"I would also suggest you drift over toward Pluto as the enemy appears to be veering in this direction. I estimate he plans on striking here afore passing inward toward Earth. If we go under, any surviving ships have been directed to revert to your immediate command. Logan is already moving in and should arrive here well before the aliens. Any help you can give would be appreciated. Good luck and good hunting. Over."

"Three scouts indeed!" snorted Duncan. It would take at least two weeks before they could even hope to reach his present position unless they happened to be right at the sector boundary. And by that time he would be roughly eight days away. Allowing for a probable higher initial velocity and the fact they would be able to anticipate his route and cut corners, it still worked out to roughly three weeks before they could be put to use. Meanwhile there was nothing to do but repair damage and wait until they could build up enough speed to overtake the rear of the enemy fleet.

A week later, the now largely repaired *Argent* and the *Azure* surveyed the ruins of Pluto. The little planet had literally been blasted apart. MacLeod was dead. Logan was dead, along with the rest of his fleet. One scout, which had been out on long patrol, survived and joined the two cruisers just inside Pluto's orbit. A utility-class cargo-fighter had somehow managed to battle its way through the hostile fleet the same way Duncan's ships had, and it too linked up with the small fleet.

But the destruction of Pluto had delayed the enemy. Within a day or two Duncan figured he would be nipping at their heels. And within another two or three days after that it seemed possible the scout detachment from Corvus might join him.

An unexpected but very welcome accretion in strength occurred when the American observation fleet commander realized there really was an alien invasion fleet. He promptly radioed the information to Earth and placed himself at the disposal of the UN fleet commander, disregarding Hamilton's furious protests that the whole thing was obviously some sort of UN hoax.

As Duncan figured it, this meant there would be approximately 117 Allied ships confronting the invaders just outside Uranus's orbit. In addition, Duncan's contingent would probably number seven by that time—for a grand total of 124 spacecraft.

A playback of the battle tapes at the instant just before the first guns were fired showed a total of 1415 hostile vessels. Subtracting the sixty lost in the opening minutes of the fight and allowing for perhaps 150 destroyed by Logan's forces and the Pluto defences, this would leave the enemy a maximum of 1200 ships at his disposal. The odds were getting better—only about ten to one—and he hadn't even started adding in the ultimate Earth strength being massed in the vicinity of Jupiter's orbit. That would probably amount to another 150 UN ships alone. Add to those the known European, Russian and Chinese ships cruising in the vicinity of Jupiter and it seemed likely the alien would face a total of more than 500 ships before he could hope to break through to Earth. And with his tactics and equipment he'd never make it.

By the second day after passing Pluto, *Argent* had the enemy fleet in sight on the long-range screens. As soon as they fell within full view of the detectors, Duncan assigned a rating to count the total and relay it on to Earth. MacLeod had indeed made a fight of it! The enemy fleet had shrunk to 1073 vessels. Over 18 percent of his fleet destroyed and he hadn't even reached the main Earth defences yet.

Even as the revised total was being transmitted to the UN command, the enemy lost more ships.

A fleet commander does not halt a thousand ships to fight one or two. When *Argent* and *Azure* each released their remaining tracking torpedoes and between them destroyed eight of his ships, he did nothing. And when *Argent* plowed into a laggard trio of ships and destroyed all of them he still could do nothing. When *Azure* repeated the maneuver at the other flank he started closing up his ranks. When the scout and utility ship slipped up on a pair of laggards he merely closed ranks a little tighter.

Later the three scouts from Corvus decided to kill off a bit of excess velocity while ripping off a chunk of his flank guard. One of the scouts was lost but even more alien ships were destroyed. Still the enemy commander resolutely ignored the terriers on his flank and rear. Perhaps with over a thousand ships he felt he could afford to; either that or he didn't know how to fight that sort of battle.

No matter what, he obviously didn't know what to do about the fleets in front of him either. At the last instant both the Soviet and the European fleets acknowledged the danger and united with the UN Uranus fleet and the Americans. The Chinese, disappointingly, pulled out of the area and moved over to a flanking position where they would merely observe.

Fortunately they weren't really needed. Using tactical data supplied by Duncan, 196 fighting ships slammed into the foe in headlong assault. When they emerged to the other side the enemy was in shambles. Over 400 derelict hulks littered the space about Uranus's orbit. Fewer than 40 Earth ships were destroyed. And now the enemy was sandwiched between the Uranus fleet behind him and the Jupiter fleet ahead—only he didn't know it yet.

Perhaps he thought he had successfully penetrated Earth's final defences and was heading for pay dirt; possibly he had even sent a victory communiqué winging home. There were many possibilities.

But when he hove within detector range of the augmented Jupiter fleet of some 400 ships he panicked. Too close to the sun to use his hyperdrive, he was trapped. In desperation he evidently ordered a mass breakout.

Some of his ships climbed. Some descended. None could stand against the uncannily powerful Earth ships with their massive armor, their heavier broadsides and their far advanced battle computers. The Earth fleet had itself a turkey shoot. Of the 1400 odd ships which attacked Earth, fewer than 200 succeeded in reaching the orbit of Pluto to escape into hyperdrive.

CHAPTER 9

The gusting north wind blew icy particles of rain mixed with salt spray into his face and Duncan unconsciously squinted as he breathed deeply against the fresh sea air. In the distance a patch of deeper blue set against the blue-grey of the lowering overcast marked the rocky crags of the Isle of Skye.

For Brigadier Duncan Campbell this was no vacation. Gregory MacLeod had been his friend. Now was his bounden duty to pay respect to the family of his friend and see him piped to a warrior's grave on Skye, although his physical body was a mass of charred and unrecoverable atoms scattered somewhere along the orbit of Pluto.

A week earlier, in Perth, he had performed the same service for his fellow warrior Logan. After a brief stay in Edinburgh, with its bustling excitement, calls for speeches, continual recruitment of new troops and myriad military duties pressing on every hand, the lonely journey to Skye, accompanied only by his personal Campbell piper and the pipe major of the Argylls, was a boon to frayed nerves.

Duncan had been mildly surprised to find himself a hero. As the only man to have survived two battles with the invader he was unique. Besides this, the playback of the tapes of the last battle showed 39 confirmed kills plus 14 probables. Those, together with the 5 destroyed in the first battle, gave a firm total of 44 with a probable 58. The only other commander even close was MacLean of *Azure*, who tallied 35 firm and 11 probable for a total of 46.

Duncan's headlong assault on the alien fleet with but three cruisers had been hailed a stroke of genius. It was pointed out that not only had this resulted in the destruction of a number of ships which could not directly be credited to the cruisers but, more importantly, it had disrupted the fleet organization of the enemy and reduced its battle efficiency during the subsequent fighting. The alien was simply not prepared for the mechanics of fielding a combat fleet of such size, and once the initial formation was shattered the task of reorganization under fire was beyond him. And lastly, the success of Duncan's initial tactics had formed the basis for subsequent strategy in the fighting around Uranus and Jupiter.

Privately Duncan considered this arrant nonsense. In fact he had come to feel it was a criminal mistake on his part not to have ordered the scouts into the fray along with the cruisers. That way they might have had at least a fighting chance of breaking out. So while others were calling him a hero and brilliant strategist he was reproaching himself as a blunderer. Naturally, whenever he tried to explain he was accused of modesty—which only made matters worse.

By now the headland loomed starkly before him and there came a perceptible lessening of the choppy swells as the boat passed close under the lee shore. A darker mass, nestling beneath a cloud-girt mountain, resolved itself into an ancient manor. Beside it filtered into view the smaller shops and homes which clustered irregularly about the ancestral home of the MacLeods of Lewis.

The engine of the launch sputtered into reverse and the little craft sidled up to the rock jetty where a waiting attendant skillfully retrieved the cast and made them fast to the moorage.

Stepping ashore, clad in the dress regimentals and flanked by his pipers, Duncan slipped naturally into the formal Gaelic as he addressed the attendant, "Will the Mistress MacLeod receive The Campbell of Breadalbane?"

The attendant drew himself erect, and replying also in the Gaelic now spoken almost nowhere else than the Outer Isles, recited the ancient formula, already old when Bruce fought and the clans forgathered: "The Lady MacLeod of Lewis bids me greet The Campbell of Breadalbane and make him welcome as uncle, brother and son. She awaits his presence within the manor on this fair and unhappy occasion. If you will permit me to escort you the gillies will be down to retrieve your equipment anon." With the formalities completed he fell into step with Duncan as the pipers paced behind. Almost as on parade the four men marched to the Keep of MacLeod.

As they reached the vast double doors, servants on either side swung them wide and the Lady MacLeod, attired in formal mourning, advanced to greet him in the old Highland custom. "A greeting, Duncan Campbell of Breadalbane, from the house of The MacLeod of Lewis. Rest yourself at ease in the love of an honored friendship and consider all within the walls of Lewis your own. . . . And now," she continued, lapsing into informal English with a wan smile, "my personal greetings and thanks for your honor of my husband. He spoke often of you, and always highly. And he said he hoped our sons would be such as ye when they reached their maturity. And now may I introduce you to the rest of our family; or would you prefer to rest from the strain of your journey first?"

"Thank you, Lady MacLeod, but the trip was relaxing. I would thank ye for accommodations for my pipers, but for myself I am quite rested and would enjoy meeting wi' your family."

Turning to a servant, Lady MacLeod said, "Warren, will ye please show these gentlemen to the guest rooms prepared for them." And to the two pipers she added, "Gentlemen, my personal gratitude for your attendance on our sorrow. The requiem services are not for two days. Until then I wish you every comfort here and in our little village. If there is aught you desire, ask, and if it be within our power it shall be yours. Warren has consented to act as your personal host during your stay. Make your wants known to him."

As Warren departed with the pipers Lady MacLeod turned back to Duncan. "If you will follow me into the library, Duncan, I will introduce you to the remainder of the family. They are most anxious to meet you."

Following, Duncan was ushered into the book-laden room and the four children of Gregory MacLeod rose to meet him.

"May I introduce first my son Donald, the new MacLeod of MacLeod."

Duncan was scarcely conscious of the firm handclasp of the fifteen-year-old heir to The MacLeod. His eye kept wandering back to the vivaciously freckled redhead standing to the rear; a bonnie lass whose formal mourning garb could not quite conceal the innate good humor and blithe spirit dancing half revealed behind sparkling green eyes.

Recovering with an effort, Duncan acknowledged his introduction to Donald. In formal Gaelic he responded: "Greetings, Donald, MacLeod of Lewis. It is a sad occasion that I must address you as The MacLeod, but wear well your name. It is honorable and your illustrious sire added much to its honor."

"Thank you, Duncan Campbell of Breadalbane. As you were my father's friend and brother I trust you shall be my friend and brother also." Then, unable to sustain the formality of the occasion, Donald burst out, "And, General Campbell, I hope someday to be able to fight under ye. I'd rather be a private in the Argylls than commander o' any other regiment in the army!"

"Donald," Duncan replied seriously. "There's a place at the academy held in your name. As for me, so long as ye shall live—and your sons after ye—there'll be a place in the Argylls for ye. Your father was one o' the bravest men ever I knew. If ye can live up to him you will ha' earned the respect o' all."

Next was the turn of nine-year-old Charles, who accepted the handshake gravely, then broke into tears halfway through the formal speech of welcome. Lady MacLeod folded him in her arms and offered Duncan an apology. "You must forgive him, Duncan. He is the child of my age and I fear he has not yet achieved his manliness."

"Why," soothed Duncan, abandoning the formal Gaelic, " 'Tis no crime to shed tears. The man who cannot cry when 'tis time for tears cannot laugh when 'tis time for laughter and is that much less a man for it. Young Charlie has much to cry for."

"Will you forgive me, Duncan? I believe I can no longer go on with the formal introductions. My eldest child, Mavis," she continued, indicating the carrot-top who had so captivated Duncan, "and my youngest daughter, Claudia," she added, nodding her head toward the remaining member of the family group.

Glancing keenly at Duncan, whose eye kept turning to Mavis, Lady

MacLeod asked, "May I offer my excuses and retire. If I may be permitted I shall leave you to the graces of my daughter and have her show you about."

"Mother!" protested Donald, "As laird o' the manor mayn't I show Duncan around as my guest?"

"No, Donald, you may not. As Laird you must attend to the duties of the manor. Mavis is the proper hostess for the occasion."

"Very well, Mother," replied Donald, somewhat crestfallen, "but sometimes I wish I weren't the new laird."

"As Duncan would be the first to tell you, my son, to be a laird is a responsibility more than a privilege. You do what you must do."

As the others departed, leaving Mavis and Duncan alone in the library, Mavis eyed him solemnly. "My own greetings, General Campbell. My father spoke often and well of ye in his letters and visits home. I wish only that we had met under happier circumstances."

"Thank ye, Mistress MacLeod. Your father lived well, fought well and died well. He was loved by his family and his men and there is none who knew him but regrets his passing. No man can ask more of life."

Seeming a bit ill at ease, Mavis looked about, then asked, "May I show you about the manor and the village, General?"

"Please, Mistress MacLeod, the title 'General' does not sit well. Your father called me 'Duncan'—and so also your mother and brother. Can ye not do the same?"

"I shall," she answered with a moue, on condition you refer to me as 'Mavis.' 'Tis a trifle less stilted than 'Mistress MacLeod,' you know."

"Very well then, Mavis. And now will ye be showing me through the manor."

By the time Duncan had been shown through the manor and they were started out to the village the shadowing of strain and sorrow was smoothing from both their faces and Mavis was showing some of the natural gaiety of manner that had been mirrored in her eyes. Both were striving valiantly to overlook the past and pretend the day was for gladness.

A bit unexpectedly perhaps, it was Mavis who was first to break the pretense. "How was it," she ventured carefully, "fighting against the aliens?"

" 'Twas not enjoyable really," replied Duncan judiciously. Brooding darkly for a moment, he continued. " 'Tis not as if we could ha' a good fight and be done wi' it. They are not good fighters, but they are a very many poor fighters. They are brave—no doubt o' that—but they lack the skill and equipment," he added musingly.

"In a way 'tis rather like a covey o' beaters who ha' been out in a farmer's croft chopping down his sheep. Each o' the beaters thinks o' it as merely another job. After all, 'tis only sheep they're butchering—and since all they ha' ever met ha' been sheep, they ha' never fretted about finding better tools for their chore. When the aliens ran up against us they were looking for sheep, but they found tigers. They had thought to give us a lesson, but they got one instead. But they'll be back. As they see it they cannot afford to let us live—not after the beating they got. And the next time they're almost certain to use their advantage o' the hyperdrive. And that will mean almost certain victory for them."

"Then 'tis more serious than we've been told," nodded Mavis as they topped the crag and stood in the salty breeze and looked out over The Minch at the grey-topped swells breaking and curling beneath them.

"Aye," replied Duncan as he steadied Mavis on the crest and stood beside her gazing out across the sea. "Aye. 'Tis worse than they ha' let on—much worse."

"Then we are being lied to?"

"Not that—not here at least. Perhaps elsewhere—among the Russkies and Americans or the other blocs—but not here. 'Tis more a problem that only a very few people can really comprehend the truth o' the matter. They look only to our victories and ignore the other factors because they're too horrid to accept. And there's the meat o' the matter."

"What can we do?" Mavis asked simply.

"I don't know. Mayhap no one knows. All we can do is our best—and do that wi' our might—and beyond that, hope."

"It doesn't seem much."

"It isn't, but 'tis the best and only thing. We cannot simply lie down and die. . . . 'Tis not a man's way to do that. We just ha' to do what we can and go on living as if life were eternal. And if that be not enough, why then 'tis not enough."

"I'm sorry, Duncan," hastened Mavis as she observed the moon of introspection and black despondency slipping over him. "Donald will want to hear all about the fighting. I can listen to such things better with him about. 'Tis no sense glooming up your stay with past memories and future fears. When you leave here I hope 'twill be with pleasant memories of a happy visit and mayhap with a wish to return again. We will speak no more of war betwixt us."

Shrugging off his gloom and breaking the spell of the Highland crag, Duncan turned back to Mavis. "I thank ye. As you can see, I am somewhat the dour Scot. 'Twould not be like me had I not a bad side

o' things to look upon. May I change the subject to one more pleasant
—yourself, for instance?"

"Now, Duncan," smiled Mavis, "I concede I may be somewhat more
pleasant a topic than war and slaying, but I misdoubt I am more interesting."

"Not true at all," objected Duncan. "A bonnie lassie is both more interesting and more pleasant than war!"

"Why, sir, I do believe you're acting the gallant. Ye have spent too
much time in Edinburgh for a simple island lassie."

"I ha' not," came the indignant reply. "I ha' but said what I
thought."

"Aye?" she dimpled. "Well, then I apologize. But 'tis time for us to
return and ready ourselves for dinner. Help me down, please, Duncan."

The following day Mavis resumed her role as guide and hostess as
they set sail in The Minch and scudded through the frothy breakers
while rounding beneath the headland they had stood atop the day before.

"Tell me, Mavis," gasped Duncan as he flinched under the impact of
the icy, wind-whipped spray. "Ha' ye spent much time on the outside?"

"Outside?"

"Aye. Away from the manor, I mean."

"Of course. I've spent many a day roving the hills and crannies of
Skye. And I've sailed my own smack clear across The Minch to the
Butt o' Lewis on the isles."

" 'Tis not what I mean, and ye know it."

"Why, then, whatever did you mean, Duncan?" she asked impishly.

"What I mean is . . . well . . . did ye ever travel to Edinburgh or
London, or elsewhere?"

"What an odd question. Whatever difference could it make?"

"Lassie," explained Duncan in exasperation, "can ye be no easier to
talk to? Ye must ken I am taken wi' ye and would like to pay court.
But how am I to do it if I can learn naught about ye?"

"Why, Duncan," she replied with a gentle smile, "am I to conclude
you wish to feel me out, as it were, and decide whether to tumble me
in the hay like some peasant girl or seduce me in the boudoir like a
lady o' London?"

"That is not what I meant," flushed Duncan hotly. " 'Tis that ye're
the bonniest lass ever I met, and I would like to know ye better. And
how am I to know ye better if I don't ask ye questions? And how can I
ask the questions when ye deliberately confuse my words?"

" 'Tis a fair question, Duncan," Mavis replied seriously, "and to be honest with you I shall enjoy your court. But mind you this, I have never entered even into the one-year marriage contract; nor shall I do so unless I am certain in my own mind that at the end of the year I shall wish to enter into the five-year pact, and after the five-year pact take the final vows. Nor would I knowingly enter into the pact with any man I did not feel was of the same mind in the matter. So if you are looking for a mate for the year please look elsewhere."

" 'Tis the same wi' me," nodded Duncan soberly. "Ye would be my first and only."

"You asked if I have traveled," continued Mavis, "and in truth I felt the need to tease a bit. But to answer . . . yes, I have traveled much, both among the UN nations and in Europe . . . and I have lived some while at the University of Paris. So to answer your question in full, I am not some peasant girl not knowing of her own mind. And should you wish to pay me court I shall be both pleased and proud. Does this reply suit ye?"

"Aye. It pleases me much."

"Very well then. I accept your court. And in our dealing with one another I shall consider you one who is suitor for me. Will you now seek the consent of my mother and brother?"

"Aye. This very evening . . . though I well ken 'tis a sad time to discuss so joyous an event."

After supper that evening Lady MacLeod invited Duncan's attendance alone in the study. Entering, Duncan wondered if Mavis had already spoken to her mother or if the matter of piping his friend to rest —due on the morrow—were to be discussed. If the latter, Duncan also wondered whether it would be possible to bring up the matter between Mavis and himself with any propriety.

"Duncan," opened Lady MacLeod after they had seated themselves, "may we speak without formality, you as the friend and me as the wife of my late husband?"

"Of course, Lady MacLeod. Consider yourself free o' all formality and I shall consider myself the same."

"Thank you," she replied simply. "I shall take you at your word." And here she paused as if seeking the appropriate opening. "Duncan," she finally commenced, "time is very short for this world. Gregory knew it, and so do you. But the fact that life is short does not mean that the living must surrender life, courage or dignity. But it sometimes occurs to me that they must compress it into a short space.

"Some time ago Gregory confided to me that he felt you would make a very desirable match for our daughter— Nay, hear me out," she gestured as Duncan started to interrupt. " 'Tis hard enough to say what I must, so let me finish." Pausing, she recommenced, "Recent events have done much to confirm in me his high regard of you.

"Ordinarily 'tis not the task of a mother to interfere so indiscreetly, but time is short. Yesterday and today, unless I permitted my hopes to interfere with my eyes, I felt you were attracted to Mavis and she to you. This pleasured me and I encouraged it by placing the two of you together as much as possible.

"Donald, quite naturally, would be overjoyed to have you as his brother-in-law, and both myself and the spirit of Gregory would be exceedingly pleased to have you for son-in-law.

"This leaves only the two most important problems: Would Mavis be pleased to have you for husband and would you be pleased with Mavis for wife? All other considerations are unimportant alongside this one. I do not expect an answer from you at this time as you have two weeks to spend with us. And under no circumstances would I do aught to cause you discomfort in visiting us either now or in times ahead.

"If you have another love, or if you cannot look upon Mavis as a suitable wife, then please disregard what I have said and the subject will never again be raised. Above all, Duncan, I would not cause you any embarrassment or any remote distress by my comments here, and it would not be taken amiss should you choose to remain silent to this conversation."

"Remain silent!" exploded Duncan. "Why, Lady MacLeod, this very afternoon Mavis and I had discussed the same matter and I had planned to seek ye out this evening to seek your permission to pay court to her!"

Two weeks later, as the launch nosed her way out, threading the coast on her journey to the Firth of Clyde and return to duty, Duncan and Mavis Campbell stood arm in arm at the fantail, watching the manor as it faded back into the mists of the Isle of Skye. Neither could help but wonder if ever again they would set eyes on the fair and pleasant land of her ancestors.

CHAPTER 10

Josiah Hamilton had swallowed a bitter pill when the American fleet put itself under the command of the UN during the battle of Uranus and Jupiter. He was resolved to swallow no more such pills. After all, had it not been for the 118 ships provided by the United States the UN fleet would have mustered only 182 vessels—plus some unimportant contributions by Europe and Russia. If the UN wanted American help in fighting their war they were going to have to pay for every bit of it. It would be perfectly acceptable, thought Hamilton, if the UN forces retained personal command over their own flotillas, but it was imperative that overall command be delegated to a responsible American officer. Additionally, this might be an excellent time to wring out a few trade concessions for after the war.

Unfortunately, a fairly large segment of the American people kept insisting this wasn't just the UN's war. They were demanding active assistance in every possible way. But marginally balanced against this group was a highly vocal collection of religious fundamentalists, America Firsters and pacifists arguing that the nation ought to get out of space altogether and leave the remainder of the world to fight its own battles. He could easily ignore them with only minor inconvenience, but they gave him a bargaining ploy with the UN. He could always pretend a reluctance to fight and demand the right to run the war his own way under threat of pulling out entirely. If he was firm enough they'd all knuckle under. No foreigner could whip a good Yankee horse trader when it came to bargaining!

Cheng, on the other hand, was moderately content. Fish scales or white skins—what was the difference? Both were barbarians. And for that matter it was even remotely possible the fish scales might be less barbaric than whites or blacks. The celestial Chinese would ultimately overcome either one. Let them fight it out like the dogs they were! Then, after one side or the other finally won, the People's Celestial Republic could step in and finish off the survivors. All he had to do was sit tight and make no concessions. He was merely an observer, although the others were not aware of it yet.

But Frankl had a problem. Europe was the heart of the civilized world. Beside it all else paled into insignificance. He visualized with cultivated horror the prospect of celaenium bombs hurtling into Paris, Rome, Dresden, Beyreuth, Spa, Florence, Venice, Naples, Madrid or any of the other irreplaceable centres of civilization. Clearly the primary task of Earth's space fleets was to protect these symbols of human glory. But how to do it? That was a very real question.

Somehow during the course of the negotiations the other power groups, including the UN, must be convinced of the necessity of concentrating the main weight of their defensive armament over Europe. Once a satisfactory number of ships and equipment was deployed there —creating a veritable Maginot Line in space, as it were—then it would be permissible to think of other matters, such as sending ships out to intercept the aliens around Pluto or Neptune or wherever they might be.

He shuddered. With impeccable distaste he considered the possibility of the baths at Spa being laid waste by a celaenium or fusion blast. It was unthinkable; simply unthinkable!

Nikolai Chebychev was worried—very worried. Yankovich, his predecessor, had failed and was now living at state expense in a village in Tanna Tuva. Nikolai's task was virtually impossible, and he knew it. But the penalty for failure was the same whether the task was possible or impossible.

The Soviet Presidium had no further illusions about the reality of the threat. Their own scientists had confirmed it. Unfortunately for Russia, while the Soviet peoples could easily be convinced it was the presence of their fleet which gave the victory to mankind, it would not be so easy to convince the rest of the world; and therein lay the trouble.

The Presidium was determined to surrender none of their autonomy of action. Either the conduct of the war would be subject to the firm veto of the Soviet High Command or no ships would be placed at the disposal of the UN in the fight against the aliens. It was that simple.

As this seemed unlikely, Chebychev was to negotiate on the basis that the Soviet Union would assume full jurisdiction over all operations. When the other nations refused to accede to this he was to maintain the position until they agreed to his minimum demands for a veto right—a right which would, in effect, allow the Soviets complete control over all operations. They would merely veto whatever alternatives the nominal command might propose until the Soviet plan was the only one left.

The trouble was, the Soviets had employed this same system of indirect control repeatedly since the nineteen-forties and the UN leadership was quite aware of the implications of any such proposal. True enough, cleverly slanted propaganda would make it appear sweetly reasonable. . . . After all, shouldn't the Soviet Government have veto power over the possibility their troops would be sent to futile and hopeless battle merely in order that the capitalists might have less to fear from them in the future. . . . The way to convince the Russians of our goodwill is to trust them. And so forth.

But the meetings had dragged on through a full month, and no concessions had been made by anyone. The Presidium had finally authorized him to announce that the Soviet Union would see to her own defences and the other nations could do likewise. It was fully realized this would lead to inevitable disaster, but the Presidium was convinced the capitalists would knuckle under and lose their nerve in the face of the threat. And under the worst of circumstances even total annihilation of all humankind was preferable to submission to the capitalist nations. It was Russia's turn to rule!

Alpin Grant had neither troubles nor worries. He had an impossibility on his hands and he knew it. How to weld together a world when each of its fragments had time and again demonstrated a total unwillingness to work together toward a common goal? He had even come to suspect that was why the dinosaurs became extinct: purely from an inability to unite against a common enemy.

True, there had been some minor advances. Sweden had joined Norway in withdrawing from the European Federation and had rejoined the UN, thereby increasing the UN fleet by some fifty spacecraft and a potential for more as production tooled up. The Union of South Africa, long violently isolationist and antiwhite after the extermination pogroms of the twenty-tens, had driven the last of the Boers into the ocean, had petitioned for admission into the UN and been duly accepted. Although they possessed only a dozen warcraft, their technology was respectable and the Zulus had repeatedly shown themselves first-rate fighters. Within a year or two they should be able to contribute several flotillas to the UN fleets.

But all this was only talking around the subject. Nothing would work with China, so it could legitimately be ignored. Europe, Russia and the United States needed to work together with the UN, but for the past month they had been sparring in fruitless rounds of endless discussion. Each was so busy jockeying for position they had little time to worry about the problem.

Alpin had finally decided this was to be his last meeting. He had too many other matters to attend to—matters which were being neglected or left to subordinates while he wasted time here. If nothing was achieved today he would withdraw from the talks and let the others fight it out among themselves. Whether they cared to admit it or not, they could still be forced into at least a limited cooperation if handled right—and Alpin knew just how to do it.

It was with this in mind that he entered the Council chambers.

"Gentlemen," he commenced, bringing the meeting to order, "do any of your nations have anything new to add to your positions of yesterday, or do matters remain as they were?"

Chebychev rose ponderously to his feet. "Mr. Grant," he began carefully, "my government has been exceedingly reasonable and patient.

We have made any number of generous concessions of vital importance to our people in an effort to avert a stalemate. . . ."

Grant tried in vain to think of a solitary such concession, but Chebychev pressed on inexorably.

"Despite all our concessions, the governments of the United States, Europe and the UN have utterly refused to reciprocate in kind. Evidently the Soviet Union is expected to make all the concessions in order that after the victory she will be left in a disadvantageous position with respect to the capitalist nations. This my government cannot accept."

Pausing momentarily for emphasis, Chebychev continued, "However, the Presidium of the Soviet Union has authorized me to make one final concession—a last appeal to reason. Veto power over all operations must be vested in the Soviet military. This way we can at least assure that no Soviet ships or troops are employed in operations not acceptable to the Soviet peoples. And I may warn you, gentlemen, if you do not accept this most reasonable condition then the Soviet people will have no option except to assume full responsibility for its own defences and trust the other nations of the world to do likewise. This is literally our final concession."

Almost before Chebychev had seated himself Hamilton was on his feet striding toward the podium. "Mr. Grant," he thundered, "the proposal of the Soviet delegate is preposterous! In the face of a veto of this nature nothing whatsoever can be accomplished. We might as well have no navies and no fleets for the defence of Earth as a hamstrung command. We must—and I emphasize *must*—have a unified defence with a competent leader given full responsibility for the success or failure of operations. And he must have all the power of command implied by such responsibility."

"Mr. Hamilton," interrupted Chebychev from the floor, "I concur wholeheartedly. This has been the position of the Soviet delegation since the beginning of these talks. And since the Soviet armed forces are obviously the most powerful and best led, then logically command of Earth's forces should be vested there. I am pleased to find you have finally come over to our way of thinking. This represents decided progress in the talks."

"Rubbish!" snorted Hamilton. "Obviously impossible. The delegate from the Soviet Union must be aware that mere superiority in manpower is no longer a criterion for military strength. I feel certain even Mr. Chebychev will admit that a horde of charging cossacks riding pell-mell across the steppes is hardly an adequate defence against a technologically potent invader such as the aliens. Patently the overall command of Earth's military forces must be assigned to that nation whose technological skill and know-how would best equip them to handle the complex operations and instruments of modern war. The United States is clearly the only one capable of assuming the task with any chance of success."

"Mr. Hamilton," called Frankl, rising stiffly to his feet. "May I suggest there is more to warfare than a bookkeeper's adding and subtracting of gadgetry. What is required, obviously, is a competent general who is capable—fully capable—of deciding between the merely desirable and the utterly necessary."

"Precisely my point, Mr. Frankl," acknowledged Hamilton. "An American general, reared in the tradition of industrial technology, would be most capable of recognizing those targets which would be of critical importance to the enemy. For example, while we all agree it would be regrettable if Paris or Rome or New York or Moscow were obliterated, it would be disaster for the whole world if Detroit or Houston were destroyed. The loss of shipbuilding capacity would be irreplaceable."

"But what is the value of saving the world if in the process everything which makes humanity distinguishable from the beasts were destroyed in the process?" rejoined Frankl. "The things of value to humanity are the distinctive products of the human spirit; the soaring temples, the works of art and genius—yes, even the comforts of convivial life. To suggest the gadgetry of your Detroit could outweigh such considerations is—is blasphemous!"

"Gentlemen," interrupted Grant peremptorily. "This discussion plainly leads nowhere. Evidently your military has failed to impress upon you the gravity of the situation. It is no longer a matter of deciding between the destruction of Rome or Paris, Detroit or Moscow, Delhi or Edinburgh. If an alien ship penetrates far enough to destroy any one of these cities there is every chance it will destroy them all.

"For the past month I have tried and failed to convince you of the seriousness of the situation. You have all seen photographs of Pluto. Your own captains have confirmed her fate. The same weapons employed against Earth will exact the same penalty. It matters not one whit whether China has declared neutrality. She still shares the common fate of all mankind. Nor will there be any left to debate the merits of communism or capitalism. They will both be merely pages in a history no one will ever read.

"To date each of your delegations has worked on the basis that they must prepare for the period after victory. This is perhaps good. A people who enters a war feeling hopeless is already defeated. But to engage in a war of this magnitude so convinced of victory that all operations are subordinated to political maneuverings aimed at assuring dominance after victory is sheer madness!

"Despite many sweeping claims of concessions by each of the interested parties, excepting the Chinese, there has still been no single point of agreement relative to the conduct of the war. I therefore propose we adjourn this conference and set about our proper business of preparing for the next battles. I suggest we make an informal agreement concerning the disposition of our overall forces and maintain an equally informal liaison at the staff level.

"The UN, as patent of their continued effort to achieve cooperation in this time of crisis, unilaterally agrees to relax all barriers on the export of critical materials surplus to our immediate needs. Additionally, we will cooperate to the best of our ability in releasing technological data to all nations.

"So far as the UN is concerned, the conference is over. If by chance any or all of you should wish to continue the talks among yourselves we will make available a conference room for as long as your respective governments desire.

"UN military liaison officers will contact your several military ministries in the near future to determine what level of military cooperation, if any, will be feasible between the respective nations. . . . Oh"—he paused as if for an afterthought—"one other item before I leave. The Chinese Government is no doubt aware of the extensive UN activity in the quadrant of the asteroid belt known as Kiang Xiu. Our government is cognizant of the fact that the Chinese people lay claim to this entire quadrant on the basis of prior occupancy of a principal asteroid. The UN has never been disposed to recognize this claim and has not in the past done so. Events of the past year have made it imperative that certain of these asteroids be converted to military bases and be physically moved from their present orbits into more favorable positions. It has come to our attention that on several occasions the Chinese Government has chosen to interfere with these operations by any of several, essentially nonviolent, methods. The danger in this is that such confrontations sometimes become more physical. While the UN is not unaware of the precedents where in the past nations have claimed entire island groups on the basis of the occupation of a single land mass, we do not feel this can be considered applicable in the asteroid belt, where positions and even family groups change from year to year.

"While we will not knowingly set foot on any asteroid which the Chinese Government has effectively occupied, we shall continue to make use of certain of these bodies whose position is uniquely favorable for plans in hand. The UN Command has repeatedly essayed to work in harmony with the several governments of Earth, and while we have made no demands of assistance from other blocs and nations we cannot and shall not tolerate active interference. I trust our position is clear in this matter?"

"Quite clear, Mr. Grant," replied Cheng through his interpreter with just the barest shrug of acquiescence. "The Chinese Government is presently unwilling to engage in hostilities against this presumed enemy of yours. But similarly, our government is also reluctant to engage in hostilities against a government of Earth. Nevertheless, we would be derelict in our responsibilities were we to submit supinely to the abduction of several thousands of cubic miles of Chinese territory."

"Just one minute, Mr. Cheng!" roared Hamilton. "The United States also has claims on the asteroid belt, and our military requirements also necessitate the use of several of these bodies. In this specific instance we must consider that an attack on the UN positions there would obviously be a prelude to an attack on our own position and take action accordingly."

"The Soviet Union also has interest in the asteroids, Mr. Cheng," added Chebychev. "Our operations for the physical removal of several of these bodies are already well advanced and we cannot brook obstructionism." Mentally Chebychev made a note to investigate what conceivable use the UN could have for these remote chunks of rock and metallic ores. How could they possibly move one? With towropes, he supposed. Well, the Soviet scientists should know—and if they didn't there were other ways of finding out.

"It would seem," Cheng murmured, forgetting his pose of being unversed in barbaric languages, "as if the present balance of power is arrayed against the Chinese people. We cannot and must not abrogate our claims to any portion of the asteroid belt. It is as much the territory of China as any village or hamlet on our mainland. However in view of the fact the immediate lives and welfare of our citizens are not essentially affected the Chinese Government will temporarily suspend her claims to those portions of the asteroid belt not presently physically occupied and on which no Chinese vessels have yet landed. When the present 'emergency,' as you term it, has been resolved the Chinese Government will immediately reassert its claim to the physical ownership of that portion of the belt. I trust this will be acceptable to your governments."

"Very much so," nodded Alpin. "May I congratulate the delegate of the People's Celestial Republic. In our month of talks this is the only genuine concession made by anyone other than the UN."

With this final comment and limited agreement the conference adjourned and the delegates returned to their respective nations. The solitary breach in the wall of disagreement was the one so casually but deliberately developed by Grant at the end of the session. Russia and the United States, by their knee-jerk reflexes on the matter of the asteroid belt, could not fail to follow up on the idea of outfitting some of them as fleet bases. And with the UN being in the position of volunteering information and data the three blocs would assuredly enter into an informal, but still fairly reliable, arrangement for manning the separate sectors about the perimeter of the system.

That much at any rate had been achieved—which made it a cut above the average summit conference.

CHAPTER 11

"Bring her down easy, Jock!"

"Damn it, man; that part's got to fit the airlock, not on the other side. What the hell you doing?"

"Hey, Sarge, how's this block winch supposed to work with no gravity? The whole bloody cable keeps slipping off."

"Keep her high and tight and she won't. Hold that flippin' tension. Don't slack off on her."

With a scarcely perceptible quiver of the surrounding lock, the battle cruiser slid smoothly into position until only the blunted nose and chin blister peeped above the surrounding rock. Overhead, a sledge loaded with canvas-lashed bales of equipment tumbled by in slow motion as it orbited the planetoid with a velocity of something like four inches a second.

In the far distance a cometlike lance of flame limned a utility ship laden with cargo beginning its braking maneuver. Nearer yet, a person who knew what to look for might have seen the dull-red glow of cooling exhaust ports on one of the new destroyer-class dreadnaughts awaiting berthing instructions.

A year ago this was officially Asteroid 2128 TA in the catalogues. Now it was the headquarters of the reconstituted Task Force Lupus, consisting of the Argyll and Sutherland Highlanders and the newly constituted Campbell of Breadalbane Highlanders.

Renamed Aileach—"rocky place" in Gaelic—the asteroid was the
future headquarters and forward base for all operations in the Lupus-
Corvus sectors. Twenty-eight miles in diameter, the whole mass was
tunneled until it resembled a rabbit warren. At the core was the resi-
dential and recreational district, a vast, vaulted hemisphere some two
and a half miles in radius with an artificial "sun" riding overhead as
permanent "noon" but dimmed to merely lunar brightness in the "evening" hours. Small cottages and playgrounds dotted the interior. Hotels
and barracks were provided for the unmarried personnel by extensions
into the rocky walls of the cavern. The area could easily accommodate
a population of thirty thousand with not the least sign of crowding,
and with only minimal further tunneling the number could be doubled
or tripled.

A half mile below were hydroponics farms to provide food for the
ship's complement. Sheep grazed placidly on newly sodded grasses, and
in an adjacent cavern herds of Angus and Ayrshire cattle browsed and
ruminated. The lack of gravity proved only a minor inconvenience
once the cattle were shod with metallic boots to anchor them to the
magnetized steel rods carefully embedded beneath the dirt and grass.

To be sure, once in a while one of the sheep would get too frisky
and bound up to the ceiling, there to float and bleat in helpless terror
until the gentle tug of the floor finally drifted it down. Or perhaps a
cow would try to find a better source of water than the nursing nipples
provided at the spigots; but these were minor nuisances and the cattle
soon learned.

The hydroponics techniques proved more difficult. At length a compromise solution was worked out whereby the water was run through a
sponge matting on which the plants could grow. It was a bit more in-
convenient than normal hydroponics methods, but it worked in null-g,
and that was what counted.

There had been a number of arguments about using the flat dome
approach for the core unit. Make the whole thing a cylinder and put a
spin on the axis and the resulting centrifugal "gravity" would be whatever was wished. The trouble with this was that the asteroid was
meant to be a maneuverable spaceship capable of accelerating at a full
g or better. Adding a centrifugal 1 g vector would be little short of cat-
astrophic to anyone inside. Additionally, trying to land and depart
ships from the surface of a small asteroid lacking an air envelope and
rotating at several feet per second was deemed an unnecessary compli-
cation.

For the time being things would be uncomfortable. Children must
be kept tethered and ropeways spanned the dome in a hundred direc-

tions. But once Aileach got under way she would be kept at a steady 0.5 g acceleration, moving on a vast arc for one half her designated track while building up to a peak speed, then being spun ponderously on her axis to spend the next half of her arc, decelerating at the same pace on the opposite vector until zero relative speed was reached. Another turn and she would be accelerating back along the same track. A person living inside Aileach would have no consciousness of motion. There would simply be a uniform "gravity" at one-half Earth norm.

Beneath the farms were the administrative offices and laboratories. Below these were production and factory areas. Aileach was a complete military, administrative, industrial and farming community within itself. And Duncan Campbell commanded it. From captain to major general in seven years. Fast perhaps, but this was war and less than six years ago the entire UN fleet numbered fewer than one hundred combat craft. Now it consisted of well over a thousand ships and was growing by about another three every day. Duncan's fellow captains were now mostly colonels and brigadiers. He was merely one step ahead of the others, but he was one battle ahead of them too.

In laboratories on Aileach, Hermes, Delhi, Baile, Weem and Wynd and a dozen other asteroids research for a hyperdrive was already being carried on. Other researchers experimented with the idea of artificial gravity. Psychiatrists and hospitals were available for the sick. Special studies in asteroidal ecology were being instituted. Schools, including small universities, could accept students through all grades.

In the factories beneath the dome complete spaceships could be manufactured from minerals excavated from the cavern walls. Given the essentially unlimited power of the cryomagnetic technology, it was possible in theory to create any desired element on demand simply by fusing nuclei of the right number together to produce larger nuclei of the desired number. Naturally most of this went for the production of celaenium—number 126 on the periodic table—but others were being produced as needed.

In ceramics facilities they were producing sleeve liners for the huge rocket tubes, dishes for the personnel aboard, test tubes for the laboratories and plate-glass windows for the stores and shops of the mall. Fabrications plants turned out everything from computers to phonograph records, from hi-fi sets to women's trews, men's kilts, space suits, baby diapers and rubber nipples.

Studding the surface of the asteroid like a giant hedgehog's quills were gun emplacements. Each emplacement was connected by an airlocked tunnel to a common platoon headquarters and relief area. Beyond each platoon headquarters, separated by yet other airlocks, were main connecting tunnels leading into the depths of the asteroid. Dotting the surface were hundreds of detecting units and their backup equipment, all providing constant electronic and visual intelligence in every direction. Anchorage berths provided secure haven for every ship, and if they needed repair a cover could be sealed over the berth and air pumped in for the benefit of the maintenance crews.

Though far from completed yet, plans were already in the works to establish an independent shipbuilding facility aboard each of the asteroids. Within a year or two Aileach and the others should be capable of turning out two cruiser-class vessels a month and one destroyer every three or four months. The aim was to make every asteroid entirely independent of Earth for all practical purposes.

But Aileach was to be only a fraction of the total defences assigned to Task Force Lupus. After it arrived on station, elements of both the Argylls and the Campbells were to be assigned to duty on fragments of demolished Pluto, plus some other asteroid swimming in the general vicinity. These fragments also were to be made self-contained and the equipment necessary to convert them into smaller copies of Aileach was already securely anchored to her surface. Ultimately both the Argylls and Breadalbane Campbells were to be augmented to roughly full divisional status mustering two space wings, or nearly four hundred ships of the line in the Lupus sector.

By now the permanent party personnel were streaming aboard. Each ship brought ten, fifty, a hundred space-suited men and women. Babies squalled lustily as they were separated from their mothers and stuffed unceremoniously into incubator boxes for transfer to the interior. Larger children gamboled dangerously and played push-away games in the null gravity. Here and there a dog or cat, boxed away for the while, whined or mewed piteously at the weightlessness.

The second battalion of the Breadalbane infantry complement arrived on two cargo carriers. The major commanding had never been off-planet before and had his men attired in dress kilts rather than trews. The battalion review was uproarious as the kilts floated defiantly upward to the obvious amusement of the female personnel present. The comments of old space hands didn't help, either. Magnetic shoes might hold the feet down, but not much else.

For Mavis this was her first off-Earthing too. And, considerate as Duncan might be, there were a few things he had neglected to tell her. For one thing, skirts were as bad as kilts. And how did you persuade your stomach you weren't falling endlessly? The doctors said it wouldn't hurt the baby, but were they really all that sure?

It mattered not that Aileach was embarking on the strangest journey in human history, there were still practical matters to think about. And for that matter, where was Duncan? He knew when she was scheduled to arrive. Probably he was too busy. She tried to understand, but she was still disappointed.

A guide met her group as they passed beyond the second airlock and were able to step out of their confining space suits. Fortunately her group of arrivals consisted only of wives and small children. Most of the women had worn skirts and slipped their space suits on over them. Had any adult males been present an embarrassing amount of southern exposure would have greeted them.

Their guide, a young woman lieutenant, had evidently encountered similar situations before this. She waited patiently while the women sorted through their personal effects for shorts, slacks, trews or whatever might be available.

One stout, red-faced sergeant's wife had none of these items and searched about desperately for something she might wear. Since none of the other women were even remotely her size, matters were at an impasse until she smiled in resolute good humor and produced a pair of mammoth garters. Slipping them around her ample knees, she drew out a handful of safety pins and ripped off the lace around the hem of a slip. Cutting the lace into short strips she anchored her dress fore and aft, then in quiet dignity lumbered off down the corridor with the others—the only woman to succeed in wearing a dress on Aileach.

As they reached the village, there was Duncan awaiting her, along with the other men whose wives were also arriving. With a small smile of joy Mavis forgot herself and began running toward him. A moment later, with arms and legs akimbo, she slammed into the hapless Duncan, coming dangerously close to driving them both off into midair. Luckily Duncan had long since developed the spaceman's trick of instinctively knowing where support was to be had so he managed to hold on to the both of them, albeit with some loss of dignity. But at least Mavis had learned her first lesson in ship's procedure: you don't run in null gravity.

Helping hands disentangled the pair. A few minutes later Mavis felt shakily secure and Duncan escorted her over to the cottage assigned them.

Now a shuddering vibration rippled through Aileach, hung on the air for a moment, then slipped down the scale of sensibility until vanishing, leaving behind only a dim, half-felt sensation hovering just below the level of consciousness. The first of her cluster of massive rockets had flared to life.

During the first minute of operation no instrument could have detected motion on Aileach, only vibration. Within an hour it had moved a foot and a half. A full day later it had moved only 180 feet on its three-billion-mile journey. Three days later it was moving at nearly a quarter mile per hour. By the fourth day the second of the great rockets came to life and Aileach passed the mile-per-hour mark.

Spaceships were still plummeting down at a rate of a dozen or more a day, each laden with supplies, personnel and equipment. The service ships were berthed and preparing for their final round trip to Earth before the distance became too great for convenience.

By the sixth day the third and fourth rockets were in place and operational. Aileach's speed had passed the fifty-mile-per-hour mark and was doubling every day. Inside the bowels of the asteroid there was the faintest feel of "down" as the tempest from the four rockets generated the first tiny sensations of acceleration.

The two remaining scouts of the Breadalbanes arrived, and next came the task of forming the regiments into fighting units rather than raw aggregates of men and equipment. As the fifth rocket chimed in with the others, the first complete flotilla of the Argylls rocketed from its berths. A jet of compressed nitrogen rammed pistons which ejected the ships at a speed of some 250 feet per second. After passing the quarter-mile mark outbound they switched to internal power and were on their own. Two years ago a full flotilla launching would have consisted of fifteen ships. Today the standard flotilla comprised four cruisers, sixteen scouts and one of the mammoth destroyers—twenty-one ships in all. With two flotillas to the regiment and two regiments aboard Aileach, Task Force Lupus consisted of eighty-four ships defending a sector which two years earlier had been manned by only thirty.

By the twentieth day of the journey the fourteenth of the massive rockets had been put into operation. Velocity was no longer measured in miles per hour but in miles per second. There was now a very perceptible "gravity" amounting to more than a quarter normal. In a few more days they would be passing through the orbit of Jupiter and in two more months they should be approaching their duty station to relieve the flotilla currently patrolling there.

Down in the communications centre was organized chaos as round-the-clock messages winged between Earth and Aileach, between Aileach and the ships of the flotillas and to vessels of all makes and descriptions plying the space routes between the asteroids. The chatter of teletypes and facsimile radio transmissions and the hiss of receivers merged into a continuing background of noise and bustle. A dozen times daily the three-bell gong announced the receipt of a priority message from Earth, so when the three-beller sounded no one really hurried. A minute, five minutes, made no difference. But eventually the transmission was plucked off the tape. An attendant put it on the tape deck, listened, turned pale, then pushed the annunciator button to headquarters. The night duty officer listened incredulously, then sounded the alarm buzzer at the general's cottage.

Groggily, Duncan switched on the light over his bed and glanced over at Mavis sleeping peacefully beside him. Then he jolted awake. The alarm communicator was buzzing. Leaping from bed he strode across the room and lifted the receiver. "Campbell here," he said tersely. "What's happening?"

"You'd best get down to administration immediately, sir," came the anonymous voice from the other end of the line. " 'Tis Earth. There's been another attack!"

"I'll be down immediately. Sound standby alert. Contact MacGillivray in the First Flotilla o' the Argylls and get him standing by at his communications. Get MacGregor o' the Campbells here immediately. Order the First Flotilla o' the Campbells to prepare for lift-off on command wi' preliminary instructions to anticipate orders to move out ahead o' Aileach at approximately twice detector range. They can start course programming now. Advise Gilchrist he is temporarily in command o' the Argylls in the absence o' MacGillivray and get him down to command immediately. Move!"

As he flipped off the receiver and turned he saw Mavis standing in the doorway blinking uncertainly at him. "Troubles?" she asked simply.

"Aye. There's report o' another attack. They may ha' beaten us to the punch this time."

"Is it bad?"

"I don't know yet. I'm going now."

"Then kiss me first. 'Twill be a long while, I fear."

"I fear so too, lass," he observed as he reached to embrace her. "I love ye."

"I love you too, Duncan. Take care."

Giving Mavis a quick pat on her bare rump and snatching up a pair of trews for himself, Duncan hurried from the cottage to the shaft leading down to the administration complex. Already he could hear sounds of aroused activity in the buildings and barracks nearby and just as he stepped into the shaft elevator the overhead "sun" switched on and 2 A.M. became bright daylight.

Lieutenant Lang and her husband, a sergeant of the Breadalbanes, came darting from their cottage. Even in his preoccupation with the aliens Duncan found time to chuckle. They would both find clothes at their respective stations. And happily married though he was, he could still appreciate a well-turned leg and trim figure—especially when exposed all the way to the neck. Night clothing had never been a strong Scots habit.

Then glancing at his trousers, still firmly clutched in his hand, Duncan abruptly realized he was in no better condition.

By the time he stepped from the shaft he may not have looked much like a commanding general, but at least he had his pants on.

An aide awaited him and the lights in administration were solidly ablaze. Staff personnel were streaming in from all directions. Far in the distance an irregular pounding rhythm denoted ships being launched into space. Burns was probably getting his ships out to standby as fast as their crews reported. It would give him a few extra minutes' edge in deployment. Smart!

Striding into his office, Duncan flipped the intercom switch. "Campbell here. MacGregor and Gilchrist are to report to my office directly as they arrive. Is MacGillivray standing by on the radio?"

"Gilchrist has just arrived and is on his way up, sir. MacGillivray standing by for instructions and reporting his flotilla four light minutes out and closing on us at point five g's from vector two hundred and thirty degrees horizontal, three thirty-five degrees vertical solar coordinates."

"Roger. Link MacGillivray to this office by remote circuit and prepare to play back the tape from Earth on my command."

"Aye, sir. The tapes are ready for your go-ahead now, sir."

"Thank ye," Duncan replied automatically as the door opened and Gilchrist entered, looking as ill prepared as Duncan for a meeting, being clad mostly in a shaggy bathrobe and floppy slippers.

Waving him impatiently to a seat, Duncan ordered up tea and waited with mounting irritation for MacGregor. Halfway through the first cup, irritation rapidly giving way to wrath, he flipped the intercom again. "Hasn't MacGregor arrived yet?" he demanded.

"Aye, sir. He's just now on his way up."

"Good."

A moment later MacGregor entered, clad in full uniform and freshly shaven. Eyeing him with barely concealed distaste, Duncan made a mental note to keep him away from future roles where he might be called on for immediate reaction. Any man who had to take time to shave and get fully uniformed in an emergency obviously wasn't qualified to cope with one. Motioning the man to a chair, Duncan went back to the intercom and announced, "We'll take the playback now, thank ye."

The men strained forward as the distinctive radio squelch whined, then a carefully impersonal voice came over the air. "UN Aileach from UN Earth. Reports just received from forward stations manned by UN, Soviet and American forces indicate the aliens appeared simultaneously at numerous positions about the periphery of the solar system approximately eighteen hours ago. Best estimates suggest as many as two hundred and fifty ships may have been involved, assuming their appearance was symmetrical.

"These ships proceeded to launch a number of torpedolike objects, most of which immediately went into hyperdrive aimed at the sun. Three of these devices were intercepted, apparently due to some malfunction in their drive mechanisms. Upon interception all three detonated.

"Analysis of the spectral characteristics of the objects indicates a lithium-hydride core having a potential two-hundred-kilomegaton capacity. Tentative estimates suppose the purpose of the torpedoes is to penetrate to the solar core in hyperdrive and detonate there, presumedly to cause the sun to enter either a flare or nova state. If so then it must be considered likely Earth will be destroyed or at the minimum made uninhabitable.

"Time required for entry into nova or flare state is unknown. The effectiveness of the attack itself is equally uncertain and some theoretical physicists opine the attack may have been merely an experimental thrust which will fail. However, we feel it would be unwise to rely too heavily on this supposition. As a preliminary measure a cadre of theoretical physicists and other science personnel additional to your regular complement is being dispatched to Aileach at maximum acceleration. Others will follow as soon as possible—circumstances permitting.

"Your present instructions are to alter trajectory and proceed to the planet Styx with all prudent speed.

"Cameron of Erracht, on station in the Lupus area, is assigned your direct command until otherwise advised. Additional personnel, including primarily families of the Camerons, will be sent to you as quickly as possible. In the event of the destruction of Earth prior to further communicaitons from here, suggest you alter course in the general direction of Corona Australis, and good luck to you.

"For your information, Hermes and Delhi have departed orbit en route their previously assigned stations. Weem anticipates departure in twenty-four hours. Wynd is to depart within the week and Baile

98 GYPSY EARTH

within two. Clach Tuill will not be readied for more than a month. All
have been directed to rendezvous at Styx and then proceed to the vicinity of Corona Australis in the event of the loss of Earth. Will advise
you of actions and courses of the other bloc asteroids as they become
available. Over . . . and again good luck."

"And, Duncan," broke in the voice of Alpin Grant, replacing the
carefully impersonal voice which preceded him, "as a personal suggestion, pile on the power as fast as your rockets will move you. The scientists say they're not sure, but there's no rational way of accounting
for the aliens' actions unless we assume this was their intent, and we
dare not bank on its failure. Don't let an apparently normal appearance
of the sun fool you. She's big and it may take her a while to belch, but
if she does Earth is dead. For the time being, and until officially informed otherwise, take it for granted we're dead back here.

"As a hint from a couple of our astrophysicists, 'tis doubtful whether
the sun has enough mass to expand much beyond the orbit of Jupiter,
so when you get out beyond Saturn's orbit the heat might scorch the
surface a bit but you'll pull through.

"We'll continue sending out asteroids as long as possible. This might
even take a year or more, but I am personally certain 'tis coming and
there's naught we can do to stop it. Good luck in case I never talk to
you again, and take care. Over and may fortune smile on you."

The tape rolled to an end and there was dead silence in the room.
No one spoke for a moment. No one could speak. Then Gilchrist
erupted angrily, "He's wrong! He must be wrong. He can't be right!"

"Shut up, Gilchrist!" snapped Duncan furiously. "Just shut up!"
Then as quickly as it rose his anger subsided. Gilchrist just happened
to be present. It wasn't his fault.

"Sorry, Gilchrist," he apologized. "You know I didn't mean it. But
Grant doesn't make many mistakes, and we daren't assume he's made
one now. We ha' to work on the premise Earth is finished and 'tis up
to us to carry on somehow."

Turning back to the intercom, Duncan flipped the switch and spoke
rapidly. "Communications. . . . I want the tape from Earth played
back just as we received it. I want it over every annunciator on
Aileach. All aboard deserve to know the facts just as we know
them. . . . And stand by to tape a personal message to follow it."

A moment's pause then, "Ready for your message now, General."

For long seconds Duncan hesitated, deciding what he should say—
what he could say. "Fellow Scots," he finally began. "Ye ha' heard the
message from Earth exactly as I heard it a few minutes afore ye. I
should like to be able to offer some words o' hope and encouragement

but cannot. We must from this moment work on the assumption our Mother Earth is dead. 'Tis only a matter o' when. If it turns out we are wrong then so much the gladder we shall be. But we cannot bank on it.

"The next few days are critical in the extreme. As Grant said, wi' Earth dead we become Earth. We must survive if man himself is to survive. We must survive to carry mankind's vengeance to our foes. This has become our solemn obligation to those left behind.

"Commencing immediately, second-shift personnel working on the rockets will be divided equally among the first and third shifts and each will work twelve hours. Berthing crews will expedite the preparation o' additional slots for ships arriving wi' more people. Tunneling crews will commence surveys for the buildings and space needful to contain new arrivals. Further orders will be given through regular channels.

"I can assure ye every communication from Earth will be relayed to all o' ye as promptly as 'tis received. Earth is the common home o' all o' us, and each o' ye deserves to know her fate as surely as I. Now 'tis needful that we survive, that we work, that we endure whatever lies afore us in order that we may keep faith wi' those left behind. For now, we do what we must."

Flipping off the intercom, Duncan turned to Gilchrist and Mac-Gregor. "Gilchrist, there's small likelihood for action at present. Therefore, in addition to your regular duties as flotilla commander ye are assigned to prepare for the arrival o' as many as sixty thousand more people. 'Tis not likely so many will be able to come, but we must be prepared if fortune smiles. This will mean contacting each o' the work shifts and engineers to coordinate plans. And do not neglect to see to the expansion o' the hydroponics system. We don't want to go on half rations. Further, all slaughter o' livestock will be cut to a scant minimum till we ha' data to determine what will be the new level of consumption.

"MacGregor, for the time being I want the Campbells to stand by as a supplementary work force. The infantry o' the Argylls will be added to your command. Retain only enough to man battle positions. Cut to two twelve-hour shifts on surface combat installations. Gilchrist will advise you on manpower needs as they arise and ye will assign personnel as needful."

Turning back to the radio, Duncan continued. "MacGillivray. Ye heard the message from Earth. Ye are now directed to proceed toward Aileach and maintain a position dead ahead at one half maximum detector range. Calder, o' the Campbells, is approaching station there

now. Upon your arrival assume command. Ye are also directed to take
what steps are needful, including the dispatch o' a scout if you deem it
proper, to establish communications wi' the Camerons out at Lupus.
We will pick them up on the fly en route to Styx. Coordinate their lift-
off so they'll be up to speed as we pass. The second flotilla o' the Argylls will be retained under my personal command. 'Tis not likely the
aliens will commence a new attack in force, but be extra alert in case
they ha' more surprises for us. Over. Acknowledge."

Eight minutes later the voice came back. "MacGillivray to Campbell.
Argylls proceeding per your instructions. Estimate time of arrival on
station approximately three days. Will advise precise time as soon as
we've sorted ourselves out. Over."

"Gentlemen," said Duncan turning back to his officers, "we all ha'
work to do, and mine is mainly at this desk. I shall want reports at
least twice daily until we pass Saturn's orbit. Any problems ye cannot
handle bring to me personally. Questions? . . . Very well, shall we set
to work."

Waving off the salutes, Duncan pushed the latch switch as they left
and locked himself in his office. Seven years before he had been an obscure captain in a utility ship, supported, however indirectly, by seven
billion people. Today he was a general commanding some thirty-five
thousand people, including the not yet joined Camerons. Was he now
perhaps the sole support of all mankind's hopes and future, charged
with the survival of a tiny remnant?

Less than three years before little Charlie MacLeod had cried over
the loss of his father and Duncan had excused him to his mother. Now
Duncan cried, and there was no one to excuse him.

CHAPTER 12

The next few days passed in numbed disbelief. The arrival of each
ship from Earth, once merely routine, became an occasion of restrained
joy and even of relief. One more ship with people aboard. One more
word from Earth. No one knew if there would be another.

Daily people congregated about the view scopes looking silently at
the sun. Was it imagination or was there a barely perceptible redden-
ing? Could that sunspot be a harbinger of a holocaust to come? Saturn's orbit was passed and Aileach was presumedly safe, but would
there be time for another ship?

Intercoms throughout the asteroid were turned to full volume, and every communication from Earth was awaited in eager anticipation and forlorn hope that the edict of doom would be repealed.

A faint cheer rippled through Aileach when Hermes, with thirty-five thousand aboard, passed Jupiter's orbit estimating Saturn's in six more days, Uranus's in nine and Neptune in fourteen. The Midlothians and Gloucestershires formed the nucleus of this group and they were to be joined by the Titan colony base as they passed.

Delhi, with the Poona Highlanders, was barely a day behind Hermes and was catching up fast. Their rocket assemblages had worked out somewhat better and they were currently two propulsion units ahead. In addition, Delhi was considerably smaller, having been designed for a single augmented brigade. The total colony barely exceeded twenty thousand.

Weem, however, was behind schedule. Her departure was delayed twenty-four hours when the first rocket tube sleeve burst in firing. It had yet to be repaired and she was currently accelerating on only two rockets, with twenty-six more to go before completion.

The news from Weem was particularly discouraging since she was another Highland asteroid, garrisoned by the MacKenzies and Buchanans.

Wynd, with the Lamonts, the Frasers and the MacPhersons added to the originally posted complement, was reported under way with one rocket firing. Two additional rockets were scheduled for completion within twenty-four hours and two more in seventy-two. With a bit of luck she'd make it.

Heartening news came from America when it was announced the asteroid George Washington, with forty thousand aboard, had passed Saturn's orbit heading outbound in the direction of Sextans. The joy was tempered considerably by the news that only slightly more than two hundred women were on board, and several of these were beyond childbearing age. The United States Government still officially denied any possibility of danger to the sun, the fundamentalist clergy there having decided that with the Lord on their side they could not lose. The Washington was supposed to continue outbound only to about the Pluto orbit before decelerating to take up permanent station there.

Word that a second American asteroid, the Thomas Jefferson, was outbound carrying another twenty-seven thousand men and only three thousand female clerical workers caused murmurs of disbelief aboard Aileach. Were *all* Americans fools?

The Soviet asteroid Nikolai Lenin, with seventy-two thousand men and women cooped up in a space only three quarters Aileach's size, was reported passing Jupiter outbound. The Presidium of the Soviet Union, declaring the event a national holiday, had taken this occasion to remove themselves and their families aboard the Lenin to "inspect" this vast triumph of Soviet technological skill and achievement. It was also pointed out with a certain malicious glee that the Soviet vessel carried seventy-two thousand while the two American vessels combined carried only seventy thousand.

Now the long-range detectors on Aileach picked up the trails of overtaking ships carrying the additional scientific personnel who were to travel with her. Hourly the blips moved nearer and nearer, then slowed their rate of closure as they commenced deceleration to match velocities.

Carefully the controllers talked each ship into berth. Suddenly every human life became infinitely precious. Not one could be wasted now.

Duncan himself came to greet the new arrivals and to ask whether they could offer a ray of hope. They had none to give. Apparently they were in unanimous agreement that Earth was doomed. The spectroscopes were even now beginning to show significant changes in the sun. The only question was when, not if.

After the scientists and their families were escorted below, Duncan wandered aimlessly about the berths. Of all the people aboard Aileach he was the least necessary. He merely took up space—space perhaps better occupied by someone more qualified to be a survivor. Turning, he saw a figure detach itself from the knot of crewmen from the newly arrived ship. It launched itself forward, forgetful of the small "gravity" aboard Aileach since it had slowed its acceleration, and descended on him in a gyrating bundle of waving arms and legs.

Instinctively Duncan reached out to intercept the plunging form and was himself swept from his feet and hurtled against the far wall. Shaking himself free, Duncan pulled himself to his feet and then turned to minister to his mysterious tormentor.

His assailant also was in the process of pulling himself to his feet. Then, seeing Duncan before him, he snapped erect and threw a salute. It would have been a beautifully executed gesture if only there had been a bit more gravity.

But there wasn't. In snapping erect the suited figure toppled itself backward and the salute, lacking proper gravity as a control, nearly shattered the plastic in the visor.

Catching him expertly, Duncan pinned him against the wall. "There now, lad," he announced firmly. "Stay there and don't move. Ye've caused enough trouble already. Now take off that helmet so I can see ye and we'll go from there."

"Duncan—sir. 'Tis me, Donald MacLeod."

"Donald! What are ye doing here? I'm glad to see ye, lad. Are your mother and the rest o' the family here too?"

"I fear not, sir," Donald replied. "They're staying behind on Skye . . . The UN is concentrating mostly on sending regiments with families plus unmarried women to match up with the unmarried men aboard."

"I'm truly sorry to hear that. But ha' ye been assigned here?"

"Not that either, Duncan. On the way out we elected to make a turnaround. The four of our ships can carry nigh unto three hundred people if we crowd matters a bit. Mayhap we can make another trip or two to Wynd before the sun burps. It's worth a try, at any rate."

"Ye could stay here, Donald. Mavis and I would be glad to ha' ye."

"Nay, Duncan. I'm still The MacLeod."

"Aye. But ye cannot be much more than seventeen, lad. Surely there're others?"

"I'm nigh eighteen, and Earth needs every man. They've emptied the academies for crewmen to man the ships as fast as they build them. We're using every minute to move every possible man, woman and bairn. I do my part."

"Ye're worthy o' your name." Duncan smiled gently. "Should ye be on Wynd or safe in space when the sun goes, come here wi' one o' the transfer ships. If ye don't make it then I promise my first son will be given the surname o' MacLeod. Your name will not die and there'll still be a MacLeod o' Lewis."

"Thank you, Duncan." Donald nodded soberly. "Say hello to Mavis for me and tell her all is yet well on Skye."

"I shall do that, Donald. And ye'd best learn how to step about in low g or the next time ye'll kill us both."

Duncan stood in the launch control room and watched until the last faint return from Donald's ship faded from the screen inbound toward Earth.

The sun was beginning to swell slightly. Her color was turning an angry, sullen red. Pockmarks pitted her surface like some ancient plague. Thule, Greenland, reported a noonday temperature of 28°C and the South Pole station recorded a temperature of only 22°C below zero in the middle of winter. It should have been 52°C below at least.

Radio reports from Earth took an ominous tone. The Chinese had launched a vast fleet of nearly 1700 ships pointed apparently at Centaurus. Rumor had it that their rulers were aboard and the ships were being manned exclusively by women so each of the leaders could dispose of some fifty women as breeding stock. It would be a sybarite's paradise. Of course there was no real certainty except the fact of the ships themselves, and since no official report had come from Earth it was probably no more than a shipboard rumor.

The Europeans were officially reported to be digging underground in the belief that the solar reaction would be only temporary and they would be able to return to the surface in a few weeks or months. A few of their spaceships, manned by mixed crews, were reported en route to Hermes. A number of others were evidently making for Neptune's moon Triton, apparently planning to hole up there in the facilities being evacuated by the Scots.

Hermes itself was nearing Saturn's orbit and probable safety. Delhi was due to pass the orbit within the next six hours.

Wynd now had eleven rockets firing and was picking up speed every minute. One more day and it would be passing Jupiter's orbit. Weem was still having trouble. Only seven rockets were firing and three had burned out. Still she was nearing the Jovian orbit.

Baile, with two rockets firing, was pulling out of orbit with forty thousand on board. Under the best of circumstances she would need three weeks to pass Saturn. Work on Clach Tuill had been stopped and the garrison was being moved to Weem.

The United States continued officially denying any danger, but the Abraham Lincoln slipped orbit with thirty-two thousand women aboard and only five thousand men. Characteristically, the government had made no effort to unite families or employ any rational selection in choosing personnel. They had merely loaded some of the women's branches of the military and added a few civil-servant secretaries to round out the figure. Still, it was to link up with the Washington and the Jefferson as soon as practicable.

The South Africans had Nairobi under way with twenty-two thousand aboard. She was expected to pass Jupiter within two days.

The Israeli Government had succeeded in equipping a small asteroid only eight miles in diameter. Named Koheleth, she carried only nine thousand. With her small mass, she passed Jupiter on the fifth day and needed only seven more to reach Saturn.

Two Moslem asteroids, the Isfahan and the Hegira, carrying twenty-eight thousand and twenty-three thousand respectively, crossed Jupiter's orbit aimed in the general direction of Lyra. One more week and they too would be safe.

The Isle of Skye was now the Isles of Skye. The melting of the polar ice caps was far advanced and millions of tons of newly thawed water flowed into the oceans with each passing hour. Already the level had risen nearly seventy feet and tens of thousands of square miles of coastal lands were flooded about the Earth.

Along the equator the temperature exceeded the boiling point of water one afternoon. India, sweltering in a heat wave of unprecedented proportions, estimated 14 million dead in a single day.

Rowboats and cabin cruisers sailed the streets of New York City seeking to save a few lives so they could be lost later.

China, left leaderless by the defection of their rulers, invaded Russia with an army of 20 million. Or perhaps it was the new rulers of Russia who invaded China. No one was really certain of anything except that vast armies were locked in mortal combat along the steppes of Siberia.

The asteroid Amaterasu, of Japan, pulled from orbit carrying sixty thousand people. Powered by supersized rockets of unique design, she was able to reach Jupiter's orbit in only six days.

Hermes and Delhi passed Saturn nearly abreast with Delhi slowly forging ahead.

Aileach passed the remains of Pluto, picking up the Camerons on the run. Steering gyros slowly tumbled the mass of the asteroid and she began her long deceleration to await the others out by Styx.

Wynd was beginning to approach Saturn. Transfer of persons from Earth had ceased on Wynd and was being shifted to Weem.

Weem, however, was still having difficulties. She had passed the orbit of Jupiter but was still running on just nine rockets and her acceleration was pitifully slow.

Baile was nearing Jupiter. The Abraham Lincoln, fleeing at near-right angles to Baile, was also approaching the Jovian orbit. Nairobi was nearing Saturn's orbit and Koheleth was safe well beyond Neptune. Isfahan and Hegira were past Saturn and well on their way to Uranus's orbit. They too could be counted as saved. Hourly it was becoming more probable that a significant fraction of humanity might make it after all.

The sun had changed into a looming horror, bulging lopsidedly around the middle and streaked with ugly black-and-red stripes as sunspots mottled the surface. The last automatic transmission from Venus had been received a week earlier and reported a temperature of 582° at the pole. Mars reported a midday temperature over 66° and on Earth an automatic thermocouple recorded an equatorial temperature of 180° before burning itself out. Three months earlier, before the alien attack, Earth had supported a population of more than seven billion. Now there were fewer than one.

Aboard Aileach no one listened to the radio or looked back at the sun anymore. It was too painful. When people passed a view screen they averted their eyes and walked more swiftly. The radios were turned off. Communicators were ignored as much as possible, and whenever one was activated to give instructions or news there was a collective pause and an inaudible sigh aboard the asteroid. Time was running out—and no one wanted to talk or think about it. But none could avoid it.

Families went for days with no words spoken, apart from meaningless grunts. Every adult aboard the asteroid was locked in a private hell —a hell as personal and meaningful as his or her own memories of Earth.

Children, not understanding, cried, wondering what they had done wrong. The tears went untended, yet the children were oddly precious. They were the new Earth; the ones who had never known it.

Earth fell silent. Possibly none of the survivors cared enough to contact the asteroids again. Possibly the heat and dense, steaming fog rising from the oceans had destroyed the radios. There was nothing heroic about Earth's death. No bugles sounded taps, no blare of bands and brave speeches.

Now a vicious burst of static erupted over all the radio wavelengths. To the watchers aboard Aileach the sun seemed the same angry, swollen, baleful horror it had become over the past weeks. Then it began to swell perceptibly. A lurid tongue of flame licked out, fell back upon itself, recovered again and reached out and then farther out. A second lash of flame followed it.

Abruptly the entire surface changed color as the sun commenced its cataclysmic expansion. Doppler effects from the onrushing surface skewed the color out of the reds up toward the violet end of the spectrum in a brilliant, intolerable burst of light. In a scant three minutes Mercury was gone. Another three minutes and it was the turn of Venus. Three more after that and Earth was gone.

Next came the turn of Mars as the scorching radiation swept out interminably, it seemed. And now a new and different burst of radio noise swept out as Jupiter, its atmosphere boiling away under the outpouring of heat and pressure from the sun, literally howled out over the decametric wavelengths. In minutes it shrank from an eighty-seven-thousand-mile giant to less than twelve thousand miles to become an airless hulk skipping along uncertainly just a few million miles above the surface of the bloated sun.

Slowly the violet color slipped away, drifting back toward red as the rate of solar expansion slowed, then stopped altogether. It was over. All that was left was a slowly shrinking sun which would perhaps take decades to recede back past whatever might be left of Earth and possibly a century or more to return to its former size.

It was that simple.

CHAPTER 13

The next weeks could have provided material for whole generations of psychiatrists. A cinematic treatment of the same topic would no doubt have depicted the survivors with some being elated at having escaped the doom of Earth. Others would be shown going mad at the agony of their loss and yet others would be shown making windy speeches and vowing eternal hate against the aliens. Actually very little of this happened.

First there was numbness. . . . The unthinkable had happened. All that was left of Earth was a vagrant, gypsy remnant, wandering aimlessly in space. They had become gypsy Earthmen.

Then there was a collective sense of guilt. What right did they have to be survivors? What was the point in it all? The abstract idea of vengeance is a sorry, pitiful thing on which to create a new future. It might be an adequate motive in a comic strip or penny dreadful, but not for flesh-and-blood humans.

It all added up to a dangerous lassitude, a sense of purposelessness. Partly, perhaps, it might be considered a sort of postpartum depression. What had seemed impossible had proved possible after all. The months'-long stress of waiting and hoping was over. The tension was gone, leaving behind only the dull ache of loss and emptiness and the prospect of a clouded, uncertain future.

No one cracked. There were no madmen shouting that God had ordained all humanity must perish and seeking to help Him along. There were not even any suicides, and no one retreated into schizoid fetality. The dominant, possibly solitary characteristic of those aboard Aileach was a sense of passive waiting—for the other shoe to drop, as it were.

This was the time for Duncan. It was his first real test. It was one thing to be a competent field commander. It was another thing to be a sector commander. But it was something entirely different to be able to take a demoralized, aimless aggregate of people and instill in them a purpose. And what made it worse was that Duncan himself felt the same way. Before the sun blew he talked of having to accept the inevitable, but he had never quite believed it. He had taken it for granted, deep within himself, that at the last minute some brilliant discovery would neutralize the attack and Earth would survive. He knew what the others were feeling precisely because he felt the same.

It was his responsibility to restructure grief and channel it into meaningful activity, to convert numbness into feeling and guilt to purpose. If he could not do this, Aileach too would inevitably join Earth in another kind of death; the ultimate death of hope. He had to do something—say something—to give his people a renewed reason for surviving.

Calling a general stand-to by the intercom outlets, Duncan began an impromptu requiem. "Earthmen o' Aileach," he began a trifle uncertainly, seeking the right words. "There is none o' us but has suffered grievously these past weeks. Even the friendless orphan has lost his Mother Earth, and that is the greatest o' all losses. . . . Nor is there any way this loss can be mended. Our Earth is gone. But in her death Mother Earth gave to us her last and greatest gift: the gift o' responsibility—the duty—to make her live again on some other planet circling some other sun. This is the gift and obligation imposed on us by Mother Earth herself.

"This gift . . . this obligation . . . this responsibility, we cannot shirk. Earth did not fail us. We cannot fail Earth! I therefore now ask each o' ye to take unto yourselves a solemn vow that Earth shall live again. We shall make her live. We shall dedicate our lives and our future to that end.

"Nor is this all. In addition to the obligation laid upon us by Earth herself, a second obligation—a *geas*—has been put upon us by those who sent us here, those who stayed behind in order that we might live. We must strike back. We must gain some measure o' revenge against those who slew wi'out purpose, who attacked wi'out warning, who set themselves to destroy us merely because we existed!

"These must be our twin goals: the one owed Earth herself that we live, and in living make her live again elsewhere; and the second to the men and women o' Earth that we not merely cower and seek escape but stand like men and fight back against those who would exterminate us. Those two goals shall mark our actions in the years to come.

"Now to turn to matters o' more immediate importance. We are not alone. On Aileach there are near forty-two thousand. By calculating the effects o' the sun's expansion on ourselves and extrapolating the positions o' the other asteroids we know several ha' survived.

"Hermes, Delhi and Wynd are definite survivors, though the continued solar interference on all frequencies forbids communications. Baile has probably survived, but I regret to say 'tis doubtful whether Weem weathered it.

"The United States asteroids probably all survived, though there is some doubt wi' respect to the Abraham Lincoln. She was roughly at the critical point at the end.

"Koheleth and Amaterasu undoubtedly survived. Nairobi, like the Lincoln, was approximately at the critical point and may not ha' managed. The Nikolai Lenin was well past the danger point and may be assumed safe. Isfahan and Hegira are both presumed safe also. As for the Chinese flotilla, we ha' no information save that they undoubtedly escaped.

"As o' the last figures, Wynd had over forty thousand aboard. Baile had near the same. Aileach has forty-two thousand. Totaled, this means over a hundred twenty-two thousand Scots ha' survived. If perchance Weem did pull through, there will be another forty-five thousand to add to this.

"About a hundred and ten thousand Americans probably survived, but only about a third are women. Thirty-five thousand English, mixed wi' a few more Scots, ha' made it. Twenty thousand Indians, sixty thousand Japanese, seventy-two thousand Russians, twenty-two thousand Africans, nine thousand Jews and fifty-one thousand Arabs and Persians made it, plus mayhap five thousand Chinese.

"In all, if our estimates hold up—and not counting Weem at all—'tis probable over a half million o' mankind has survived. The Chinese, Russians, Japanese, Americans and Arabs we shall never know about since they were moving out in other directions and are many billions o' miles away by now. The Jews are another question. They were rising on the plane o' the ecliptic in our general direction so we may yet hear from them if fortune smiles and they are not out o' range by the time radio interference lessens.

"As for Aileach, Baile, Wynd, Hermes, Delhi and Weem if she survived, our present plans are to rendezvous in the vicinity o' Styx and assess the situation afore making any final decisions. Aileach has enough additional equipment and supplies guyed to the surface to outfit another asteroid, so if the total surviving population is enough to justify doing so we may make use o' Styx itself or one o' the other asteroids certain to be found in the area.

"To that end we are currently reducing speed so we can take up orbit about Styx and await the others. In the interim the first flotilla o' the Camerons is to be dispatched to Styx to survey the area for suitability and to make certain tests I ha' in mind. As for their families on Wynd, transfer will take place at Styx.

"Wi'in the next few days I intend to speak to ye again wi' respect to the future o' our group. As your general I can assume control only o' the military aspects o' our situation. I cannot, either in justice or honor, also assume any rulership over your lives, your fortunes or your futures. That must be your prerogative and I cannot interfere save as it affects the military status o' Aileach. However, until such time as we ha' received more complete information regarding the other asteroids I shall continue to exercise full powers o' command.

"And now I say, let us be o' good cheer. . . . Despite our loss we must and shall survive. We *will* accept our responsibility. We shall not shirk nor shall we be found wanting. Let us work to do that which must be done—and there is much to be done now—afore we meet wi' the others at Styx. So let us now be to it."

For the first time in months the muted thunder of the giant rockets was stilled. Aileach whipped in tight orbit a scant 140 miles above Styx. Delhi, moving in a higher, slower orbit, circled at 225 miles. Wynd nestled tightly against a pitiful mite of a moonlet only seven miles in diameter orbiting some 280 miles up. Hermes spun in silent solitude at 360 miles and Baile coasted serenely at 500 miles.

Ships plied busily in the space between the asteroids, transferring passengers from one to another. Wynd, carrying everything the UN fleets could cart away during those last hectic weeks, contained an incredible 27,000 more than Duncan's initial estimate of 40,000. Baile turned up with 8000 extras. Hermes had 14,000 extras over the estimated 35,000. Most of these were families of the Camerons, but at the last moment a dozen ships carrying Brazilians had scampered aboard and some thirty-two ships from Sweden were in escort. Delhi was only 6000 above its original complement, but among these were 250 Danes who had been surveying Jupiter's moon Io when the sun started to go.

The total number of survivors looked to be perhaps 550,000 of the 7 billion who had inhabited Earth a year earlier.

A few days before slipping into Styx orbit there had been a brief contact with Koheleth, but no one aboard the asteroids spoke fluent Hebrew and the people aboard Koheleth flatly refused to speak any other language, so nothing was gained from the contact and she quickly sailed out of range.

The first order of business following the sorting out of personnel and equipment was a joint meeting of the commanders of the several asteroids. Wynd was selected for the meeting, and on the appointed day scouts from each of the asteroids converged for what would possibly prove to be the last summit conference of mankind.

General Dyananda Nanak of Delhi, was first to be piped aboard. Then came Duncan of Aileach, General Sir Harold Desmond-Phillips of Hermes, and last of all General MacAuslan of Baile. General Ritchie of Wynd, as senior officer, hosted.

"Gentlemen," he announced calling the meeting to order after the usual introductions and swapping of experiences were complete, "I suppose each of you has ideas and plans. Since this may well be the last meeting of this sort for humanity I feel it our duty to explore every possibility and examine each idea before leaving this place. There can be no arbitrariness in our decisions. The very future of what is left of mankind may easily depend on what we say and do here. Each of us is sovereign commander of our own vessel and as such is peer with all. As such I see no recourse but to consider each of us as representative of an independent nation as it were. For that reason my only exercise of authority will be as moderator. Is this acceptable to all of you?"

"Entirely acceptable, General Ritchie," replied Nanak. "To tell the truth, I had wondered how the question of authority would be treated and could see no solution save that advanced by you at this time."

"Then I take it we are agreed? . . . Very well, I shall stand as chairman but no more than that. To get down to business, I have been in communication with General Campbell over the past weeks and he has a number of thoughts it may be to our advantage to hear. I give him the floor now."

Rising, Duncan surveyed the men around him. "Gentlemen," he began, feeling for the proper words, "the alien is not done wi' us yet. . . . He cannot afford to be. He knows this as well as we. Given the overwhelming advantage in numbers in two open battles we still whipped him decisively on both occasions. We humiliated him. We refused to die when he demanded it o' us. He attacked us wi'out warning or provocation, and wi' every advantage on his side, yet he was compelled to destroy our whole solar system since he could not conquer it!

"Knowing this, he must also know that should any o' us survive 'twould be merely a matter o' time afore we would seek him out and demand atonement. Therefore the very galaxy itself is too small for the two o' us.

"But he still has the advantage o' the hyperdrive—and that becomes a greater asset to him now than it ever was. For example, suppose we decide to go to the nearest star, Alpha Centauri, and we take off after the Chinese. Now if we're to get a gravity aboard ship we must either continue accelerating for the first half o' the trip and then flip over and decelerate for the other half or we would ha' to restructure the asteroids to allow for a very small acceleration, together wi' a spin to give a centrifugal sort o' gravity.

"If we do the first and simply accelerate outbound, then wi'in about a year—depending on our rate o' acceleration—we will ha' speeded to a point where time compression becomes a factor. The voyage will take perhaps five to ten years outside time, but 'twill take only about two point five to three point five years in our time—assuming we spend two o' these years in the acceleration-deceleration stages. Only six months or so will be required once we reach time-compression speeds.

"Now this is all to the good so far as our own lives are concerned. We would not ha' to spend generations cooped up in our little asteroids. But on the other hand, it gives the aliens *more* time to prepare against us. He has mayhap six years to build new ships, to develop new tactics and devise new gadgets. We would ha' only two or three years. We would be donating time at a ratio o' two to one.

"Nor can I imagine the alien being so foolish as to ignore the chance some o' us ha' gotten loose. He will begin checking out all the nearby stars wi'in the next few years, and he'll be overreaching us at every turn. If he does not find us first then mayhap he'll find the Jews, the Russians, the Americans or any o' the others. And once having found the first asteroid he'll know what to look for and be sure to commence a systematic search to root out every survivor.

"We could easily rove all eternity from sun to sun, seeking a new home, only to find the alien ahead o' us at every turn!"

"How about heading out toward some star group a thousand light-years distant?" ventured MacAuslan. "With the time-compression factor in our favor we ought to be able to manage it well within a single lifetime aboard ship."

"That leads us to the heart o' the matter," argued Duncan. "We could get there wi'out difficulty. Given time compression, the physics people aboard Aileach ha' calculated 'twould take a shade over seven years internal time to go a hundred and fifty light-years—exclusive o' the time needed to get up to speed and down again. In brief, it would take about six months at speed to go four point five light-years but only about seven years to go a hundred and fifty light-years. A thousand light-years could be covered in less than a half century, internal time.

"The problem in this is the same as I mentioned earlier. We might ha' perhaps fifty years o' research time and study en route, whilst the alien would gain a thousand years. Assuming we are essentially even today—wi' us having the edge in battle skills while he has the hyperdrive—when we arrived at our destination he would be some nine hundred and fifty years ahead o' us.

"Gentlemen, I do not think we can afford so great a difference—not when our enemy has already shown an implacable hostility toward us. We cannot merely hope that a hundred or a thousand years hence he will ha' mended his ways and be sweetly solicitous o' our welfare."

Nanak broke the silence first, murmuring, "So it is not done. . . . We should have known so. The wheel has yet another turn to make."

Desmond-Phillips blurted an angry retort, then choked it off midway and faced Duncan. "Confound it, sir, you have given us a knotty problem. You say we cannot escape without giving the enemy time to move so far ahead of us we can never catch up. Is that your only contribution or have you more bad news to offer?"

Duncan nodded briefly, then continued, "As a matter o' fact, I do ha' some ideas. And they will take your cooperation to put into effect. Will ye gi' me your ear a while longer?"

Eyeing the mute acceptance in their faces, Duncan went on. "Prior to our arrival here I sent the Camerons out wi' special detection equipment—equipment designed to record the passage o' ships in hyperspace. These were essentially the same detectors we ha' been using since before the battle o' Jupiter, but refined to gi' some indication o' direction and speed. Since then we ha' obtained three tracks o' vessels where they tripped three or more detectors in a straight line. These detectors showed the vessels to be tracking wi'in some five one-thousandths o' a degree o' one another. Extending the tracks backward gives us a point o' origin at oh one seven degrees from the sun plus oh one three degrees above the ecliptic. Computation o' the time between successive detector trips indicates the craft were moving at a speed o' about a hundred and fifty times light—give or take five or six.

"Since the time between the second and third assaults on Earth was about two years, the reasonable assumption is the aliens could not ha' originated from any point more than a hundred and fifty light-years distant—allowing barely time for one round trip. The probability is that the alien craft did not originate from a point more than a hundred light-years out. This would allow time for a return to their origin wi' news o' their defeat, a month or so for them to make a decision and reprovision their strike craft and then lift off afore setting out to Earth again.

"Detailed analysis o' the star charts in that area, plus direct telescopic observation wi' Aileach's fifty-inch Schmidt camera, reveals a star o' type G-two located almost squarely at the right place at a distance o' some sixty-three light-years. Presumedly this is at least a staging base for the aliens and possibly even their home planet."

"Just from curiosity," interrupted Nanak, "has this star a name?"

"No. 'Tis only a number on the charts," replied Duncan.

"Then may I make the suggestion we assign it a common name—possibly Shiva, as emblematic of the god of death and destruction. It would be considerably simpler to call it by an agreed-upon name than to refer to it by a number or call it by colloquialisms which soon would become proper names used by different worlds. The latter would inevitably lead to confusion."

"I am perfectly agreeable," remarked MacAuslan. "It would certainly be appropriate, and as you say it would avoid confusion."

Noting the murmur of consensus, Ritchie broke in. "Very well, Shiva it is."

"I fail to see where this is leading us," argued Desmond-Phillips. "The fact that we know where our foe originates may be useful in the long run, but it can be useful only if we survive long enough for someone to make use of it. And everything I have heard so far merely increases my doubts of our survival. I would like to hear something bearing on this issue."

"I am coming to that, sir," replied Duncan. "I believe our problem can be minimized only if we are prepared to approach it on several fronts. For one, I feel we cannot afford to abandon this solar system entirely. I think we must prepare a base here on Styx and leave the bulk o' our science personnel behind."

"Preposterous!" blurted MacAuslan. "This is certain to be the first place the aliens look when they start checking to see whether any of us survived. They'll come straight to the sun and commence fanning out. They'll check all the outer reaches of the system on the assumption any survivors will most likely have moved out there. We'd be discovered immediately and then we'd lose all our science people—not to mention the rest of us."

"I'm not suggesting we all stay here," argued Duncan. "Nor am I suggesting we set up fortifications on Styx. I merely feel we must take a calculated risk and establish a deep underground scientific base here. But if done properly I do not believe it will prove an unacceptable risk.

"Consider the problem," Duncan continued inexorably. "If we all go away in separate directions in order to maximize the possibility o' there being at least a few survivors, then if any one o' us discovers the hyperdrive there will be no way o' informing the others. But if we keep a base here and make it our home port, as it were, then if anyone should discover anything o' value it can be relayed back to be sent out to the others.

"Even more to the point, a base here will not suffer time compression. A year o' working time here will be a year o' working time for the aliens too. Wi' *any* other solution we will be giving the aliens precious time we can never hope to recover. We *must* establish our science base here. I am totally convinced o' that.

"What we should do is place it far underground, in an area o' heavy-metal deposits and enough natural radioactivity to bollix any surface detection devices. The planet will not be equipped to fight, only to remain concealed even if the alien lands to search us out."

"This is interesting," conceded Nanak. "But it can be feasible only if the requirements for concealment are met. I presume you have checked into the matter?"

"I have. There are at least a dozen such places on Styx, so the alien could not become suspicious o' any one. I ha' even begun a test drill down twelve miles so far. I intend to take it down to fifty miles to make certain 'tis feasible, but so far the results are encouraging. And even if it fails here, there are still several thousands of smallish planetoids like Styx in this general vicinity, so one at least ought to work."

"Perhaps you'd better tell the rest of your scheme, Duncan," interrupted Ritchie, "before matters get too far astray."

"Very well. The next thing we must do is try to find some way o' confusing and hurting the alien. I propose we take yon moonlet Wynd is hooked onto, convert it into an assault vessel and then head directly to Shiva. 'Twill take perhaps seventy years objective time to arrive there, but if we can deliver a massive blow to the alien on his home planet we can probably slow some o' his technological development and chop him down a little closer to our size."

"Do you believe it can be done?" pressed Nanak.

"Aye—and I think it *must* be done—for several reasons. If we are intercepted along the way, for example, 'twill force the alien to divert a considerable part o' his fleet for the protection o' his home planet. He simply will not be able to afford the risk that Earth had launched a dozen or so asteroids before the blowup and will therefore ha' to assume more are on the way.

"If some o' ye are intercepted, on the other hand, 'tis likely the enemy will not stop to consider the possibility any craft would be heading straight toward them. They would figure we're scattering and neither expect nor prepare against a blow to their homeland. So in that event our attack might well be made easier. Either way, 'twould seem this must be our strategy."

"Then to sum it up," commented Desmond-Phillips, "you would propose we leave the bulk of our science personnel here to continue research and also provide a communications centre, scatter the rest of the asteroids by moving them along predetermined tracks toward relatively empty regions of space and then convert our small moonlet out there into an assault ship to worry and conceivably even cripple the alien's homeland?"

"Precisely," nodded Duncan. "As I see it any other result leads to probable disaster."

"And am I in error to assume you would like to captain the assault ship?" ventured MacAuslan.

"You are quite correct, sir," replied Duncan. "We all ha' a score to settle wi' the alien but we cannot all do it individually. Since the idea is mine I think I should be allowed to carry it to its conclusion."

"You have justice on your side in the argument, but I certainly would have appreciated the opportunity to carry it through myself," said Nanak. "Personally I believe you have developed an excellent plan. I dislike splintering the remnants of humanity so much, but the military necessity is urgent and I feel it is undoubtedly the best available option. . . . But may I make one personal request if your plan is ultimately approved?"

"By all means," replied Duncan.

"I should like to feel that India too assisted in the counterstroke against the alien. Since I cannot personally accompany the ship I should like to offer one destroyer, complete with crew and families, and ask that it be made part of the mission."

"I am proud to accept the offer," nodded Duncan. "And if the plan be approved ye ha' my guarantee India shall ha' a post o' honor in the attack, sir."

"England, of course, cannot be omitted from the honor of striking back either," harrumphed Desmond-Phillips. "The overall plan appears rational and is almost certainly the best option. I too would like to offer a crew and destroyer. And may I also make the suggestion the asteroid be given a name suitable for the mission."

"Aye," decided Ritchie. "Your plan seems acceptable to all. I therefore propose each o' us tender a destroyer wi' crew and families for the mission. 'Twill be more like Earth herself striking back if done that way. As for a name, how would 'Vengeance' or perhaps 'Revenge' strike you?"

" 'Wolf' would be another good name," suggested MacAuslan, "especially since the aliens come from the Constellation Lupus, which means 'wolf.' "

"You know," spoke up Desmond-Phillips, "those names all seem good, but somehow lacking substance. My ancestors fought against you Scots for many centuries. During that period we acquired a healthy respect for the claymore. I confess a goodly number of my forebears died under it. I think it would be entirely appropriate to name the ship after the sword of Scotland—the 'Claymore.' "

"Our Highlander regiment would appreciate that too," agreed Nanak. "The Poonas received their tartan and colors from Scotland, and in view of the recent events it would seem a most appropriate name—one ship setting out to defeat a world. It even sounds like a Highlander assault."

"Then 'Claymore' she is," decided Ritchie. "And may she be a strong right arm for mankind!"

"A toast, gentlemen," ordered MacAuslan grimly. "A toast to Claymore and the ability to strike back!"

CHAPTER 14

By the second week after the conference the preliminary shaft into Styx leveled off just over fifty-three miles beneath the surface of the Mercury-sized planet. Conditions were gratifyingly close to expectations. The natural, pressure-induced temperature was 20° C. The rocky walls were mainly fusible iron oxides, capable of supporting extensive caverning while producing oxygen as a by-product. Everything was go, at least for the first phase of the plan.

Wynd, having debarked the personnel who were to remain, fired her massive rockets and began the long journey into nothingness carrying a cargo of forty-seven thousand of humanity's small remaining fragment.

Delhi slipped her orbit the next morning with twenty-eight thousand aboard. Departing tangentially from Wynd at an angle of 85 degrees, she too began her trek into the unknown.

Baile and Hermes were to orbit Styx another two months before starting out and Aileach, which would be traveling under the command of General Menzies of the Camerons, was to remain until Claymore was fully outfitted and started on her journey.

Additional to the destroyers assigned Claymore, each of the asteroids detached two cruisers, two scouts and five utility-class fighter-cargo craft. Five of the cruisers, all of the scouts and all but three of the utility ships were to be berthed on Styx for possible conversion to hyperdrive when and as the technology was discovered.

Styx was to have no defence; that had been agreed upon from the start. Her only hope was strict concealment plus good intelligence of any alien activities in the vicinity. Cleverly concealed on the surface of the planet were small detector devices designed to reveal the passage of any ships in hyperdrive. A ship landing on Styx would be certain to be detected well in advance no matter what the direction of approach. And once landed the odds were high that it would be under immediate observation by one or more of the tiny scanners carefully recessed into the rocks surrounding the most likely landing areas on the planet.

The ships assigned to Styx were carefully dug into the rock face of the planet in areas of high magnetic activity so any survey from above would show no anomalies to excite suspicion. The mouths of the tunnels were carefully placed in areas remote from normal landing sites apt to be selected by alien explorers, and after the last of the asteroids had departed ground crews on Styx were to obliterate all traces of the tiny fields by strewing boulders and scree about them.

As a "play within a play," a half dozen of the Danish ships were to serve a decoy function by not being berthed on the planet at all. Over the coming months they would visit dozens of the similar planetoids in the general vicinity, set up camps, strew debris about and then depart. Styx was to have two such campsites, both located on the most obvious landing sites—coincidentally, those being used mainly by the personnel digging into the surface.

If time permitted, the nomad fleet would visit hundreds of the remote rocks, then gradually work its way back toward the inner zones of the solar system—possibly as far as Jupiter—not only to confuse possible alien exploratory ships but also to seek out any pockets of humanity which might have found sanctuary on moons circling the outer planets. Some educated guesswork, based on fragmentary reports of the last climactic days, suggested that as many as thirty to fifty thousand people might have made it there.

When the decoy work was completed, not only would the enemy find hundreds of misleading clues, he would also be led to the conclusion all this activity was prior to the death of Earth and the forces involved had been withdrawn.

The preparations of the Claymore were, if anything, even more complex and elaborate. Every source of radiation was carefully shielded so it might be better able to escape detection once the rockets were shut down. The rockets themselves were patterned after the giant thrusters developed for the Amaterasu by the Japanese. The magnetic scoops, designed to suck in the raw hydrogen from interstellar space ahead of the speeding asteroid so it could be converted into reaction mass, were both narrowed and fine tuned to make detection of their field more difficult. Automatic shield dampers were placed about the magnets, utilizing the galactic magnetic flux for the main drive system.

The five destroyers, five cruisers and three utility ships posted to Claymore were carefully clustered about what would be the bow of the ship and an auxiliary control console was actually built into the command room of one of the destroyers so the whole asteroid could be maneuvered and fought from this one position if need be.

The village mall in the core of Claymore was quite small, being only a quarter mile in diameter. Just over two thousand people were to fight her, and wherever possible wives were to fill in as part of the operational structure. In all, slightly fewer than five thousand humans of all ages would set out with her.

The hospital facilities were large in proportion to the population but the hydroponics area was fairly small, being barely adequate to provide for a total population increase of 50 percent.

No conventional manufacturing facilities were installed and reliance was placed on the inclusion of numerous spare parts plus a tooling shop where items could be handcrafted as needed. To make up for any deficiencies, a dozen highly skilled patternmakers were added to the ship's complement.

But if conventional manufacturing was omitted, the lack was more than atoned for in the weapons-making capability. Rather than a single celaenium-producing facility three were installed together with a weapons-production shop which rivaled those of the larger asteroids.

The surface of Claymore was studded with a bewildering array of defences and special devices. With a surface area of some twenty-two square miles to work with, it was planned to install over four thousand separate torpedo launchers plus over eleven thousand of the 44 mm machine cannon.

Claymore's interior was just as impressive, though not so obvious. Where the other asteroids were intended primarily as support bases, having limited defence capability, Claymore was an attack ship intended to take punishment. Miles of corridors, layer upon layer deep, contained hundreds of individual airlocks. Whole miles of tunnel were drilled, then filled with carefully fused nickel-iron ore extracted from nearby asteroids of the transplutonian belt. When complete, Claymore looked from the outside like a conventional asteroid, but the miles of fifteen-foot diameter fused nickel-iron gave her an internal strength and rigidity a hundred times greater than any ordinary chunk of space flotsam.

As a final item, eight special torpedoes, identical to the others in outward appearance but with a special inertial homing device instead of a warhead and a chain of booster clusters to drive them, were seated squarely amid the fifteen massive propulsion rockets. These torpedoes were constantly homed on Styx and carried a special memory unit. Should it be possible for Claymore to capture an enemy ship, if only for a few minutes, a battery of specially trained technicians would enter and record everything in sight with cameras slaved to the base computer system. As the torpedo memories were also slaved to the same computers, they would record and file the same data. All written or printed matter would be included and as soon as the process was completed one of the torpedoes would be fired back along the rocket exhaust to return to Styx.

As a last precaution against the aliens stumbling across one of the torpedoes and using it to home in on the Styx garrison, each torpedo carried a special guidance sensor mechanism. A random pattern of radiation would not affect it, but any fixed radar tracker not properly coded would activate a special circuit and cause it to home in on Earth—or where Earth would normally have been—rather than on remote Styx. It was felt this would mislead the aliens into concluding that Claymore had been sent out well before Earth's destruction, so they would not look further into the matter.

Just before completion of the main connecting tunnels into Styx, Hermes and Baile commenced their long trek; Baile following in the wake of Wynd and Hermes, striking off on her own. Only Aileach remained with her cargo of sixty-five thousand humans, twenty thousand of whom were ultimately to be transferred to Styx and five thousand to Claymore.

As Claymore neared completion a trickle of men and women began to drift aboard, among them Mavis and her two-month-old daughter Celia—one of the very first of the new generation of humankind who were born after the death of Earth. Then the trickle became a minor flood as all five thousand crowded aboard, and then abruptly the flood ceased.

Duncan and Mavis returned to Aileach briefly for a final conference, reception and ceremonial review of the troops. As a special for the occasion Aileach's engines fired to life and they thrust outward at one quarter g for the evening. For one all too brief moment a bit of the gaiety of old Earth was recaptured at the brilliant ball, resplendent with regimental tartans, clan tartans and the whole vivid panoply of the

Highlands. Duncan felt a familiar surge of pride as the ranks of Highlanders—until only recently his men—passed before him attired in their dress trews. The pipes and drums struck up the clan air of the Breadalbane, "The Carles," followed by "The Thistle" before finally rolling into "Scotland the Brave" and "Scots Wha' Hae'," and he found himself standing stiffly at attention with tears streaming down his face.

The next morning Duncan and Mavis returned to Claymore and the first of the vast rockets fired, hesitatingly at the start and then with the raw, beautiful flame that signified millions of pounds of brute force. The second rocket sputtered momentarily, then added its thunder to the first. Then the third, fourth and fifth added their voices to the soundless cacophony and Claymore began to move with elaborate deliberation.

Inside Claymore the very walls whispered muted thunder which rose in crescendo as the sixth, seventh, eighth, ninth and tenth rockets added their roar to the symphony of noise. As the eleventh and twelfth rockets added their own basso notes, the first twinges of weight were felt. At first only a few ounces, it multiplied into a pound, then two, three, a dozen. Then it became fifty, a hundred and more. Inside the bowels of the asteroid a new noise intruded itself as the very structure of the ship commenced a nerve-racking groaning and cracking as pressures built up inside rock which had not known stress since the beginning of the solar system.

Claymore was accelerating at nearly 2 g's by the time inertia was overcome and the rockets were developing full thrust.

Behind her were Aileach and Styx, standing nearly motionless in space and perceptibly fading from sight. Aileach would remain in her orbit another month or so until Styx was fully equipped and in operation. Then she too would commence her own journey.

By the time Aileach departed Claymore would be speeding at an appreciable fraction of light. Two months at 2 g's would be nearly sixty-three thousand miles per second. Another month would bring them halfway to the speed of light. Within six months, provided the rockets held up and could overcome the increasing inertia scientists predicted would appear with a closer approximation to the velocity of light, they would be moving at 97 percent of light speed and be well within the time-compression zone predicted but never before actually encountered by humans.

But the 2 g acceleration created its own problems. To a people who had been living at fractional Earth gravities for the better part of a year the abrupt transition to double normal gravity was agony. Merely breathing was a painful chore, yet work had to go on. Preparations had to be completed, munitions to be stockpiled and the installation of the guns and torpedoes finished.

Work was at first assigned on a four-hour, six-shift-per-day basis. It was all a man could force himself to manage without collapse. As the weeks passed scarcely a soul aboard Claymore, Duncan included, had not keeled over at least once under the pressure of the ceaseless acceleration.

By the end of the fourth month the speed had passed 127,000 miles per second with no end in sight. The fifth month brought them up to 159,000 per second. Then a new and unexpected hazard appeared. Despite the massive nickel-iron cores running through the asteroid, a whole series of cracks and fissures began showing up in the rock walls of the asteroid as the unending vibration from the rockets exacted its toll.

Crews of space-suited men were sent through crawlways to check the conditions of the torpedoes and machine rocket guns. A number were found to be damaged or misaligned by the shifting and fracturing of the underlying rock. When they got to speed and could throttle back there would be work to be done, but for now it was enough that there was no indication of serious danger.

Still the acceleration continued.

At last the rockets themselves began to strain under the increasing resistance to further acceleration. Power was chopped to 1.75 g's, then to 1.5 . . . to 1.0. Finally, as the terminal velocity approached 185,920 miles per second, the rockets were stabilized at 0.3 g, or just enough to compensate for a certain slowing effect which had not been predicted by the physicists. Evidently at these speeds there was not only an increased resistance to further acceleration, there was also an apparent modification in the laws of momentum. This was a novel effect, one which the technicians felt might conceivably be important to the main research staff back on Styx. On this basis it was decided to send one of the torpedoes winging back.

With acceleration reduced, Claymore got down to work. Given their existing rate of time foreshortening, they would have a little more than twenty-six months of subjective time before they had to commence deceleration. Shiva, on the other hand, would have sixty-three years to prepare for them. They would have time for one attack only—if that much. It would have to be good.

Daily belt after belt of the 44 mm rocket ammunition spewed from the weapons shop. With 11,000 guns aboard, each capable of firing 600 rounds per minute, a single minute of concentrated firing would consume over 6.5 million rounds of munitions. Production at a rate of

250,000 rounds a day would be required to bring the supply to an acceptable stockpile.

Within two weeks after the shops went into full production they were turning out nearly 330,000 rounds a day.

Parties of space-suited men and women scoured the surface of Claymore, checking the torpedo-firing mechanisms and installing warheads, each of them with a 50 kilomegaton rating. Twenty of these, if fired against a planet the size of Earth, could wipe out a small nation. Two hundred would obliterate a continent. Claymore carried four thousand!

Twice in a single week the magnetic detectors placed fore and aft on Claymore registered the passage of a ship in hyperdrive. In both instances the bow detector tripped first, indicating a ship en route from Shiva to the solar system. Four days later the detectors picked up two separate ships passing from Earth toward Shiva. Calculations showed Claymore was just over twenty light-years into her journey.

Then came a period when for several days the detectors were in almost continual alarm, indicating ships presumedly passing from Shiva toward Earth. Had Styx been discovered or was this the start of an extensive search operation for human survivors—or both?

One thing at least was to the good. The enemy had acted far more slowly than they had assumed. They had waited over twenty years before starting their search—if it actually was a search. A twenty-light-year search sphere is four times as big as a ten-year one. This almost certainly meant the aliens would focus their attentions in the direction of likely target areas. There was simply too much volume of space to do otherwise. To cover the whole area effectively would require literally billions of ships. And with the UN asteroids carefully plotting their courses away from any nearby systems, there was probably a relatively small chance any of them would be discovered. As for the non-UN asteroids . . . no use speculating.

Considering the matter, Duncan grinned complacently. The enemy was sending ships looking for survivors in places the survivors would most likely be. And if he was doing that he would almost certainly not conceive of an asteroid heading directly toward his own homeland. He would be working on the assumption that any survivors would be heading away in mad, desperate flight for safety. But then he recalled his own actions a few short years ago and his grin faded. Basically he was even now merely repeating his own tactics. The enemy, remembering the headlong charge of three cruisers against his massed fleet, might very well consider the possibility of the same thing happening again and be preparing for it. It might even be written down in his war book as a standard human tactic.

Even if it were, though, it was far too late to do anything about it. All they could do is let it ride and hope for the best.

Another month and two more light-years passed. The detectors seldom went a day without indicating the passage of one or more of the aliens. On one such passage the stern detector slipped completely over and attempted to register two directions at once. The only explanation anyone could offer was that the alien ship had physically passed through the detector!

There was brief debate on the advisability of sending a second torpedo to inform Styx of this characteristic of the hyperdrive, but it was decided against. There were only seven of the homing torpedoes left and they might be more urgently needed later. The information was merely coded into the torpedoes, where it would wait until there was more to say.

By now all four thousand torpedoes were armed and cradled in their launchers. Three separate sets of computers were installed in parallel to service the 44 mm cannon. If any one of them failed the other two would be in line to take over. And if the capabilities of any one system was exceeded the overflow would automatically be shunted to the second, then to the third if needed.

Two separate computer systems controlled the torpedoes. And in addition to all this, every torpedo and every gun carried a manual firing mechanism. Even if all the computers were blown Claymore would not be helpless.

Added to the capabilities of Claymore herself were those of the five destroyers, the five cruisers and the three utility ships. Combined, Claymore and her associated fleet wielded more than twice the destructive capabilities of the whole Earth fleet during the battle of Jupiter.

During the second year of the trip Mavis gave birth to their second child, a boy who was promptly named Donald MacLeod and titled The MacLeod of Lewis. Their next son, they decided, would become the next Campbell of Breadalbane.

Donald's birth had been eagerly awaited by the doctors—a waiting which seemed vaguely obscene to Duncan and Mavis. While they both understood the reasoning underlying the medical anticipation, it certainly did nothing to lessen their natural fears. The doctors simply wanted to know whether a child conceived and carried under a 2 g acceleration and born at .97 light speed would be normal in every essential respect. After all, in terms of outside objective time Mavis had been pregnant for nearly eighteen years!

Fortunately for Duncan and Mavis, Donald was quite normal, so the doctors subsided with the merest hint of discontent. They would probably have been happier if he had been born with two heads. It would have given them something to write about.

More months passed. Claymore completed her preparations. The weapons shops slowed to a halt for lack of storage space for more munitions. The check-out of guns, computers and all the other essential gear aboard Claymore had been repeated for the third time. Physically there was simply no more to do.

For three whole weeks Claymore celebrated. There were games, dancing, piping and all the other revelries they could dream up. There were even a couple of determined efforts to distill some good Scots whisky. It was woefully unsuccessful, so they all called it bourbon and let it go at that.

Then came the countdown. Already the star of Shiva was the dominant object in the sky. Earth's sun was merely another star in the heavens, nearly sixty-three light-years away. Five days before commencing deceleration. Time for one last fete with a couple of days left over for recuperation.

Majestically, the gyros tumbled Claymore and the rockets commenced their full-throated rumble. Again came the agony of months of deceleration at two gravities. Five months . . . three months . . . one month. At last Claymore hovered silent in space, six billion miles from Shiva's sun, almost twice the distance at which Pluto had once swung in orbit about Earth's star.

The easy part of their journey was complete.

CHAPTER 15

Inertialess, the central mall was vacated as the tiny garrison moved into connecting tunnels. Crews physically moved into their ships, where they remained on semialert status against discovery. While it was considered unlikely they would be discovered at so great a distance from the central regions of the star system, no one was willing to take the chance.

Next came the role of the technicians. While Claymore stabilized in space an array of long-range electromagnetic spectrum detectors was put into operation. A pair of liquid-helium maser antennae were spread two miles to either side of Claymore, producing a dish over seven miles in diameter. The fifty-inch telescope, with image intensifier attached, scanned the region about the star in search of planets.

They found them. Six in all. The first one, close in to the sun, was scarcely larger than the now-vanished Mercury. The second, somewhat the size of Earth, was located at about the same distance out that Earth had been. No trace could be found of a planet which might correspond to Venus. The third, fourth and fifth were methane giants. The sixth, orbiting about as far out as Neptune, was scarcely asteroidal in size and located roughly 50 degrees out of line with Claymore. Conceivably there might be some other planet on the other side of the central star in its orbit, but save for the inevitable minor planetoids, to all intents and purposes this was the system.

Since the distance of Claymore to the sixth planet was well over 4 billion miles—a third again the distance Pluto had once orbited from the sun—it was felt safe to move in closer. The likelihood of anyone chancing to look in the specific direction of Claymore—and being able to detect her even if he did—was so slim as to be virtually negligible.

Moving in cautiously, only a few miles per second, the people aboard Claymore worked shift and shift, examining every bit of data they could glean from their instruments. As expected, the EMR apparatus showed intense activity emanating from the second planet. One enterprising technician isolated a fairly wide-band radiation squarely in the middle of the old Earth VHF TV spectrum. Computer analysis and rectification indicated that the aliens were transmitting with 1728 lines to the inch. While Claymore maneuvered in closer a receiver was rigged.

The results were disappointing, as broadcasts from a dozen different channels transmitting on the same frequency were picked up simultaneously. Even when efforts were made to differentiate between stations and eliminate unwanted data, the best they could obtain was occasional fuzzy images incapable of revealing anything of importance. Possibly things would improve as they closed on Shiva, but for the time being it was hopeless and the effort was abandoned.

The other EMR devices proved more rewarding. Intermittent radio and radiation signals were received not only from the sixth planet but also at relatively constant 60-degree angles about its orbit. Evidently the alien had elected to make use of the L4 and L5 stability slots around Shiva, probably as transfer stations.

Farther out on the perimeter of the system were other constant radio signals. From their foci it was concluded that they were probably defence or traffic-control bases on approximate equilaterals around the orbit of the outermost planet. A continuation of the survey also established the existence of two similar rings with inclinations of 60 degrees to the plane of the ecliptic. Apparently there were some eighteen monitoring stations in orbit about Shiva, with their orbits so interlaced that there would be little point in trying to rise above the plane of the ecliptic to slip in closer. Their work was going to be cut out for them.

Telescopic observations coupled with spectrum analysis revealed occasional ships penetrating into or emerging from overdrive. The distinctive celaenium spectrum was simply too obvious to miss if you had a good idea where to look. By plotting the positions of these ships over a period of several weeks, a pattern developed. For the most part these vessels entered or emerged at one or another of eleven points. Extending the points from Shiva revealed eleven stars, all within a radius of thirty to seventy light-years.

Significantly, Shiva seemed to be the centre of this activity, and Earth would have been a twelfth star radiating out from the same hub. Equally significantly, all the destination stars were of spectral type G and rotations on the order of thirty days, the same as the sun and Shiva's star.

The symmetry and consistency of the pattern was taken as suggesting a fairly high likelihood that Shiva was the actual home of the race and not merely an outpost. If correct, then in all probability the alien had not possessed the hyperdrive for any considerable length of time or it would have arrived at Earth markedly sooner. Assuming this reasoning was correct, the odds were pretty good that a decisive strike at Shiva would constitute at the minimum a temporarily crippling blow at their society, perhaps even allowing the remnants of Earth a breathing space to catch up.

Of course, it was only speculative and everyone aboard Claymore knew it, but at least it was reasonable—more reasonable than any other alternative they could arrive at. The fact that it was also hopeful was merely an added benefit.

Careful monitoring of the locations and orbits of the perimeter stations showed the intervals between stations on the same orbit to be in the neighborhood of 1.5 billion miles, with similar points of maximum separation between stations at differing inclinations. The mean orbital periods of the stations appeared to be somewhere in the vicinity of 260 years, but this was only an average and the stations were rather obviously not all at precisely the same distance from their sun. The actual periods varied from 253 to 267 years and there were currently three different positions about the perimeter of the system where existing gaps exceeded 60 degrees. These minor gaps offered the optimum chance of slipping between the Shivan defences undetected.

There was only one difficulty: the rockets could not be operated that close to the Shivan system without virtual certainty of discovery and annihilation. Claymore's present distance of 3 billion miles from the nearest observation station was so great it would take a stroke of fantastically bad luck for them to be discovered. Someone would have to be using a powerful telescope deliberately aimed at the exact location of Claymore to detect their rocket exhaust. But if they were to slip between the defences they would have to come within .75 billion miles—and that was simply too close for comfort.

Briefly Duncan considered the advisability of launching a few hundred or even a few thousand torpedoes programmed to drift in until they approached the orbit of Shiva, then orient themselves and rocket into the planet. Unfortunately, while this was almost certain to cause damage to Shiva, it most likely would not cause enough. Almost certainly one or more of the torpedoes would be intercepted on the way in, and as soon as the first was intercepted there would be an immediate systemwide alert, with a good possibility virtually all of the missiles would be stopped. Besides, it would forfeit any opportunity of obtaining an intact hyperdrive ship.

The same objection weighed against any plan which simply involved backing off in order to gain space to build up speed, then plunging in headlong, relying on a presumed inability of the enemy to scrape together a fleet large enough to destroy Claymore before Claymore destroyed Shiva. Conceivably they might get away with it, but Claymore's purpose was to damage Shiva, not merely to frighten it in some kamikaze attack.

Yet another possibility Duncan considered and rejected was the idea of dispatching a destroyer or a cruiser on a wide circuit of Shiva with orders to pick up momentum on the way to a breakout area for hyperdrive ships, then chop engines while still out of detector range, drift into the breakout area and fire up as if they were a new arrival. While conceivably this might work and the ship would be allowed to join the traffic pattern en route to Shiva, the odds weren't too good. It was altogether too likely any arriving ship would be required to give identification data and receive tracking instructions from one of the stations. The ship would be detected as an impostor and destroyed—and in the process the likelihood of any further surprises would be reduced.

After some consultation with various of the technicians, Duncan finally decided on a plan which seemed to offer the best prospects of success and the greatest flexibility of response if things went awry. The gyros spun Claymore on her axis until she faced broadside to the Shiva system. One of the great rockets was unshipped and the firing tube recessed nearly a quarter mile deeper into the rock. The wall was then funneled out slightly and the rocket reseated into the deepened well. As added concealment a conic baffle was erected as an extension of the firing tube and carried out an additional two thousand feet. When it was completed, the exhaust flame would be invisible from any angle except that of an observer situated within 5 degrees of the stern. Claymore could now maneuver with small risk of detection from her rocket exhaust.

It would take time—possibly as much as a year—but by cautiously picking her way in, disguised as a routine small asteroid of the sort found in abundance around any stellar system, they might be able to position themselves directly opposite one of the minor orbital gaps they had discovered. Then the sleeve extension on the central rocket could be cast off and the five central rockets, plus the newly recessed central one, would fire intermittently for from three to five days until they achieved an essentially "normal" speed for a free-falling outer asteroid. Since Claymore herself would be between the rocket exhaust and the outer satellite stations during the brief firing interval, the danger of detection would be negligible.

As soon as the desired velocity was achieved Claymore would chop power and coast between the stations on a trajectory designed to bring her immediately in behind the fourth planet—the largest of the Jovian type. Using it as a gravity brake and employing steam jets to make small corrections in the trajectory, they ought to be able to slip into a moderately tight orbit about the planet.

It was chancy, but not too much so. Assuming this planet, like the Jupiter of old, had a number of moonlets, Claymore might well be able to elude detection indefinitely. After all, a small, seven-mile planetoid is barely noticeable even under the best of circumstances, and Duncan intended to do everything in his power to make these the worst of circumstances.

Once they had penetrated the outer perimeter of the system and approached the planet, the sole remaining hazards stemmed from the possibility that the aliens had observation or research bases on one or more of the planet's inner satellites, or the physical possibility the planetary magnetosphere would be too intense for the shielding in Claymore. In case the aliens had observation bases there was still a reasonable chance they would not notice a tiny chunk of rock the size of Claymore. In case the magnetosphere was unacceptably hazardous they could still divert and commence an all-out assault on Shiva with the added advantage of starting from a point far inside the outer perimeter.

Admittedly the whole project was iffy, but it was better than any of the other alternatives. And if Claymore was detected she could still fire off her torpedoes and follow up with a headlong assault, so nothing could be lost by making the effort, and there was a potential for considerable gain.

Cranking Claymore up to yellow alert status, the destroyers, cruisers and utility ships kept their command stations manned around the clock. Everything was ready to fight on a moment's notice. If discovered, the fleet could be launched within two minutes. The full battery of torpedoes could be launched within five minutes and her thousands of rocket cannon could commence firing within thirty seconds after the fleet had cleared berth.

Next followed four tortuous months of cautious maneuver and careful research. Each change in the inclination of the asteroid was checked and double-checked in advance. Radio monitoring was continual. Even though they had no idea what the aliens were saying to one another, it was fairly predictable that the total volume of radio traffic would jump abruptly if Claymore's existence was accidentally discovered and suspicion was aroused.

A major alert occurred around the middle of the second month when a fleet of more than seventy ships was detected heading outbound from Shiva toward them. They didn't know whether to be worried or relieved when it passed the outer satellite station and went immediately into hyperdrive. This was the logical departure point for any expeditions aimed at Earth or at tracking down Earth survivors. They would almost rather have had it continue onward to attack them; at least that way the waiting would be over and they could act.

Finally they were moved into position. Everything was in readiness. The final compilation of all available data was fed into one of the seven remaining homing torpedoes and the message was sent winging on its sixty-three-year voyage back to Styx.

The muzzle shield was blown away and the six centre rockets slammed into action in a series of short, staccato bursts designed to nudge Claymore into the few feet per second expected of a minor asteroid at that distance from Shiva's sun.

They were on their way in.

CHAPTER 16

Almost before the final burst from the rockets ceased and the last gasp was belched, work parties swarmed through the airlocks and tunnels to inspect and repair any odds and ends of minor damage that might have occurred during the three days of erratic jolting as Claymore's aim was trued and speed was built up.

Additional shielding was placed around the giant reactors to reduce still further the already minimal danger of detectable leakage. Defective and even doubtful wire was ripped out wholesale and replaced with new lengths. More backup equipment was installed. Battery-powered slave motors were tied into each block of weapons so a failure of the main power system would not leave Claymore helpless. Personnel were assigned to duty stations where they could manually trigger entire banks of weapons in emergency.

The fifty-inch Schmidt was fixed continually on Shiva and smaller telescopes were focused on the rapidly nearing stations. Since little was known about the enemy's detection systems, and as he had had sixty-four years to improve on what little was known, all but essential power was curtailed inside Claymore. A community kitchen burned wood from the small grove of trees which had been transplanted from Aileach, and candles were used for ordinary lighting. Hot water for bathing became a thing of the past. In the hospital a small hydrogen motor with a shielded spark provided power. The celaenium reactors were damped and only enough power was developed to maintain the computers, the central control room and the hospital emergency room. Inertly Claymore plunged inward.

By now the sun of Shiva winked malevolently in the sky and had begun to show a perceptible disk. They were nearing the orbit of the stations. Still there was no sign of undue activity.

When they slipped ghostlike between the ring of stations a subdued cheer went up. A haggis was brought out and the carefully hoarded supply of Scots whisky was broached and a dollop distributed to all hands. The pipers serenaded in the passageways where they had moved just before the acceleration was canceled and the ancient songs were sung under an alien sun in zero gravity conditions.

Still undetected, Claymore slipped within the orbit of the fifth planet. By now she was closer to Shiva than to the satellite stations.

Then came the first bit of bad luck. The fifty-inch telescope was trained on the fourth planet. Within a few hours seven satellites were discovered orbiting her, and on two of these the EMR detectors found evidence of occupation. A hasty calculation proved the feasibility of employing the steam jets to warp her into orbit just beyond the main satellite orbits. There would still be a good chance of eluding detection, particularly as there was a considerable amount of debris already in orbit throughout the system. The major problem was the expenditure of water required for the steam jets. It would critically deplete the supply available for hydroponics. But there was no real choice, so the data were fed back into the computers and shortly a barely perceptible shudder filtered through Claymore as the first of the jets fired.

A long month later Claymore drifted across the orbit of the fourth planet in a gently curving trajectory. They were within scant days of taking up their wished-for orbit.

Alarms jangled! Battle alert! They were under radar observation.

With practiced confusion men and women raced to their appointed stations. The children were gathered into a trio of specially constructed padded cubbyholes just outside the main village dome. A dozen supervisory adults hurriedly locked them into restraining couches, a dozen or more children to each separately airlocked niche. Other women sped to the hospital to serve as emergency nurses. Yet others stood by in administration and command to serve as runners should communications fail. The majority of the women joined the men racing to man gunnery stations or emergency repair crews.

With silent clicks the arming fuses on the torpedoes slid from their safety locks as four thousand torpedoes armed for launching. Belts of ammunition slipped into the machine rockets. Automatic relays slid the bolts to half cock, then to full cock. Claymore was ready for war.

Moving into his control couch, Duncan flipped the main battle vision screen and strained to discover the source of the alarm. There was still no absolute certainty they had been discovered, and he hesitated to employ an active detection system lest Claymore's radiations should expose her. This left only telescopic observation and passive detection devices.

Unable to see anything, Duncan hazarded increasing the total radiation emission from Claymore by turning on the main spectral-analysis machinery and feeding it onto the screen. There it was: a ship, heading almost directly toward them.

Tersely he flipped the intercom and advised all personnel, "A single ship, apparently en route from Shiva, heading directly toward us. Approximately two hours distant at present time. Hold fire until the signal is given. If he lands this may be an opportunity to seize a ship."

Still bearing straight toward them, the ship sped on at an ever-accelerating pace. It should have been slowing if it planned to investigate. Could it be an unmanned vessel sent to destroy an unwanted chunk of debris? If so, interception was essential.

Duncan checked the chronometer anxiously. The alien was far beyond the critical slowing point and still accelerating. It must be unmanned. No other answer seemed probable.

Flipping the intercom again, he spoke calmly, "Prepare to fire when the alien comes wi'in five minutes' interception range." Claymore was committed.

At almost the last possible second before firing, Duncan spotted the least imaginable deflection from its head-on course. Calculating rapidly, he opened the intercom and ordered, "Hold fire!"

With agonizing slowness, even as Duncan debated the wisdom of his decision, the alien ship skewed slightly sidewise and passed within some ten miles astern and continued heading out into space.

Back in the solar system Duncan's ships had often done exactly the same thing. The computer would spot a bit of debris and automatically plot a smooth, easy trajectory around it. Probably no one aboard the alien ship was even aware of the nearby chunk of rock they had so narrowly missed. Hastily Duncan ran a projection of the alien track, then decided it was en route to one of the outlying stations, either for relief and supply or for transit to some other system.

Tension once built up is hard to release. For several days afterward the most trivial incident would evoke gales of laughter or streams of tears. A cross word would provoke a fight and a tender one a reconciliation. The fact all aboard reacted so strongly to what was, after all, a minor incident was a measure of the stress they had all been under over the past years.

A final burst of precious steam erupted from the bow steering jets and Claymore at last steadied in orbit about the fourth planet. As a mean distance of just over nine hundred thousand miles and with a period of just over eleven days, they had eased into an orbit which would take them high over the two occupied satellites for the first half dozen conjunctions.

The next morning Duncan called a battle conference with his principal commanders. Now that they had achieved their primary goal of penetrating the outer defences undetected it was time to take stock and decide on their next moves. For the first time the people aboard Claymore felt they honestly had a better than even chance of completing their primary task of launching a crippling blow against Shiva. Their secondary task of obtaining hyperdrive data was far less than promising . . . perhaps one in ten at best. Their third task, getting out again, was something no one was even willing to think about.

Present at the conference were Colonels Chandra Krishman, Stephen Holmes, Andrew MacPherson, Duncan MacPhail of the destroyers; Lawrence Oliphant, a brigadier by Duncan's appointment, commanded Claymore's defences. Wallace Chisholm and Allen Layton, representing the scientific and technical personnel, completed the roster.

"Gentlemen," Duncan began once they had sorted themselves out, "We ha' achieved our first goal. We are well behind the enemy's outer defences and are presumedly both undetected and unsuspected. The next problem is, what do we do now? Almost certainly we can launch our torpedoes and do grave, if not fatal, damage to our enemies on Shiva. Conceivably we might even be able to launch our torpedoes in silence and then remain precisely where we are, evading detection for an indefinite period.

"But this would still not solve our long-range problem. So far as we know, Styx still has not solved the hyperdrive question. And they may never do so. Mayhap they've been detected and destroyed. Mayhap the whole hyperdrive concept is so outrageous it could only be stumbled on by accident. And if either o' these be the case, then though we may destroy Shiva herself we will ha' but scotched the snake, not destroyed it. Their people will remain on their other planets and continue their advances. Ultimately, wi'out the secret o' the hyperdrive, we face certain destruction as a race.

"This sets the purpose o' our meeting. Ha' any o' ye any ideas how we might go about obtaining an enemy ship? 'Tis no easy question and it may well be we shall ha' to consider the matter several weeks afore we finally arrive at a decision. So we may take our time and invite suggestions from anyone aboard should it turn out that we ha' no acceptable ideas amongst ourselves. . . . So wi' that note, gentlemen, ye ha' the floor."

Allen was the first to break silence. "I don't know whether it would be feasible," he mused aloud, "but as we are already within the main defences of the system the alien probably wouldn't be particularly suspicious if a utility ship came in bold as brass and landed square in the middle of a spaceport. He'd very likely figure it was just an unfamiliar model and let it go at that. If we landed next to one of their spacers there would be at least a chance we could capture it intact and cut out with it before anyone knew anything was wrong."

"Unlikely!" snorted Chisholm. "How would you take off in her? You'd have no idea how the controls were laid out and it'd be pure luck if they were anything similar to ours. There'd be maybe four or five minutes before the aliens caught on and then the cat would be out of the bag in earnest. For that matter, it's entirely possible we'd not even be able to find the control room in that length of time. We might not even find out how to open the airlock door."

"I'm afraid I must agree with Chisholm," Krishnan nodded. "Think how difficult it would be for you to walk inside a Soviet ship and fly it without prior knowledge of the language and control setup. And there we at least know something of the theory of their ships. Here we wouldn't even know that much."

"I concur with that," agreed MacPhail. "As a last resort, if nothing else offers any prospects of success, we might give it a try, but only as a final hope."

"Well," Allen shrugged, "I suppose that shoots me down. I withdraw the suggestion. Anybody else with an idea?"

"I'm no military man," Chisholm ventured, "but personally I figure our best bet would be to drop in next door and see about getting a ship from there."

"How do you mean that?" demanded Krishnan.

"We've been monitoring the transmissions of the two satellites beneath us. Apparently they send out data every second or third day, always in response to a transmission from Shiva herself.

"Some of my lads have run both ends of the transmissions through the computer to see what might come out. It's fairly certain the innermost satellite is automatic, but variations in the transmission pattern from the outer station suggest they've got a manned operation going.

"With nine different sets of transmissions to work with, we've got a few ideas anyhow. No idea what they are saying but at least the start of a pattern. We've assigned numerical values to the material and have been looking for repetitions and correlations."

"I fail to see how you could get useful correlations from a language you know nothing about," objected Oliphant.

"It's not as hard as it sounds," shrugged Chisholm. "We started with the assumption that the station is there for a purpose—a purpose primarily connected with the planet itself. So whenever there was a transmission from Shiva we looked for signs of activity on the planet which might prompt it. In each case we observed a correlation between the transmission and a burst of activity from the planet in the four-to-twelve-millimeter band. Additionally, by back-checking we were able to determine that there were no such bursts which were not accompanied by an exchange of messages. I would say the correlation is pretty conclusive."

"It would seem you've made a pretty good case," conceded Oliphant, "but I still fail to see the significance."

"I'm coming to that," Chisholm continued imperturbably. "From the few carcasses recovered during the battles around Earth we know the alien has six digits on each hand—twelve in all. His numbering system is therefore most apt to be based on this. Now, each of his transmissions has contained certain initial points of similarity but with some variations suggestive of a date-time group. Given another week or two I believe we will be able to juggle things around enough that we could temporarily take over their transmissions without arousing suspicion."

"I fail to see what purpose that could achieve," objected Holmes. "Even if we could translate their language completely I doubt seriously whether they would be kind enough to radio us their data on the hyperdrive."

"Right. But what I have in mind is a trifle different. Suppose we were to remove the warheads from a few spare torpedoes and expand the cannister area. There would be more than enough room for a fully equipped, space-suited man in each one. A few technicians, properly equipped, could land on the back side of the satellite, move around to the alien's base, cut their antenna leads so they couldn't call for help, capture the base and take possession. If there's a ship already there we could study it at our leisure for a couple of weeks while sending out faked data. Even if it wasn't hyperdrive-equipped, we might still be able to use it to hop down to Shiva and cut out one of their starships.

"Even if there are no ships on the satellite we might still be able to fake an accident and cause enough damage to have them send out a relief-and-repair ship for us to capture. In effect, we would be asking them to send a ship out to us rather than us having to go out and get one."

"Permit me to withdraw my objection," nodded Holmes. "I find the idea most attractive."

"It seems quite good save for a couple of technical details," admitted Krishnan. "I believe it would be essential to establish a reliable means of communication between Claymore and the landing party. We would have to know almost immediately whether the attack was successful; otherwise there would be a distinct possibility the enemy could be alerted without our even being aware of it."

"I agree with Krishnan," seconded MacPhail, "and I should like to add a point of my own. We have no real guarantee their satellite station is even manned. The whole thing could be automated, and if so there is a good possibility it would be left airless. It would be terrible if our men went out and were successful in their primary mission only to die for want of air."

"Your points are well taken," agreed Duncan. "Ha' ye any remarks to make concerning them, Mr. Chisholm?"

"Yes. With respect to communications, we already know the alien base is on the side of the satellite permanently facing the planet. As such, for at least a few hours after our arrival we would have the whole bulk of the satellite blocking radiation. Using directional transmitters set at minimum power we could talk back and forth without alarming anyone. Later, after we've gotten out of alignment, we'd have to go to real tight-beam stuff, but by then we'd either have succeeded or failed anyhow.

"As far as oxygen and other supplies are concerned, it would be no problem at all. Rig a few additional torpedoes for the other items needed and send them down as drones. The satellite's gravity is hardly enough to fret over. I'd weigh just about a stone down there—and fourteen pounds is nothing. Any of us could easily circle the entire moonlet in six or eight hours while loaded with two hundred pounds of added gear."

"And how'd you expect to find the supply rockets in all the rocks jumbled down there?" demanded MacPherson.

"Set them up with infrared whip beacons and use our goggles. We could also use infrared for our own lights until we got close enough to the alien base, where they might spot us."

"I thought infrared was invisible," objected Holmes. "If so, then why not use it all the way through the assault?"

"It's invisible to us," admitted Chisholm, "but we're not sure it would be invisible to the aliens. It might be plain as day to them. We have to take some risks, but there's no sense in taking more than absolutely needful. Besides, the light from the planet should be more than enough to see by."

"How many men, and what types, will ye need?" asked Duncan.

"Myself and at least two other rocket technicians. A couple of electronics techs and two xenologists who are acquainted with several Earth languages—preferably like Bantu or Basque or Chinese—something as foreign to Celtic and English as possible. In all seven men."

"Ye know the seven?"

"Aye. I know exactly who would be best for the job."

"Then ye ha' them," decided Duncan. "But in addition ye'll ha' a squad o' the Argylls scout platoon to help in the fighting and as may be needed otherwise. They'll be under your orders but I suggest ye confer wi' the sergeant wi' respect to scouting or fighting. 'Tis his specialty, just as the other technicians ha' their own areas o' expertise. Make use o' them. . . . Now, how soon do ye figure to depart?"

"It would be advisable to wait a couple of weeks until we've had a chance to monitor more of the enemy's communications and tape the responses. During the while we could get the project readied and the torpedoes prepared. I would suggest we plan on departing in about seventeen days—provided I recall the orbital elements of the satellite and Claymore correctly. . . . Certainly within a day or two of that, at any rate."

"Then we'll do it. Oliphant here will assign ye your squad wi'in the day. They'll be detached from all other duties to work wi' ye until further notice. The other personnel ye need are to be similarly detached and assigned to the operation. Ye'll ha' full use o' all the facilities o' Claymore save for any matter requiring unshielding o' radiation sources. For these ye're to consult either wi' me or Oliphant first. Is this agreeable wi' ye?"

"Very much so. 'Tis more than I really expected. So if you have no more need of me I'd like to start putting things together."

"I think we're all o' us done for the while," nodded Duncan. "We've come to our decision. Now 'tis time to follow through wi' it."

CHAPTER 17

Eighteen days and three hours later Chisholm and the nineteen men of his command clustered together just beneath the outer skin of Claymore. One by one they stepped into their torpedoes and were lofted into the tubes. Last-minute data was slaved into their guidance systems from Claymore's computer and the umbilicals fell away. In a simultaneous burst of compressed nitrogen the forty torpedoes, twenty carrying men and twenty with additional equipment, launched outward toward the second satellite of the massive planet.

To Chisholm and the others the experience was eerie and improbable. Scant minutes before they had been in the relative safety of Claymore. Now everything was reduced to a solitary coffin-sized cannister drifting slowly toward a giant ball of variegated brightness they had named Jove because of its resemblance to ancient Jupiter.

Within moments Claymore was invisible against the inky background and no sign of their destination lay ahead of them. Their sole safety lay in the programmed guidance system locked into their torpedoes' computers. Should any of these fail by so much as a single decimal point, their fate would be a fiery plunge into the depths of the planet below.

Chisholm had never considered himself a coward. But then he had never really thought of himself as brave, either. Both ideas were foreign to him. He merely did what he thought he must and that was all there was to it. He felt he had to captain this mission. It was his idea, therefore he had to risk it. But right now he felt very small and lonely and more than a little frightened. He was alone as man had seldom been alone.

Somewhere out in the darkness were nineteen other men, each as isolated as himself, but the mere knowledge of their existence did little to bolster his courage. He was frankly and honestly afraid, and frightened as only a man can be who realizes he is working at the thinnest margin of his capabilities in a desperate and possibly hopeless gamble.

It could have been no more than a few minutes after the launch that he began to realize just how inadequate their plans had been. Locked inside his spacesuit and sleeved tightly within the torpedo, he was pinned to the walls. There was no way he could even lift his arms, and his fingers were imprisoned within the mitted gloves of his suit.

He itched. But there was no way to scratch.

The journey was to take six hours. Abruptly he discovered there was no way he could know exactly how long he had been traveling. It might have been only two or three short minutes, but then it could just as easily have been two or three eternal hours. He simply did not know.

He decided it must have been an hour at least. He was certain he couldn't last five more. He tried counting . . . slowly . . . one to sixty. Then again . . . one to sixty. And again and again. Five whole minutes. Only four hours fifty-five minutes to go. He'd never make it—not sane, at any rate. Briefly he retreated within himself, concentrating on his mission. Would he actually be able to meet an alien face to face? Would the plan succeed? How well would he handle himself if there was fighting? Did he have the leadership ability needed for the job?

He tried sleeping. Desperately he closed his eyes and forced himself to go limp. He still itched.

It didn't work. Wearily he opened his eyes again, hoping against hope that he had actually dozed off for a few minutes.

Reluctantly he decided he must have been traveling for hours—for days, possibly. The satellite must be just beneath him, but he saw no trace of it. . . . Nothing but the overwhelming view of the ever-enlarging planet below . . . or was it getting larger? Was he even moving at all, or had the guidance system failed and sent him drifting in eternal orbit about Jove? There was no weight. He had no bodily sensations. His muscles had long since cramped into utter numbness. There was no room to move in the confined space. Every square inch not occupied by him and his suit was crammed with equipment.

He decided he had probably been traveling about an hour. But no, it couldn't have been that short a space. It must have been a week at least. But then it couldn't have been a week because he hadn't gotten hungry yet. . . . Yes, he decided he really was hungry. In fact, he was completely famished!

He also had to use the bathroom. And paradoxically, while none of the big things of the universe seemed to help, that little, everyday, mundane need did more to reassure him than anything else could have. "Let's see," he muttered to himself in defiant effort to clear the cobwebs from his brain, "I used the jakes just before getting suited. And I haven't had any water since. . . . Christ, I'm thirsty! . . . So I figure 'twould take at least three hours before I'd have to go again. . . . Make that four, to be needing to as bad as I do now. That'd mean maybe two more hours to put it off 'cause there's no way to turn the spigot in here, what with my hands tied the way they are."

He was so worried about the condition of his bladder that he scarcely noticed when the torpedo spun sharply and a series of small, precise bursts gave him momentary weight. Then there was a tiny, almost imperceptible crunching sensation, a slow rolling and a final jolt as the explosive bolts of the nose cone burst, freeing him from the straitjacket that had been his home for the past six hours.

Numbly he wriggled himself out onto the surface of the satellite to lie there helplessly for a good ten minutes as he tried to coax life back into leaden limbs. Surprisingly, now that he was down and able to open the petcock, he discovered he no longer had the need. The urge had left him completely.

Staggering to his feet at last, Chisholm adjusted his infrared goggles, turned back to the torpedo and commenced fumbling through his equipment, using a tiny red-filtered light to see by.

Soon he had the torpedo emptied and the equipment laid out alongside it. Next he rummaged about until he located the extensible whip antenna carrying the three red beacons which signified the main assembly point. Climbing to the top of the largest nearby elevation, he mounted it, then turned to survey the jumbled terrain surrounding him.

Instinctively he stumbled back and gasped in alarm at the ominous shape which abruptly rose menacingly beside him. Then with a scarcely audible sigh of relief he nearly fell into the arms of one of his companions, who had been climbing the same elevation for the same purpose.

Two of the twenty were together, so a second whip antenna was placed beside the first, this one carrying only two lights. Then two more showed in another direction, followed quickly by an answering double beacon just above the nearby horizon. A third figure walked up to join them. A moment later a single flashing beacon commenced winking off and on—an unmanned torpedo mounting an automatic flasher on an extensible whip.

Another beacon showed, so far in the distance it was barely visible over the curve of the moonlet. Then came two more supply beacons. Another space-suited figure moved up to join the party and they were four. Two more beacons raised. Three winking supply beacons came to life almost simultaneously, followed by another personal light.

By now the other beacons were beginning to converge on the command post as the suited men bundled their gear together and, carrying their beacons along with them as identification, moved in on Chisholm and his party. Nine men accounted for so far. Fifteen of the supply torpedoes in sight. Within another ten minutes all twenty supply torpedoes were accounted for, but no more men . . . and no more beacons showed.

Wearily they set off by threes to bring together the supply torpedoes, but none of the eleven missing men appeared.

One of the anonymous figures first put it into words. " 'Tis not likely they'll ever be found," he announced gloomily. " 'Twas unco' lonely out there and there's naught to hold a man together save what he's got inside himself. Were it not for the hate of them as brought me here I'd not have made it myself."

"Aye," commented another wonderingly. " 'Twas the same that pulled me through. I got to dreaming about back on Earth. . . . A small stream where I used to fish. . . . 'Twas so real . . . a hot sun, the smell of the greenery about, the feel of the water running cold. . . . 'Twas exactly as if I was there and I didn't ever want to leave again. It would have been so easy to stay forever."

"Why didn't you?" demanded one of the other suited shapes.

"I got to thinking of my mums and sister back in Glasgow and what the aliens had done to them and Earth. Then I lost everything and all I could do was have hate for them for doing it."

"It was different with me," admitted Chisholm. "I got to fretting about having to go to the jakes."

"Me too," grunted another. "It seemed I had to go forever."

"I fear you're right about the others," chimed in yet another voice, one Chisholm recognized as that of Bethune, a physicist who had spent most of their journey jotting equations he hoped would lead to a principle of a hyperlight drive. " 'Tis likely a strong hate or other emotion needed to make a man forget himself was what was needed to survive."

"I didn't figure you to be that emotional," grunted another, evidently also recognizing Bethune's voice.

"The fact I think does not imply I cannot feel," came the cool rejoinder. "I have as much hate for the alien as any other man. It's just I can also see him as a puzzle that needs solving."

"This gets us nowhere," decided Chisholm. "No matter what, we have to get down to work. Now to see who's here. Identify yourselves. I'm Chisholm."

"MacIlhose of the Argylls," told off one.

"Sergeant Currie of the Argylls," snapped the shrouded figure who had been first to voice their common dread.

"High Private Forbes," announced a third.

"Downes. Electronics."

"Bethune. Physicist."

"Private Glennie o' the Argylls," piped a youthful-sounding voice still laden with the distinctive burr of the Outer Isles.

"Lance Corporal MacCondy of the Argylls," called another.

"Kirkpatrick. Electronics," came the final reply.

"No xenologists. I was afraid of that," commented Chisholm. "It occurs to me that a xenologist would be too curious about his enemy to hate him greatly. Well, we must make do. . . . Downes, how soon till you can have communications in operation?"

"Soon as I get this faceplate off the torp, sir."

When their radio was set up, Chisholm had a hurried conversation with Duncan aboard Claymore. The loss of eleven men was disheartening, but there was nothing to do but continue the operation. Either they succeeded or they were dead men. Not one of them could endure a return to Claymore in the torpedoes—not after the trip down—and with the difference in orbital period between Claymore and the satellite any rescue ship would be certain of detection any time within the next fourteen days.

Closing down the radio, the little party packed up and commenced a stumbling odyssey over the rocky and nearly gravityless surface, leaving behind them a dimly seen marker beacon, a transmitter and some twenty supply torpedoes all neatly clustered together.

Somewhere in the darkness behind them a man huddled, lonely in a black, invisible torpedo, sobbing hopelessly. . . . Wouldn't the torpedo ever land? In yet another torpedo, not two hundred yards distant, another man lay with eyes wide open and staring, a beatific smile on his face. He was back home on Earth with his family. In other torpedoes were men catatonic in their stupor, and in one there was an already chilling corpse of a man whose brain had literally forgotten to order the heart to keep beating.

Single file, the tiny party half bounded, half picked their way around and over the maze of rocky pinnacles and jagged craters. Occasionally one or another of the party would leap high over an obstacle and gaze briefly at the giant planet hanging ominously just over the horizon. A while later it no longer took a high bound. Crossing each small mound they would catch a fleeting glimpse of Jove's sultry face. At length they stood full under the unwinking gaze of the methane monster.

Personal lights were extinguished lest they reveal their presence. Radios were switched off and the pack antennae disconnected to prevent accidental transmissions.

Sergeant Currie bounded forward to confer with Chisholm. Putting helmets together so the sound could be transmitted through the plastic contact, he commented, "Mr. Chisholm, sir. I'm thinking we'd best send a couple of men up ahead a bit as scouts. We're most likely pretty near the center of the asteroid and 'twould seem probable the base must be located somewhere near here. I'd hate to have us stumble over them and maybe give them a chance to send off a message."

"Good idea, Sergeant," Chisholm acknowledged. "Take any measures you feel needful. The only thing I ask is that if any fighting comes you try to destroy as little enemy equipment as possible. We need every bit of data we can collect. Also, if you see any chance of picking up one of the aliens alive, 'tis worth much to do so."

"Aye, sir. I'll take a party on ahead. You wait here with the others till I wave you up." Turning back, Currie motioned to MacIlhose and MacCondy. A few minutes later the three of them were advancing with low bounds closer to the centre of the satellite. Moving up to a small ridge they peered over the top and studied the terrain on the far side. Then one of the three turned and waved the rest of the party up.

Cautiously Chisholm and the other five with him moved forward. When they arrived at the ridge Currie motioned for them to remain there and then took off again with the two scouts. Then came another wave-up. Leapfrogging this way, it took nearly two hours before Jove hung directly overhead. Still there was no sign of the base.

Now the group wearily laid down their burdens while Currie sent the two scouts out in different directions. Soon both were lost to sight amid the maze of rocks and over the short horizon.

Putting his helmet next to Currie's, Chisholm asked worriedly, "Any chance of them getting lost? I don't think we could stand to lose any more men."

"Not anybody of my section," replied Currie complacently. "We're the scout platoon of the Argylls. There's not a man of us but could find his way through this blindfolded."

Privately Currie was not so certain, but the answer did much to relieve the rest of the party.

Two hours later MacIlhose returned. He'd found the base not a half mile distant. Now there was nothing to do but wait for MacCondy to make it back. When the latter finally conceded defeat and returned, nearly five hours after MacIlhose, the party picked up their gear and set out on the last leg of their journey.

Within twenty minutes MacIlhose motioned them down and waved up Currie and Chisholm.

Wedging his helmet between the two of them, MacIlhose said, "Peek careful over the top of the rise. 'Tis just on the other side."

Lifting his head cautiously, Chisholm peered over to find a small, leveled field with a trio of connected domes rising perhaps five feet above the terrain off on the other side.

Pulling back, Chisholm tucked his helmet uncomfortably between MacIlhose and Currie. "You find a way to get us around to the domes without being seen?" he demanded.

"Aye," replied MacIlhose with a touch of asperity. "Of course I have!"

Ignoring the note of irritation, Chisholm continued, "Very well. Lead on, MacDuff."

"The name is MacIlhose, sir," replied the literal-minded soldier a trifle huffily.

"Very well, then. Lead on, MacIlhose."

Skirting the vacant landing apron, the party was soon hunkered down among the rocks a scant ten yards from the domes. Two men were sent up to cover the area with their submachine guns, a type of weapon which had survived essentially unchanged for nearly three centuries. The rest of the party went into conclave behind a rock outcrop.

Their first concern was the antenna outlet. If the aliens kept to the same schedule, there would probably be no incoming calls for at least another twelve to fourteen hours. To be on the safe side the antenna should be back in service within eight hours.

A study of the complex showed that each of the domes had a single, porthole-type window. Between the trio of domes were numerous odds and ends of electronics gear and several antennae. It was fortunate, thought Chisholm, that the electronics men had survived. Otherwise they'd have to guess which wires to cut.

Covered by the guns of the others, Downes carefully crawled forward to a blind spot beside the domes. Moving cautiously around the rim of the nearest dome while taking care not to touch it, he stepped between two of them and vanished into the electronics area. A few minutes later he emerged and returned to the party.

Putting his head between Currie and Chisholm, he announced, "It's cut. They can't communicate now."

"Good," Currie replied simply. "Does this mean we're safe to use our suit radios now?"

"Probably. But I'm not absolutely sure. Too much stray radiation might leak into the sets simply because we're so close."

"We're getting to a point where we need the capability of talking over the suits," persisted Currie. "Hand signals might not be quite enough if something unexpected comes up."

"Then put the antennae back in the suits," shrugged Downes negligently, "but order everyone to keep their suit radios tuned to receive until ordered otherwise."

"Does that sound good, sir?" Currie asked Chisholm.

"I think we have to take the chance. When we get finished here, go ahead and set it up; but make sure everyone has the word about not using their radios until we give the all-clear."

Turning back to Downes, Currie added. "Did you take the time to peek inside the domes?"

"I didn't think to do it," Downes replied sheepishly. "I was too busy trying to figure out which wires to cut."

"How long till they send a man out to check on why their antenna isn't working, do you think?" asked Chisholm.

"Unless they happen to look at their monitor panel—which I doubt —they'll not think to do it till they fail to receive their next expected signal," opined Downes.

"Is there even anyone inside the domes?" persisted Currie.

"I don't know, I tell you," shrugged Downes.

"Then, sir," continued Currie to Chisholm, "I suggest I go up and take a look myself. Cutting the wires to bring them out isn't apt to do much good if they aren't there to begin with."

"I suppose you're right, Sergeant," agreed Chisholm. "Do what you think best. That's your department."

Before Chisholm had a chance to say more, Currie was scurrying out to the domes. Several feet back from one of the ports he stopped, then cautiously raised his head and angled a peek through the first of the portholes. Slowly he moved closer until he could peer full in. A moment later he backed away and went to the second dome's port and started to repeat the process. This time he did not bring his head up against the window but contented himself instead with a hasty glance from a distance.

Moving back to the first port, he looked in again before turning back to the covering force. Lifting one arm above his head, he brought it down to point to one of the Argylls, then brought it back toward himself.

A trooper disengaged himself from the rocks and hastily bounded up to the sergeant. They conferred for a moment, then Currie started around to the remaining dome while the trooper stood off to one side with his eyes fixed on the port.

Reaching the window of the third dome, Currie moved up again and peered in. Satisfying himself, he moved out of the line of sight of the third window and walked erect around the front of the domes, stooped over briefly to take a hasty look at something invisible to the rest of the party, then cautiously moved back to Chisholm.

"There's four of them in there," he announced. "The first window I peeked in was the bunk room. Nobody was in there, but I counted four bunks. The second room contained gadgets and there were three of them in it. The fourth was in the third room, which looks like a general living-and-eating area. The front of the gadget room contains an airlock, plus a second port which we didn't spot earlier. It faces at a little different angle from the airlock proper, so it oughtn't to be much of a problem. The dome construction is concrete or something like it and is about two feet thick. The ports are laminated and look as if they're layered in about four plies. . . . Makes me think they may worry a bit about meteorites."

"What do you figure is the next step?" demanded Chisholm.

"Well, if 'twere me I'd move a couple of men out to cover the airlock door—keeping them offset so they can't be seen from any of the portholes. The rest could move up inside the dome area to where all the outside gear is located. Downes could clip a couple of more wires or something whilst I pick up a rock and slap it down on the dome. 'Twouldn't be enough to crack it or anything, but 'twould sound unholy loud inside. When their receiver goes off at the same time they'll probably figure a meteorite did it and send a man or two outside to check for damage. Them we shoot. With no air to carry the sound it won't disturb anybody inside. This'll give us a chance to slip a couple of men into the airlock and maybe get inside before they can figure out what's going on. With some luck we can maybe even take them prisoner, but if they come up with any weapons or try to make a fight of it, we'll have to kill them too."

"Then let's do it," Chisholm decided. "Campbell said this is the sort of thing you're trained for, so I don't figure to be able to come up with anything better."

Minutes later the plan was in motion. Chisholm and four of the group moved into the central compound and off into the shadows. Setting out separately, Glennie and MacIlhose scrabbled a pair of shallow holes a few yards in front of the lock so they would have a clear field of fire. Currie hoisted a medium-sized boulder which would have weighed a smart ten stone on Earth, then stood by to smash it down atop the dome on signal. Downes, the remaining man, moved over to the electronics complex, studied the various pieces of apparatus for a minute before bringing his cutters up, then nodded over to Currie.

The rock caromed against the dome. Wire cutters snipped and the job was done.

The came an unpleasant surprise: the entire dome area was immediately flooded with light.

Chisholm cursed himself for not anticipating this development. Obviously they would have to have lights available for repairs and adjustments, and while the light reflected from Jove's face was enough to cast a subdued, ruddy light on the surface, it would hardly be sufficient for exacting work. This could be a problem.

But before he could act the entire rear bank of lights flicked off, leaving only the front of the compound still lit. Looking over he saw Downes triumphantly waving his wire cutters.

That turned matters to their advantage. The aliens would have to peer out into the darkness while themselves being framed against the light.

Minutes passed. Tension mounted. The exterior lock wheel rotated and a pair of space-suited figures emerged. Leaving the lock door open behind them, they moved purposefully into the compound.

No sooner had the aliens turned their backs on the lock than Glennie and MacIlhose bounded from concealment and slipped into it. Shutting the door behind them they dogged the lock and then turned to the inner door. MacIlhose cursed briefly as he spotted a window looking through the inner door. It meant anyone could see them if they looked. No matter, though: most likely the two left inside would be busy studying their instruments in the second dome. Either way, he and Glennie were committed.

Studying the lock control panel intently, MacIlhose muttered in disgust. Two levers. One was obviously meant to control the entry of air, so the other no doubt opened the inner door. If he pulled the wrong one first he'd likely sound an alarm somewhere. And there was no way he could be sure which was which!

No time to waste trying to decide. He pulled at the lever which looked as if it "ought" to release air and in a moment was rewarded by a vague hissing sound as pressure began to build up.

Just as the hissing ceased, a startled face appeared at the window. Swinging the inner lock lever over before the alien could react, MacIlhose and Glennie burst into the dome. A gun-butt to the head abruptly cut short a half-formed cry of alarm and Glennie darted into the second dome. There was sound of a brief scuffle, a moment of silence and Glennie backed into the first dome dragging an unconscious alien to join the other. The dome was theirs.

An hour's work was needed to tidy things up and repair the severed circuits and external lead-ins. When completed there was no external evidence anything was amiss within. Later they would have to send parties back to the other side to bring in food and other supplies, but for now they rested . . . and also took their first good look at the aliens.

It was almost a disappointment. No horns, no fangs; just a pair of virtually humanoid people. Two arms, two legs, a head and a torso. Looked at closely the hair could be seen to have an almost feathery quality about it, with each strand branching into several distinct, smaller strands. The hands were not unlike the human type except for six rather than the conventional five digits. The scaly character of the skin, noted from the biopsies of aliens killed in the battles around Earth, was virtually invisible to the naked eye. A medium-sized microscope could spot the difference immediately, but no casual glance would notice.

A certain fluidity in the way their bodies handled suggested the possibility of a somewhat more efficient ball joint in the elbows, wrists and knees, but it was not something to jar the sensibilities of the unsuspecting. Either of the aliens could have walked down the street of an Earth city without evoking the least attention.

And that was the most disquieting thing about the whole affair. Monsters who would destroy entire worlds filled with people without ever making an effort to talk or to learn ought to look like monsters. They shouldn't look much like anyone else. They would be far easier to hate if they slithered about like venomous snakes or possessed slashing fangs like sabre-toothed tigers and drooled at the sight of human flesh. To someone the least bit inclined to introspection it suggested the possibility humans weren't above the same sort of thing either.

But no matter what, they were here for now. With luck they might be able to stretch their stay for a month or more. And during that stay they had to learn every possible fact they could about their foe.

CHAPTER 18

For the past two days the tiny party had been watching anxiously as the alien ship applied reverse thrust for its landing. Starting yesterday as a faint blip on the aliens' radar, it was now a vivid streak of flame a scant few miles overhead.

Chisholm's group had spent nearly six weeks in the dome. Downes and Kirkpatrick could reproduce every alien circuit by heart. Chisholm had studied drawings in alien books and magazines until he was nearly blind, seeking to glean every possible scrap of information from them. Bethune had examined every dial, every doorknob and every gadget in the domes. He had even spent a solid two hours in the kitchen twiddling and twisting everything in sight. Though no one would have suspected it, he had proved himself a pretty keen psychologist in a pinch.

It had been his idea to chop off in the middle of a routine transmission some three weeks earlier and then stay off the air permanently. His estimate that it would take the aliens about three weeks to decide there was something wrong and then send a ship out to investigate had proved uncannily accurate. He had also predicted—and how they hoped he was right on this one—that the aliens would assume there had merely been some accident on the satellite station and send up a repair-and-rescue team—not a military force.

The afternoon before the ship edged into visibility was Chisholm's day of glory. He had their undivided attention as he presented his observations and made recommendations.

"One thing you'll almost certainly discover everywhere aboard their vessel is that all gauges and dials are reversed from what we would consider normal. On their radios, for example, the on-off switch is located on the right-hand side and turns counterclockwise. On their stove you turn the knob to the left to turn it on. If a doorknob turns in a single direction 'twill most likely be to the left. If you have a bank of levers or dials to look at you can figure the first one to worry about is the one to the extreme right.

"With the actual working of levers, though, you can figure it's exactly like the workings in our own system. If you find a lever, simply do what seems natural and you'll most likely be right. If you read a gauge, however, remember the zero will always read from the right unless it's a vertical gauge like a thermometer, in which case read it normally.

"I would also suggest you spend the next few hours until their ship arrives boning up on their numbering system until you've got it down pat. It could be any one of us will have to try piloting it in alone, so you should be as ready as you can.

"As any technological race must, they have a cyclic numbering system and positional notation. Their numbers run from one to twelve, with distinct symbols for each digit below twelve. Then they go back to their original digit and add a dot where we'd put a zero. Their first two-digit number is therefore twelve. Their first three-digit number becomes one hundred and forty-four, and so on. It's simple and efficient. As a matter of fact, before the computers came in there were a number of suggestions that we ought to convert to the duodecimal system because of its convenience for division and other numerical processes. Some of you may even have toyed with the system during your lower forms. But just remember, here it's no game. The aliens really use it, so any mistake can kill you."

More hours of waiting as the alien ship twice circled the little moon, apparently bleeding off momentum from braking jets at the bow. Evidently this ship, at least, was not designed to tumble and use the main rocket for its critical maneuvers. It suggested an inefficient use of computer potential, which could tie in with a surprising lack of small electronic-type calculator-computers inside the dome.

The alien ship settled back, her engines chopped power and she drifted the final three or four feet before coming to rest on the barren landing pad just outside the main dome.

Even before her hatch lock was fully opened, three space-suited figures, one of them carrying a fourth, dashed from the dome and up to the lock. Immediately as the door swung open the four figures darted inside. Chisholm cast a quick glance about and spotted the interior controls for the hatch, waited until the last of the four was aboard, then spun the door closed as expertly as if he had done it all his life.

Moments later they began to hear the hiss of air as the atmosphere within the lock thickened. Glennie, standing next to the inner window with his face averted, propped the body of a recently killed alien prisoner on its feet and swung a limp arm about his shoulder.

As the inner door swung open he gave a slight shrug and the alien slipped forward, pitching headlong to the floor. The three unsuited aliens inside hastily bent over to tend to their "injured" comrade. Glennie's arm swung twice in rapid succession and two of them slumped inertly to the floor. Forbes's fist lashed out just as the third alien looked up uncomprehendingly and the three of them were laid out cold.

While Chisholm shuffled the three aliens and the body of the fourth into the airlock, Glennie and Forbes raced cautiously forward. An alien opened a compartment door just ahead of them and stepped into the corridor. His face registered instant shock and amazement, but before he could cry out Glennie's hand brushed by almost negligently and the alien reeled back, his throat torn out by a triangular-bladed trench knife.

The delay was enough to allow Chisholm to come up even with the two of them. He had opened the outer lock. It was up to the others to follow as fast as they could.

Taking the lead, Chisholm burst into the control room and launched himself headlong at the unsuspecting pilot, who had scant time even to pull himself to his feet before being rammed by the plunging Scot. A gauntleted fist unleashed itself and the pilot slumped unconscious to the floor.

Leaving the alien to the tender mercies of Glennie, Chisholm glanced out the port to see how things were proceeding outside. There were five of his men busily hauling the neatly bundled books and notes salvaged from the dome, plus sufficient food and water for the next few days. As he watched, the rest of his men emerged from the dome, and a moment later he felt a queer thump as the surface beneath the ship jolted and with almost a tinge of regret watched the three domes expand queerly, then collapse upon themselves in soundless explosion.

A few loops of adhesive tape secured the still-unconscious alien pilot and he was unceremoniously dumped against the cabin wall. Chisholm then moved off to the side of the passageway entrance so he could intercept anyone who might try to enter while Glennie and Forbes were making their way back to the airlock.

A few minutes later all eleven Earthmen were safely tucked inside. Not a word had been spoken, nor would there be until they had made certain there were no more aliens inside and no radios could be transmitting back to Shiva.

Fanning out silently by pairs, the men systematically searched every compartment and cubicle of the ship. Another alien was found relaxed on a couch in the engine compartment. He was captured and trussed before he even knew what was happening, and the ship passed into the complete control of the attackers.

Downes and Kirkpatrick silently examined the pilot's console while Chisholm and Bethune studied the engine room. As they were completing their inspection of the engines Downes's voice came over the intercom. "You can speak now. All radios are off and there's no danger of transmitting anything out over the air."

Fully relaxed for the first time, the group congratulated themselves and completed a thorough examination of the ship.

"Well, Chisholm," Bethune asked as they emerged from the engine room after finishing their survey, "what do you think?"

"The drive system is enough like ours we'll not have too much trouble piloting her. Unfortunate she's not equipped with the hyperdrive, but then that would have been a mite much to expect. It means we'll probably have to figure on a raid on Shiva to cut one out, but that's apt to be chancy."

"Agreed," Bethune remarked drily. "They'll be expecting to hear from this ship, and when she fails to report they'll start getting nervous. If it's maybe some university-owned tub it might take a while for the word to get around, but my guess is it's most likely a standard government-owned ship and they'll start wondering in a hurry."

"It doesn't sound too good, then?" persisted Chisholm.

"Not very. I figure the best thing we can do is get under way immediately as I can figure out the controls. The faster we get back to Claymore the more time we'll have to do whatever's needed."

Turning to Currie, Chisholm ordered, "Get the four prisoners into their galley or bunk area, whichever you prefer. Then take the rest of the men and have them start collecting every scrap of writing aboard. I want it all in one place and ready to be carried onto Claymore as soon as we berth."

"Aye," replied Currie, "but I'd like to keep two men detailed to watch the prisoners—just in case."

"Do as you think best, but hurry."

"You can handle the con," Bethune added after Currie left. "I'd like to stay down here in the engine room unless you feel you'd like some backup. Maybe I can pick up an idea or two from the feel of the way they've put things together."

"You don't think I'll have any problems with the controls?"

"I doubt it. If you do just give a call on the intercom and I'll head up."

Leaving Bethune, Chisholm moved back into the controls section. Conferring briefly with Downes and Kirkpatrick, he was soon able to eliminate the radio controls and other nonessential gear from his survey of the ship's instrumentation. That left him with merely two or three dozen miscellaneous gauges, levers and buttons to worry over.

Taking his time, Chisholm studied the control hookup. Even in an alien ship there was still a certain logic in the arrangement. There had to be or they would never have gotten out into space to begin with. It was merely a matter of defining it; but that was easier said than done. After more than two hours' study he felt himself ready for some cautious experimentation. Flipping up the intercom switch, he called out, "Brace yourselves, lads, I'm going to try to start the beastie and I'm not for certain which way she's going!" Then he reached out and gingerly pushed a lever forward, one notch at a time.

Nothing happened.

Returning the lever to its original setting, Chisholm studied the board intently another couple of minutes, then reached out to flip a switch. This time when he touched the lever he felt a faint rumble in the stern and a slight grating along the belly of the ship as it inched over the rough surface of the satellite.

Satisfied, Chisholm added power and simultaneously pulled back on the main steering yoke. The flames of the small bow jet lighted the ground briefly, then faded as the alien ship swung away from the surface in a tight turn. Carefully, with short, even erratic bursts of power, he jockeyed the craft around the satellite and lifted her toward the higher orbit of Claymore.

As he gained confidence in his ability to handle the ship, his next job was navigating her back to the asteroid without the aid of specialized computer input. None of the men aboard knew enough about the alien's psychology to start punching computer buttons at random. It would have to be seat-of-the-pants navigation coupled with whatever help the men aboard Claymore could give them. And that would be very little through most of their trip.

Punching the intercom so he could talk to Bethune, Chisholm outlined his problem. "Let's see if we agree," he figured aloud. "When we landed here we were almost dead under Claymore at an inclination of roughly twenty degrees. Now Claymore has an orbital period of some two point one nine times that of the satellite. We were there for forty-one days. As I figure it, this means Claymore's about seven days ahead of where she was when we landed, or about two twenty-five degrees advanced in orbit. On our part we're one day, or roughly seventy-two degrees, advanced. So Claymore should be some one hundred forty-five degrees ahead of us in orbit—almost square on the other side of Jove. Does that check with you so far?"

"Aye. I'm following you, but you're roughing it a bit much. I'd say 'twould be more like a hundred fifty-two degrees ahead. What have you got with respect to the innermost satellite—the one with the other alien station?"

"I figure it's about eighty degrees behind us and catching up fast. As a guess it would seem best if I cut the corner of Jove a couple of thousand miles above the surface and used the planet's gravity to skew us around as we pass perigee. That would make for the fastest run and still give us the best chance of eluding detection. How does that sound?"

After a minute Bethune came back over the intercom. " 'Twould be even better if we could clip the corner on Jove within five hundred miles. Think we can do it in this craft?"

"I can try." Suiting deed to word, Chisholm completed his tight orbit of the now abandoned satellite, widened the throttle setting and plunged toward the left rim of the planet beneath them.

Slamming forward in a 2.5 g acceleration, the alien ship leaped like some startled behemoth. Bulbs shattered. Crockery smashed somewhere in the bowels of the ship as ominous creakings and grumblings accompanied the acceleration.

Hastily Chisholm retarded the settings. The ship had obviously never been constructed for battle maneuvers. Compared to Earth ships it was a flimsy eggshell. No wonder their warheads had done so little damage to Earth ships if they were set to do battle against ships of their own class.

But the aliens had had nearly seventy years to improve their shipbuilding technology, he reflected, and this was most probably some superannuated, semiretired old clunker used exclusively for short servicing hops. If so, perhaps the aliens would not be too surprised when she failed to report back. He wouldn't bet on it though.

Fourteen hours later, accelerating at 1.5 g's, they approached pericentron with Jove. By now the planet loomed a sultry yellow through more than three quarters of the sky and looked like nothing so much as some outrageously inflated balloon. It filled the entire bank of starboard ports, half the forward ports and part of the aft repeater screen and was growing by the minute. Then in a scant few seconds it slipped off the forward port entirely and vanished to the side. They were past pericentron and heading outward toward Claymore.

Since most of their approach would have to be visual and by hand radio, all lights in the control room were dimmed and they used only the infrared suit lights they had brought aboard with them. In the meantime Downes suited up again and headed out the airlock while Chisholm chopped acceleration. Minutes later they heard his heavy magnetic boots clumping eerily along outside the ship as he worked his way toward the bow carrying a small homing radio pretuned to Claymore's frequency. There was some risk of alien interception, but it had to be. At least this was better than trying to figure the range, frequency standards and calibration of the alien radios.

There were more clatterings from outside as Downes anchored himself to the ship and stuck a graphite seal to mount their radio to the hull. Another minute and they were back in direct communication with Claymore.

Using the lowest power possible and operating on a wavelength seldom used by the aliens, the ship and Claymore carried on a guarded conversation. "We've got you on the scope, Chisholm, but you're coming in too low. You'll miss by a considerable margin. Start reducing speed at one point zero g deceleration. Now bring the nose five degrees to port. . . . No! Make that starboard. Up five degrees. Maintain present heading and decelerate for three minutes at one point zero g's, then chop power so we can get a better reading on your trajectory."

A few minutes later: "Lower the nose one half degree and bring her five more degrees to starboard. Maintain course. Increase deceleration to one point five g's. . . . Now hold her. . . . Steady as she goes. Chop power. You'll pass within a quarter mile of us within thirty-five minutes at fifty-three hundred miles per hour relative speed.

"Apply one point zero g deceleration for ten seconds. Bring the nose one quarter degree to starboard and hold. . . . One point zero g deceleration for seven minutes. . . . You're thirty-eight minutes to contact now, making a relative speed of thirty-four hundred miles per hour.

"Bring the bow up one half degree. Hit one point zero g deceleration for five minutes. New contact time thirty-four minutes at twenty-two hundred miles relative.

"Course steady. Six minutes deceleration. New contact time thirty minutes at relative velocity of one thousand miles. . . . Bow up three degrees. Port your helm six point five degrees. One point zero g deceleration for six minutes thirty seconds. Contact time now fifteen minutes at relative two hundred fifty miles per hour.

"Give us one point zero g deceleration for ten seconds. . . . Hold her. . . . Steady. . . . Stand by for boarding party. You are three hundred feet above Claymore with zero relative. Good job!"

A metallic clank rang on the hull as the first grapple was applied. Then another and still a third.

There was a knock at the door.

The pipers of Claymore ushered them back aboard as virtually everyone not actively on duty turned out in greeting. And almost as soon as they cleared the hatch, scientists and technicians swarmed aboard the alien craft, filching every scrap of written material, photographing every rivet and seam in the vessel and examining each detail of construction and design.

The physicians and xenologists hauled the aliens away to perform whatever rituals their science demanded, while a second team of computer specialists vanished into the depths of the ship's computer room —only to emerge disgusted several hours later. This ship certainly wasn't rigged for even the most elementary battle maneuvers. There wasn't the slightest doubt on that score.

A second set of computer men busily converted all the data into duplicate sets of tapes for the benefit of the people back on Styx. Time was now of highest importance. With every passing hour the certainty of detection increased. The aliens were bound to react to the double loss of their station and ship. There were simply too many alien bodies lying about. Claymore had to act before the aliens got their wind up too far.

Hours after Chisholm's party returned Duncan called a battle conference. Matters were coming to a head. The radio-frequency monitor reported apparently continuing efforts to contact both the satellite and the ship. Very possibly another ship was already en route. If so, discovery was at most only two weeks away—assuming the follow-up ship needed just time enough to arrive at the base and radio back its findings. The time might be even shorter if they happened to have a ship in the area which could be diverted.

Of course, there was no way the aliens could be certain of the precise cause of their troubles. But they would certainly consider the possibility of a sneak attack by another race. After all, they had done the same thing to Earth less than a century ago.

Possibly they would miss Claymore, or fail to recognize her for what she was if they did find her. But no matter what, they would certainly be on the alert for anything out of the ordinary for the next couple of years. And Claymore could not afford to lurk in orbit that long, waiting for another crack at an alien ship.

Chisholm and Bethune were the first to arrive at the conference, followed closely by an uncomfortable-looking Private Glennie. Bethune in particular was openly jubilant and Duncan couldn't blame him in the least. It was a first-rate coup they'd pulled off. Then came Krishnan, looking grave and just a trifle worried. Holmes arrived, looking belligerent and spoiling for a fight. Duncan could not help but think of him as a sort of latter-day British sea dog: grim, determined, totally reliable and utterly humorless. Then in quick succession came MacPherson, MacPhail, Allen and Oliphant to complete the roster.

With scarcely a note of greeting Duncan called them to order. "Gentlemen," he prefaced, "useful and important as the raid may ha' been, it still does not present us wi' a sample o' the enemy's hyperdrive device. To that extent it was a failure. Now we are faced with the possibility o' quick discovery so we must come to an immediate decision."

Bethune's grin became even wider as Duncan continued. "Now, gentlemen," he added, "I ha' invited Private Glennie to sit wi' us since for the past seven weeks he has been in direct contact wi' two alien prisoners, seeking to learn as much as possible o' their language, their thoughts and their ways. I invite ye to pay heed."

Looking nervous, Glennie rose to his feet, cleared his throat a couple of times, then began. "Well, sirs, I really didna' learn much from the aliens themselves. They wouldna' communicate wi' me or even make an effort. 'Twas almost as if I didna' even exist save for once when I got too close to one o' them whilst trying to feed him—and then he tried to lunch on my arm. . . . See!" Pulling back his sleeve, Glennie revealed a freshly healing row of needlepoint incisions running midway between the wrist and elbow. "Hurt like the very devil too, I might add."

Pausing, Glennie looked about seeking approval or criticism, then brought out a small handful of booklets before continuing. "At first I figured they were most likely scared, so I tried to figure out something o' their way of thinking. I rummaged about in their books till I found what looked apt to be casual reading things—not textbooks or whatever —just something to read in their spare time. I thought mayhap 'twould make them open up a bit. At any rate, here are a few o' them ye might like to take a look at."

"Just tell us about them for now," urged Duncan.

"Aye, sir. Well, they had a couple o' comics sort o' book which showed them out fighting amongst the stars. O' course, we could expect them to be winning so I didn't think much o' that. But what seems significant to me is what they do to their prisoners in the strips. Mind ye, I'm no xenologist, but what wi' all ours being lost on the way in I guess the rest o' it sort o' fell to me. . . . But anyhow, it struck me that they always show their prisoners being cut up or burned, or whatever. 'Tis not like any Earthside comic strip I ever saw. To judge by their comics they cannot just capture or kill their foes; they ha' to torture and mutilate them."

"One moment, son," interrupted Krishnan, "In the seven weeks you had custody of the two aliens was there no progress in communicating with them?"

"Hardly any, sir. They both acted as if I wasn't human—if ye know what I mean."

"No. I don't quite know. Would you help me?" persisted Krishnan.

"Aye, sir. They just totally rejected everything. 'Twasn't just fear o' what we could do—they never showed any o' that so far as I could tell —it's just they weren't even *interested*. Like maybe some tiger back on Earth would grab a man and haul him away wi'out killing him. The man might try to find some way to get out—or mayhap to kill the tiger. But he wouldna' try to communicate wi' it as a rational being. The fact we had space suits and other equipage, which showed we were able to think and go into space, just didn't mean anything to them. We were still vermin—little bugs to be squished!"

"Are you certain this is not merely a reflection of your personal feelings toward the aliens and their destruction of Earth?" continued Krishnan.

"No, sir," replied Glennie straightforwardly. "I'm not. I had two sisters and a brother back on Earth. Yes, I hate the bloody bastards— but I've tried to gi' ye an honest accounting. If I've misthought 'twas not for want o' trying to say it right."

"I'm sure you have, son, but I wanted to be certain," nodded Krishnan sympathetically. "But let me ask this of you also. Were any of the beings shown being tortured in their comics recognizably human?"

"Aye, sir. . . . But not all. Not even most. As near as I could see they ha' three, maybe four different monster types which keep showing up in their books."

"And you say all of these go through the torture scenes?"

"Aye, sir."

"I have no more questions," decided Krishnan.

"Nor I," agreed Duncan, glancing about the room. "If none o' ye gentlemen has any more questions o' Private Glennie, I believe we can go on to other matters."

Hearing none, Duncan continued, "Now our next question is what —if anything—can we do about getting our hands on a hyperdrive ship? 'Twas the main reason for our raid and I would hate to overlook any opportunity to pull it off so long as there's a fighting chance. Suggestions?"

"May I speak?" asked Bethune.

"O' course. Say your will."

"Very well," replied Bethune with careful blandness. "We have the hyperdrive."

"What!" exploded a half dozen voices in unison.

"Aye," he confirmed. "One of the computer techs taping data for Styx discovered it less than an hour ago. The manuals aboard the alien craft contain all the material. Apparently it's a general-issue manual and the technician noted it because it showed star representations and had a diagram showing calculations from their sun to various points outside the system proper. The technician figured it would represent the method of calculating safe distances for jumping into hyperdrive.

"Once he'd concluded that, he took time off and thumbed through the whole book. It contained several hundred pages showing circuitry and schematics. When he took it to one of the engineers, the man was easy put to recognize the basic data relating to their celaenium-drive engines. But following that section of the book were fifty, perhaps sixty, pages of diagrams which could only apply to the hyperdrive. It will naturally take some time to translate properly, but it's morally certain we possess the hyperdrive data."

"Gentlemen, this puts a different complexion on things," exclaimed Duncan. Turning back to Bethune, he demanded, "Has all this been taped for Styx?"

"Naturally. I've had two torpedoes filled with the data. That way we double our chances of at least one getting through. I would suggest firing one just as we are set to go into battle and the other not till we're either about to be destroyed or just getting loose from the system."

"Good," Duncan replied simply. "Wi' the drive in our hands 'tis no use pussyfooting about anymore. We'll move to the attack immediately, before the aliens can get their wind up any more than they already have. Claymore is coming around Jove in a good attack angle right now. Unfortunately, Shiva has moved ahead till 'tis almost on the opposite side o' their sun, so 'twill take longer than I'd like for us to get there. But the course corrections won't be too hard. . . . Oliphant!"

"Aye?"

"How long till we can get everything battened down and be ready to slip orbit?"

"Six hours maybe. Certainly no more."

"Good. Then I'll want us pushing out at a steady one point zero g acceleration as soon as ye can get fired up. . . . Krishnan, ye're to be in command o' destroyer division one. Ye'll move out to the left at extreme detector range wi' two destroyers and three cruisers. MacPherson will be your second aboard the cruisers. Figure to be starting out in about twenty-four hours. Ye're to take enough o' all needed parts and supplies to sustain isolated action for up to five months. Strip your crews to the minimum consistent wi' effective combat capabilities and use the added space for food and munitions. . . . Holmes, ye command the second division wi' three destroyers and two cruisers. Same basic instructions, except you're to move to the right flank. Allen is to be your second.

"MacPhail, ye're to second Oliphant in command o' defences. . . . Oliphant, ye second me. I'll handle the torpedoes from the central control and command screens. Ye're to pass us by their sun as closely as ye can wi'out endangering either Claymore or the ships wi' us. Set up a grazing trajectory to pass wi'in a hundred and fifty miles o' Shiva. Base it on a one point zero g acceleration until some twenty-four hours out from their planet, then at zero point seven five g's till passing her. That will gi' everyone aboard a chance to be as rested as possible through the battle. It's apt to be long and I don't want the men exhausted afore we ever get there.

"Wi' any luck we may ha' one or two days' acceleration afore the alien realizes just what's happening. 'Twill take about a week afore we can get to Shiva, so every few minutes' extra time we get gives them less time to react. And if they miss seeing us for a day or two this whole affair may turn out to be a piece o' cake! At any rate, I can hope so.

"Start your preparations, gentlemen. And if there are any delays I want to be informed immediately."

CHAPTER 19

Alarms jangled as Claymore sprang to life after her long months of darkness and null gravity. Technicians made last-minute checks, reexamining for a final time the equipment they had checked a hundred times before. Crews swarmed over the catapults beneath the fighting ships, manhandling stores and cargo aboard. The computers ran automatic interrogation signals over hundreds of miles of wiring to make certain all circuits were fully operative. Casks were filled with water and distributed in strategic locations throughout the ship. Then the mains were emptied so a chance hit could not flood vital electronic control mechanisms. Chinaware and other breakables were stuffed hastily in chests anchored to floors. Everything capable of falling or sliding was strapped down to bolts driven deep into rocky walls and floors. In a scant three hours Claymore was ready.

The rockets burped—gently at first as they probed for possible malfunctions; then with a rising crescendo as each proved out.

Claymore shuddered throughout her vast bulk, shaking herself like some prehistoric behemoth rousing itself from a long sleep. Small pebbles jarred loose from the roof of the village mall, hung there briefly and then hailed down in a gentle rain as Claymore lurched forward. In a few more minutes a similar pebble jarring loose would pellet down like a shot.

Slowly, majestically, Claymore slipped orbit and commenced her long acceleration toward Shiva. The attack was under way.

Nine hours after she pulled free the ten giant catapults rammed forward and the destroyer and cruiser divisions hurtled off into space, where they commenced fanning out into battle array.

In the electronics room radio jammers stood by. If the inner satellite chanced to spot Claymore and tried to radio Shiva, the message would never make it. For that matter, if at all possible Shiva herself was to be effectively isolated from her satellite stations. Special jammers attached to high-frequency oscillators would send wavering shrieks and groans up and down the wavelengths as soon as traffic picked up on Shiva. True, the interference would immediately add to the alert there, but the potential benefits to be gained by disrupting communications would more than outweigh the minimal disadvantage of permitting the enemy a pinpoint location for the source of the interference. Any of a dozen other methods would provide the same information anyhow, so there was nothing to be lost.

The aliens had fought one type of war against Earth. Very well, Claymore intended to fight a wholly different kind of war. In their assault against Earth the alien had relied on a single area of absolute technological superiority conferred by possession of a device Earth lacked. Now Earth hoped to show the aliens how to use commonplace devices both sides had possessed for centuries. Duncan intended to make Claymore a strict taskmaker.

As Claymore cleared her orbit, picking up speed by the minute, he programmed a torpedo section and punched the firing stud. Three dozen torpedoes winged out on collision courses toward six of the orbital stations far behind them. Claymore's mission was destruction. The aliens had destroyed Earth; now it was Earth's turn to strike back. And if more excuse was needed, the torpedoes should be just arriving at the outer stations about the time the attack on Shiva was reaching its climax. Having their sentinel stations on the far side of the star system abruptly destroyed might convince the aliens a second assault was under way and cause them to divert some of their fighter craft to defend against the new threat. And every ship diverted would be one less to challenge Claymore.

Aboard the asteroid, muscles long unused to work protested violently at first, then acquiesced grudgingly as their owners demanded obedience. The personnel assigned to backup gunnery duty under Claymore's skin crawled back and forth through their assigned stretches of tunnel, checking out each gun to their satisfaction, examining airlock seals, moving up added stores of munitions—anything they could think of to improve fighting ability.

Airtight locks isolated every tunnel in a hundred places. The village was abandoned and sealed off lest a hit crack the surrounding rock and permit the air to escape. Clustered in groups of ten and twelve, the nonessential people and children moved to sealed shelters possessing automatic airlocks and oxygen supplies adequate for a month or more.

In the electronics section the radio monitors sprang to abrupt life as alien voices began gabbling on a dozen frequencies simultaneously. The jammers flipped into action and frequencies up and down the spectrum were filled with a cacophony of grunts, wheezes, shrieks and groans. To make matters more enjoyable for the alien, one of the radio techs serenaded them with a whole set of choice bagpipe selections featuring massed bands in review.

The telescopic monitor on Shiva was little help as yet, since the planet was very nearly in line with their sun and at the opposite extreme of its orbit, but relaying photos from one of the flanking destroyers suggested traces of celaenium spectral emissions erupting around the planet—undoubtedly ships. And almost certainly a good many of them, to be detectable at that range. Still they had gained nearly two full days before the first real sign of mustering resistance. Only six more days to go before they would be passing Shiva itself.

Patching together a laser communication relay with the flanking destroyer of the second division and adding a photomultiplier, they were able to pick up a reasonably detailed idea of the Shivite fleet dispositions. Apparently they were milling about in the vicinity of the planet trying to group themselves into a recognizable order.

As far back as the battle of Neptune they had experienced obvious difficulty in maintaining their fleet dispositions once they were disrupted —and then the Earth fleets were not even trying to jam communications. The aliens were obviously still having their problems in that area.

At length the monitor showed a solitary streak as one of the ships headed out toward Claymore on its own. Then a couple more followed and finally the remainder, grouped haphazardly, trailed along after. It was unfortunate that Shiva's atmosphere reflected so much of the jamming; otherwise the whole planet might have lost all but landline communications.

Now other ships could be seen rising about the planet's surface, being picked up by the telescope and photomultiplier as streaks of bright, celaenium-blue light as they emerged from the atmosphere. The computers at Duncan's side showed the aliens had passed the 150 mark for ships up; and this with Claymore four full days out of effective range. The numbers would mount steadily now. It was going to be a fight—no doubt of that!

Claymore's repeater screens sprang to life as the first alien ship came within electronic detection range of the destroyers and was rebroadcast to him via tight beam. Only one ship. Within minutes it had sailed into range of the flanking destroyer. A moment after that it commenced the familiar expansion and vanished from the screen.

"Scratch one ship!" came the jubilant cry from Krishnan's flagship. "It was probably a cutter type—light armed and en route to Jove to find out what was going wrong there."

"At least 'tis a good start," acknowledged Duncan. "Did ye take any fire?"

"Some small stuff. Probably a couple of twenty-millimeter popguns from the size of it."

The computer tab on the ships rising from Shiva passed the three hundred mark with a shade over three days remaining until interception.

The few ships which had fumblingly taken off earlier swam into range of the destroyers and cruisers. There was no fight. The destroyers' guns simply blasted them out of space on the first salvo. Again probably only light armed patrol ships not equipped for battle, Duncan decided.

With two and a half days to go more than seven hundred alien ships were now showing on the screen.

Abruptly the TV stations on Shiva cleared. Where before the Claymore had been unable to disentangle the transmissions from hundreds of different stations carrying different programming on the same channels now there came a brief interval when some government proclamation had preempted regular programming. Delightedly the electronics technicians taped the image of Claymore as seen from Shiva. A follow-up portion of the transmission, which showed the Shivites manning ground defence installations, was immediately passed on to Duncan. One of the devices was clearly recognizable as a neutron cannon!

Duncan could scarcely restrain a chuckle. That would be like trying to aim a peashooter at the moon and expecting to hit it. Claymore would never pass within a hundred miles of such a weapon.

With fewer than twenty-four hours remaining until contact with their main forces, the enemy had more than a thousand ships in space and the number was rising by the minute.

Flipping the communications switch, Duncan broadcast his final message to the people aboard Claymore. "Fellow Scots, English and Indians," he began, "we ha' long awaited the time when we could extract payment for the loss o' Earth. That time is fast upon us. Tomorrow we will come wi'in range o' the leading enemy warships and battle will be joined. Within another three days after that we will be skirting the atmosphere o' Shiva herself. In six days we will either ha' moved beyond immediate pursuit, have been destroyed ourselves or ha' eliminated the enemy fleet.

"Though each o' us has a firm determination to avenge ourselves for the loss o' Earth, we must not fail to gi' our foe full credit for his courage. Time and again he has shown his bravery. 'Tis this selfsame bravery which now constitutes our gravest danger. All gunners must expect suicide runs trying to ram us. 'Twould be what any o' us would do under the same circumstances if we felt 'twould help save Earth. Mayhap such a suicide run would not destroy Claymore, but 'twould possible cripple us. Should enough such runs occur it would destroy us.

"To be wholly honest wi' all o' ye, I doubt our eventual survival in this battle. But each o' us, myself included, can count it a life well spent if by our actions we can help mankind survive and gain a measure o' atonement for the vandalism o' Earth.

"My salute to ye all, and should the god o' battle smile on us, why then I shall greet ye again after the week to come."

Flipping off the set, Duncan leaned back and idly noted that in the few minutes he had been speaking the enemy fleet had grown by forty ships. " 'Twould be a good time to rest," he muttered to himself. "There'll be scant time for it later."

When he awakened the enemy fleet had passed twelve hundred ships, and even as he looked the computer tally spun over another six digits. A message from electronics informed him the enemy TV stations had all gone off the air. The foe still had been unable to devise effective counterjamming action. Most likely he had never encountered that particular problem before and wasn't entirely sure how to go about neutralizing it—not in so short a span of time, at any rate. This meant his fleet would be uncoordinated. It also boded well for the future of Claymore.

The repeater screens in the control room showed faint blips speckling ahead as the advance elements of the foe swept into extreme detector range of the destroyers and cruisers. A survey of the aft screens showed, as expected, only blankness. The combat-readiness panel glowed solid green save for the two lights representing the kitchens and hydroponics areas. They were to be shut down at the last possible minute.

A report from the damage-control division arrived as Duncan was eating. Each of the airlocked sections had spare oxygen bottles and food and water adequate for a week. Hospital stores had been distributed and were available in each section. With the manual disconnects and firing systems this meant a man could be totally isolated from the remainder of the ship and still continue manning his weapons bank for a full seven days. It would not be nearly as efficient as computer-directed firing but it would be reasonably effective for the sort of battle they'd be in and it would be immeasurably better than the alternative.

He glanced at the clock and ran a rate of closure. Twelve hours to go for Claymore. Ten and a fraction for the destroyers and cruisers. . . . Too long a gap. It would allow the enemy to concentrate on each group in detail. Tersely he ordered the advance and flanking ships to close to within ten minutes of Claymore.

The computer showed over fourteen hundred ships in space.

Electronics reported that the enemy had massed several transmitters together on 301.4 megahertz and was attempting to ram messages through the jamming. One of the screechers was taken off the general-frequency jamming and assigned to that channel. It effectively squelched the matter and shortly the enemy quit trying.

With less than four hours to go the enemy had scarcely added another dozen ships to his fleet. Apparently he had passed his peak and would level at a figure of somewhat less than fifteen hundred ships. Idly Duncan wondered whether the Shivites had done the same thing seventy years ago. Had they simply taken every ship in their fleet and massed for the attack, or had they simply never quite made up for the losses they had suffered in the battles of Jupiter and Saturn? Then too, perhaps this was merely their reserve fleet and they had the bulk of their forces out looking for possible survivors of Earth. He recalled the days on their way here when the detectors had reported continuous flights of ships passing by them in hyperspace, all aimed for the sun. Was Claymore perhaps the last of humankind, with the other fleeing fragments already exterminated?

With fifteen minutes to go before the lead ships entered the fray,

Duncan ordered acceleration aboard all ships cut back to 0.5 g's. Then he reconsidered. Flipping the intercom he called over to Oliphant. "Can ye gi' me a trajectory to graze Shiva at only zero point two gravity? 'Twill lessen fatigue if we can cut the acceleration to the bone."

"Aye," came the reply after a moment's calculation. "No problem at all. Shall I chop power now?"

"Aye," confirmed Duncan. "Reduce acceleration to zero point two g." Turning to the radio he relayed the instructions to the destroyers and cruisers. A brief moment later his muscles relaxed as the apparent gravity was cut back to a bare minimum consistent with efficient operation of the ship.

Battle joined!

The destroyers opened it with a concerted salvo of the 550 mm guns aimed squarely at the centre of the approaching enemy fleet. Ten of the 20 megaton missiles sped toward the point where the ships were clustered most tightly. With a force of 200 million tons of TNT the missiles detonated almost simultaneously, literally atomizing every object within a fifty-mile radius of the centre. Over a hundred alien ships, including several dozen whose momentum carried them into the blast area, were annihilated by the unexpected onslaught. Apparently superartillery was also a weapon they had never bothered developing.

Then the destroyers and cruisers vanished into the confused maelstrom of fighting ships. Lights flashed in the darkness as ships erupted in flaming salvos. Ships exploded and burst into brief flame as their oxygen boiled away into the void. Hurtling fragments of steel armor plate spun wickedly into previously unharmed ships, adding to the carnage.

Duncan, almost alone of all those in the battle, could see what was happening and to some degree control it. Now a green blip on the screen vanished as one of his cruisers was destroyed. The computer on the desk had reversed its spin. The reading was now fewer than twelve hundred alien ships as the first freshets of the swirling wave of combat washed over Claymore.

Abruptly the asteroid shuddered strangely as eleven thousand machine cannon erupted in a litany of destruction. She was become a veritable sphere of fire as the first salvo blasted into the ranks of the enemy. But now little pockmarks spread across her surface as enemy guns ranged in on a target which could not maneuver out of the way and was too big to miss. Chips and fragments flew off into the void as precious inches and feet of her slab-rock sides were blasted away.

Red lights began appearing on Duncan's console, each indicating a torpedo damaged and unable to fire or a machine cannon out of operation. Damage-control parties scurried about making such repairs as were possible. A few of the red lights turned green again, but other red lights took their place. With the battle only a few minutes joined, the damage-control system was already being overwhelmed.

The computer tally reeled down toward a thousand of the enemy. Another green blip vanished from the screens—one of the destroyers of Krishnan's group. More salvos given and received rocked Claymore. A whole bank of machine guns flared red on the console as their wiring was cut. The lower green buttons flashed on to indicate that the trooper in the section still survived and was manually triggering his weapons.

The computer showed 997 enemy ships. Ten percent of Claymore's torpedoes were inoperative. Should Duncan fire the rest of them now? He decided to wait. More red lights flared as another bank of guns failed and were not being triggered manually. The tally of the enemy slipped below 900 as the pace of battle slowed. A few of the enemy were behind Claymore now and out of the fight for a while at least. The dangerous ships were the ones which had angled in from the flanks. They had no excess relative velocity to kill and could press their assault home.

A bank of weapons which had gone completely red turned green again on the lower register. One of the reserves in a suit, thought Duncan. An explosion rocked Claymore as a direct hit on a torpedo jammed the safety mechanism, allowing the warhead to detonate, though not with anything like normal efficiency. It was more of a squib burst, Duncan imagined.

An enemy suicide ship exploded at the last instant as the computer found the range. Another green blip vanished. One of Holmes's ships, Duncan decided; though by now both divisions were so intermixed it was impossible to tell for sure.

The computer showed 832 enemy ships with fifty-two hours yet to go before passing Shiva. More red lights flashed onto the console and the battle status display showed 3317 torpedoes remaining of the original 4000. Fewer than 9800 machine guns were operational.

There was neither time nor space for tactics. This was bull ahead and fight. To make certain of doing some damage, Duncan launched 400 torpedoes at Shiva. Claymore herself lurched as a lucky hit destroyed one of the torpedoes only a few miles away. Lights showed red all along the flank, but there was no enemy ship to follow up the momentary advantage, and within minutes the board was sparkling green again. Forty-six hours to close approach and 712 enemy ships left.

Damage-control parties toiled to repair the fighting strength of the ship. Expended torpedoes were replaced by new ones in the tubes. Another green blip vanished from the screen. Claymore shuddered with the impact of a shell as it made a direct hit on one of the three utility ships remaining aboard ship and its nose jets exploded.

A thunderous roar jarred Claymore from stem to stern as an alien suicide ship rammed full tilt into one of the massive rocket tubes and exploded there. Three more aliens tried to follow the track of the first but were blasted before they could get within range. A group of six aliens moved directly ahead of Claymore, then turned in toward her, accelerating at full speed. All six were destroyed by the guns, but shattered fragments of metal and flesh pelted down to the surface, smashing several torpedo tubes and guns.

Forty-two hours to passage and the tally was 659. The enemy was starting to change his tactics as small groups of ships would make a run in from the flanks while firing desperately, then peel off to make another run. The console lights were gleaming ever more wickedly red. The status display showed only 2831 torpedoes available. There were 9048 machine guns operational, and an entire bank of weapons shone redly on one flank.

Another shock jolted Claymore as an enemy pilot rammed into the port side throwing two full banks of guns into the red and annihilating twenty torpedoes. Still another green blip vanished from the screen ahead. Thirty-six hours to go and 587 of the enemy between them and their objective.

Duncan fired another 400 torpedoes at Shiva, then commenced a rhythmic stabbing of the individual firing buttons, sending out torpedoes at intervals of two, three or four seconds, a half dozen at a time —all winging their way to the still-distant planet. The damage-control parties were not so fast in replacing the torpedoes this time, Duncan noticed. They had their hands full all over the ship. Only 2114 torpedoes left and slightly over 7000 machine guns still working.

A light showed red on the secondary console. The air of the village was escaping! Another alien rammed Claymore, and two more banks of guns showed red along with a dozen torpedoes. The light for the village turned back to green as damage control sealed the leak. Thirty hours to go; 504 enemy remaining.

Another 100 torpedoes arrowed out at short intervals: 1422 left. And 5956 machine guns were still firing. There was now a blind spot on Claymore. The enemy had not found it yet, but he would. One more of the green blips went into oblivion. The little fleet of destroyers and cruisers was nearly gone now. A row of green lights flashed to life squarely in the centre of the blind spot. Mentally Duncan congratulated damage control. They were still in there working.

One of the screens went blank for a moment, then returned to life as the backup system went into operation. The relayed view of Shiva disappeared permanently as the fifty-inch Schmidt was smashed. Another red light flared on the secondary console. The reactor areas this time.

The 0.2 g acceleration ceased as Claymore's drive rockets sputtered out. Then the interior lights winked out and were supplanted by emergency circuits. The computers and consoles faltered momentarily, then resumed their steady clicking. Another of the green blips had disappeared during that brief interval.

Duncan fired another 200 torpedoes.

Twenty-six hours and 422 enemy ships. Claymore was reeling from the pounding she was taking. The reactor room was still red and the hospital area had been added to it. There were 823 torpedoes left operational and 4413 machine guns still showed green, more than half being manually fired.

By now the first of the torpedoes should be striking Shiva. Duncan wished he had a view screen to observe the damage, if any.

Electronics reported over the communications net. Whole groups of the enemy's ground radio stations had gone off the air. A member of a damage-control party stated that a sergeant manning one of the bow gun banks had reported observing several dozen bright flashes on Shiva. Probably torpedoes hitting.

Now the enemy redoubled his attacks. Claymore was hurt, and hurt badly. Fewer than 300 torpedoes remained. Only 3800 machine guns were firing. Nineteen hours and 306 enemy ships remained. The question was, could Claymore endure those few more hours?

A further report from the bow established beyond doubt that Shiva was in trouble. A man was sent forward with a small hand telescope and radio so he could give a report. Duncan spread the word throughout the ship. They might all die, but it would be with the satisfaction of a job well done.

Claymore lurched stumblingly twice in succession as two enemy ships plunged into her from opposite sides. An ominous hiss in the administration room told him air was escaping. The secondary console glowed redly before him. His own section was damaged. Everyone had donned space suits before the battle, and Duncan was no exception. He snapped on his helmet and plugged the feeder tube into the local oxygen system to conserve his portable supply.

Then another red light flashed on the secondary console. The village again. Only hydroponics, communications, weapons and stores were left. Even as he watched, the stores light changed to red. It couldn't be much longer now; not at the rate things were going.

Only two green blips, besides Claymore, remained on the screen. The weapons-status lights were almost solidly red: 207 torpedoes and 3165 machine guns left. Fourteen hours and 219 enemy ships remaining—218, noted Duncan, as Claymore shuddered through her bulk when another ship rammed her. More lights flashed red from the impact.

Communications died, and with it the consoles. Duncan was left in darkness. Not even the torpedoes were left to him. They would all have to be fired manually.

Strapping on a pair of extra oxygen bottles, he took his hand torch and departed the administration tunnel for the surface. Switching on his helmet to general frequency, he alerted the gunners. "Attention. Campbell here. Communications is out. We ha' approximately twelve hours to closest approach, when I propose to fire the remaining torpedoes. The responsibility for firing them will rest wi' the individual gunners as all controls are out. I will advise my presence every half hour. If I fail ye are to assume I'm dead and use your best judgment unless instructed otherwise by Oliphant or his designated second."

Switching to damage-control frequency, he asked, "Do ye need any personnel for manual firing? If so, consider me available for this or such other orders as ye may ha'. I am unreservedly at your disposal."

"Aye, General," came the immediate response. "We need a gunner for bank three, section two. 'Tis urgent."

"I'm on my way. And thanks."

Stumbling half blindly through the littered passageways, he weaved carefully through regions of almost unimaginable destruction. In one spot, previously a full half mile beneath the rocky surface, he clambered through a wrecked airlock and found himself briefly on the surface itself! Reaching his destination, he discovered he was not the first replacement. Three men had already died there keeping the guns firing. As he shifted a body to reach the central firing solenoid he realized he had been wrong. It hadn't been three men. It had been two men and the wife of one of the sergeants in his command.

Was Mavis also on the firing line? The question was meaningless. Everyone was on the firing line. Nine guns of the fifty originally in the bank were operational. Linking them en banc, he flipped the solenoid and fired blindly into space. There was nothing to see unless an enemy came close enough for a proximity fuse to go off.

A brilliant series of flashes burst against his eyes and he automatically swiveled his guns toward the source. Then three successive blasts illuminated that portion of the sky as an enemy ship on a suicide run roiled up in smoke. "If only he hadn't fired," thought Duncan, "I never would ha' seen him. Two hundred and seventeen to go!" he thought wildly, ignoring the probability that other ships had been destroyed since he had left the administration centre.

Slamming down the solenoid trigger, he systematically swept the whole sky segment covered by his guns. Then he changed sweep patterns to try to confuse the enemy. He spelled out the letter A in bold arcs. Then B and C and D, right through the alphabet. Twice during this period he was rewarded by seeing a ship erupt into nothingness. He ran out of ammunition and hastily reloaded the last of the 20,000-round cannisters. Then he worked out a compound French curve in the sky and tried out a sine wave. Going back to the alphabet, he saw another ship go.

A pattering rain of bright flashes spitted across the surface, the nearest flashing only a yard away. Spinning his guns around, he commenced a wild search pattern for the enemy ship. A moment later he was half stunned by the lurching impact as the crippled alien plunged into the surface a hundred feet away. He dimly realized through a haze of fatigue that the guns were empty. How long had they been that way?

Running stooped, and scrabbling for hand holds so he would not fly off into space, Duncan searched dazedly about the rubble until he discovered the remains of a demolished machine gun. But it had a nearly intact 20,000-round belt still attached to it. Heaving the cannister ahead of him, he inched it back to his gun section and commenced firing again.

Another few minutes and once more the guns fell silent. The cannister must have been emptier than he thought. Numbly he shuffled back into what was left of the support tunnel until he uncovered several of the smaller, 2000-round ammo boxes. Wrestling several of these into position, he levered the ammunition into the breeches and commenced firing again.

Another shuddering jolt rocked Claymore from one end to the other. It was followed almost immediately by a jarring, wrenching impact as an enemy ship plunged headlong into Claymore's bow. Splashes of light pocked across the surface beside him and he dimly sensed the flight of rock fragments as they whizzed through space around him. A small boulder smashed into his side. He scarcely noticed it. He was simply too tired to feel anything. His fingers were glued to the firing solenoid. . . . Down through the alphabet again, stopping twice to change ammunition belts.

An annoying light loomed to his right. It interfered with his already limited vision into the blackness. Instinctively he held his hand out to shield his eyes. Then he paused to wonder what it meant and peered fully into the ball of light as it swam into full view. It was Shiva! They were passing into near approach.

Wonderingly his eyes took in the pattern of desolation beneath him. He couldn't recall how many torpedoes he had fired but knew it must have been well over a thousand. Four hundred should virtually sterilize a planet. But from three to four hundred must have struck this side of the planet alone. Vast, roiling clouds of undulating smoke obscured every part of the surface. He might have been peering at the sun for all the detail he could see.

Was that a speck? Yes. A ship. A ship coming in to the attack while silhouetted against that background. A fool! Never come in with the light behind you. He fired and watched the ship disintegrate and slip down into the background.

He searched about and found the remains of a torpedo tube . . . empty.

Scrambling out onto the rubbled surface, he spotted a relatively un-damaged area by the weird light of the dying planet. Inching his way across the debris he searched for torpedo tubes, and found one. Working back to the hatch area he finally located the firing switch. One more torpedo for Earth. One last torpedo for Earth.

For a final moment the exultant madness lingered as Duncan gazed with grim satisfaction at the destruction below him. And then the moment passed and the battle madness was gone. He stared again at the ball of seething death with sadness and even a touch of regret. Vainly he tried to recall his hate of a scant few minutes ago. Whatever Shiva had done, Shiva had paid for.

If another ship had shown up now Duncan could not have fired at it. He couldn't have fired if it meant the whole of Claymore. He was only weary—desperately weary. Stumbling over the rubble, he turned back into the darkened bowels of the ruined asteroid.

CHAPTER 20

The torpedo Duncan had fired at dying Shiva was the last of the battle. As they passed close approach, the few remaining enemy ships broke off the combat and apparently landed to attempt whatever rescue operations they could. Either that or the torpedoes blasting their satellite stations far at the other end of the Shiva system alerted them to the prospect of a second assault. Either way, the last of them turned back and Claymore was left a broken hulk spinning helplessly out into the remote reaches of space.

Gradually the damage-control parties began getting some of the areas of Claymore back into repair. The guns and torpedoes came first. Duncan was isolated among his lonely bank of guns, but then so were many others. Frankly, damage control had forgotten he was even out in the guns area. It was a lance corporal who had sent him out there to begin with, and the corporal was long dead.

A few hours later the lights flickered on in the section of passageway where Duncan lay. Rousing groggily, he looked about in renewed interest, only to realize he had absolutely no idea where he was on Claymore. The lights were only pinpoints reflecting thinly along the walls so he knew there was no air in the corridor. A check of his oxygen gauge convinced him he had better move fast. Less than twenty minutes' air supply remained and the regeneration unit in the suit had already passed its rated capacity.

The corridor he was in ended in a caved-in rubble on either side. The supplies of reserve oxygen must be on the other side. Testing his helmet radio on all frequencies, he heard nothing. Yet they were alive in there or the lights would never have come back on. It must be his radio at fault.

Searching back along the corridor, he found the hatch he had used to gain entry and climbed back onto the surface. Shiva was a brilliant disk far back in the distance. Not enough light from her to see by, and the sun was evidently on the other side of Claymore. His hand torch was gone. Nothing to do but return to the tunnel and try to dig through.

Reentering the area he had just left, he commenced digging through the rubble. With no effective gravity he had only the inertia of the rock to worry about, and within a few minutes he was able to wriggle through the caved-in area only to find another immediately ahead of him.

Bobbing his head in mute acceptance of the fact, Duncan continued digging until he worked himself a crawl space and could twist into the next area. Not even the dim, airless flicker of light tempered the darkness on the other side. Duncan groped his way in utter blackness until finally stumbling into yet another caved-in area. Fumblingly he threw aside the rocky debris until he could slip over onto the other side.

There was no other side. The caved-in area dipped slightly and he was square up against another dead end.

His breath was coming in huge gasps now. The tank was empty and only the air-regeneration unit kept him supplied with a trace of usable oxygen—and the unit had long since exceeded every design limit built into it. Sobbing in angry frustration, he tackled the next cave-in area, sliding the rubble around behind him as he toiled, twisting himself around the larger boulders and on one occasion even sliding under an inverted pyramid of massive rocks. Then his hand felt nothingness ahead of him. He was through into the next section of the tunnel. Far ahead glowed a dim red light. An airlock door.

Beside the airlock was a supply of spare oxygen bottles, water and other foods. The oxygen he could use, but how do you drink water through a space suit? Grasping two of the oxygen bottles and a pair of regeneration units, he quickly strapped them on and breathed deeply of the life-giving air.

The red light meant there was no air on the other side of the door. That was its designed purpose. Battery powered, it contained a diaphragm which would rupture and complete a circuit whenever the atmospheric pressure slipped below eight pounds. According to that, recalled Duncan, there should also be a red light on the opposite side of the lock to inform anyone over there that this side had no air. If it was still working it should give at least a little light to see by. It was.

But there were also other lights as well; the dim pinpricks denoting an airless space. Duncan permitted himself a short, barking laugh. There was no air anywhere save what he carried under his arm and on his back. He was the last surviving creature in the universe. There was nothing else anywhere. He'd wager his life on that. But no matter: there was another airlock ahead.

Slipping through the double doors, one after the other, he entered the next passageway. It too was caved in at several points. Stopping to look back at the door he had just passed, Duncan cursed himself for a fool! He was in bank seven, section one. He was circling Claymore when he should have been seeking out connecting passages to get below.

Straining his memory, he recalled the layout of the weapons tunnels: 150 feet between airlocks; floor locks leading below at fifty and a hundred feet along the tunnels.

He had to dig between two caved-in areas before he found the fifty-foot lock. The recessed light was not lit. Presumedly there was air below. Spinning the hatch, he stepped into blackness. Fumbling for holds, he spun the hatch back and dogged it shut, then searched for the hatch beneath him. His groping hands found it, spun it open and he emerged into even deeper blackness, if such is possible.

No red light showed on this side either.

Was he in air or wasn't he? Instinctively he used the old spaceman's trick of clapping his hands together. The only sound transmitted was the vibration up his arms. There was no air.

Straining his memory, he tried to recall the layout of this tunnel and couldn't. The only thing to do was crawl until he reached a hatch or lock of some sort and see where it might lead.

Carefully counting off each crawled foot, he passed along the corridor, only to come up short against another cave-in. Turning back, he counted the other way until he felt the rungs leading up to the airlock he had just descended, then commenced counting off in the other direction. This time he was successful and came up against a lock door.

Passing through the second door he was momentarily startled by the dull gleam of the red bulb above him. There was an odd scraping sound. Something was wrong. Then he realized. He was hearing. There was air. Cautiously he loosed the valve of his tank and his nose was assailed by the stale air of the corridor.

How long he slept there Duncan never knew. He didn't even quite recall falling asleep. For that matter he couldn't remember whether he'd managed to sleep anytime during the battle. And he didn't even know how long the battle had lasted except that it must have been at least four days.

When he finally awakened he was conscious only of a terrible, throbbing head and neck ache. Every muscle and joint in his body felt as if it had been wrenched apart and haphazardly reassembled. His side felt as if it had been mangled in some forgotten accident and he had a strong suspicion some ribs were broken. Dimly he recalled being struck by a flying rock toward the latter stages of the battle. He was hungry. He was thirsty. He had to go to the bathroom. That, at least, he could do.

Picking up his remaining spare oxygen tank, he proceeded cautiously down the black corridor. His foot kicked something soft and yielding and he fell down. Somebody was lying there in the dark. Feeling carefully about the motionless figure, his hands groped at the waist. Sure enough, there was the standard torch hanging there.

Gratefully Duncan recovered it, then flashed it briefly over the body of one of the ratings, a spreaded pool of clotted blood smearing out from the stump of an arm.

With the light his progress was quicker. Twice more on his descent he had to reattach his air hose to the tank when the flutter valve to the outside refused to open, indicating lack of air. In the fourth level of the B layer, normally about two miles down before the aliens had peeled their thousands of feet off Claymore, he found himself once more in a lighted area, this time with air. As he passed into the next lock he was met by a damage-control party.

His strange odyssey was over. Within an hour he was back at the heart of Claymore.

There was no rejoicing over their victory. There was only death, sorrow and work. Their asteroid had been so brutally damaged there was real doubt she could ever be repaired. Scarcely a family but had lost one or more members. Duncan and Mavis themselves mourned the loss of young Donald MacLeod, their son. But Celia had somehow survived in her own space suit even though her security section had lost its air. Mavis, though a full six months pregnant, had manned a section of guns for almost half the battle.

The hydroponics section was still basically operational and communications had been partially restored. Administration was alive again. The reactor area was too hot to enter. Weapons had been almost completely destroyed and the village was still without air. No damage-control parties had even been able to reach the hospital area yet, so there was no word on it. Two of the destroyers had survived and were jury-berthed on the surface. One of them was currently supplying power for the whole of Claymore.

As Duncan surveyed their situation he was astounded at the helplessness of their craft. Of the fifty-one hundred people—including children—who had lived on her at the start of the assault fewer than twenty-two hundred still survived—nearly 60 percent casualties. The weapons-status consoles, back in operation now that power was returned, showed only four torpedoes and nineteen guns operational.

One utility boat had somehow managed to come through unscathed, so they now had a total of two destroyers and one utility craft. The captured alien vessel had vanished without a trace.

Claymore herself was clearly incapable of any sort of resistance.

That was obvious. At the same time it was a virtual certainty that the aliens would react. Probably it would be rather disorganized and slow at the start, but when it finally came the reaction would inevitably be augmented by the fury of despair.

The one free destroyer was resupplied as well as possible and ordered off in close support. The utility craft was sent forward as a scout. Damage control was set to mapping areas of available oxygen. The wounded, the children, the few remaining doctors and nurses, along with a small scattering of lightly injured women to serve as aides, cooks and provisioners, were moved into the hydroponics area. All other personnel were placed at the disposal of damage control.

A team of rocket specialists wormed their way back to the powerful propulsion units and soon reported three of the rockets could be made operable. A jury control was rigged and one of the rockets sprang to cautious, tentative life. Then a second rocket fired and Claymore eased into a 0.1 g acceleration. A shunt around the third rocket provided limited amounts of power as the heat was used to generate steam and electricity. The second destroyer then disconnected her tie-in with Claymore and went speeding off to join her sister ship.

Search parties scoured the debris and rubble. With Claymore under way at a constant, if limited, acceleration, boulders could be carried up to the surface and hurled into space, where they would soon fall behind. A queer bucket brigade was organized to lift the rubble from sections where it was impeding operations, and shortly the ship's trajectory was marked by a stream of trailing rock.

Boxes of unexpended ammunition uncovered beneath the rubble were moved into the open. Occasional machine guns were discovered and brought into a central reassembly area where lightly injured women pirated parts from the more heavily damaged guns, turning two or three unserviceable weapons into a single operational one. Possibly not all the weapons so reconstructed would work properly or long, but some would, and it was at least a start.

Three torpedoes were uncovered intact in their launching tubes. The catapults were repaired and the wiring tied into administration. Now there were seven green lights winking amid 3993 red ones. Nine more torpedoes were discovered lying askew and buried in the rubble. The tubes themselves were damaged beyond repair, but there were plenty of undamaged ones around. The torpedoes were shifted into these and nine more lights winked green.

Communications, reporting for damage control, advised that forty-two machine guns had been repaired and armed and were in position on the surface. No attempt had been made to slave them in with the master console at this time. If they were to be operated a gunner would have to do it.

A radiation party succeeded in penetrating the weapons section. It was reported a shambles and the task of recovering usable machinery was begun. The secondary console light denoting the hospital was shifted from red to green. Three doctors and sixteen patients had survived in an airlocked wing of the complex. The bodies of the alien prisoners were found in the research wing of the building. A xenologist had evidently been attempting to lead them to an airlock when the penetrating hit fractured the walls allowing the air to escape.

The party working on the rocket tubes reported a fourth rocket ready to fire. As the acceleration built up to 0.2 g a section of the roof collapsed, crushing a fortunately unused area of the administration complex. Acceleration was promptly reduced to 0.15 g and stabilized there.

A pair of melters were assembled from the ruins of the weapons room and put into operation. Flamed on the surface of the rock along a crack, the rock would melt and flow into the fissure, effectively and permanently sealing it. They were ineffectual against major cave-ins and gaping holes, but the innumerable lesser cracks were rapidly repaired.

Gleaming red lights on the secondary console began changing to green as sections of the tunnels were sealed and air was pumped into them. Almost a third of Claymore now had air.

One of the larger melters was returned to operation and moved onto the surface. Soon whole acres were being cauterized. Buckets of rock were dumped atop the newly melted areas and the melter applied a second time, adding to the thickness of solidified rock above the living areas.

They were approaching the orbit of the sixth planet and the satellite stations. Claymore was in no condition to fight her way through. The destroyers had to do it for her. They moved out in the van, leaving the utility ship as rear guard.

The aliens aboard the station were well armed and certainly prepared, but they had never dreamed of a 550 mm gun. Their largest weapon appeared to be something in the vicinity of a 155 mm gun. The simultaneous eruption of four 550 mm rounds, each of 20 megaton rating, enveloped the station with the combined force of 80 million tons of TNT and Claymore sailed serenely through the gaping hole in the satellite defence ring.

With a steady 0.15 g acceleration adding momentarily to the 5000-mile-per-second velocity she had built up during her wild plunge on

Shiva, Claymore had by now accumulated a modest speed in excess of 7000 miles per second. Each day more of the red lights vanished from the panel and were replaced by a healthy green. But reactors was still red. So were the village and weapons.

Sixty torpedoes were now operational, most of them taken from the reserve stock and mounted in spent tubes; 172 machine guns were functioning and tied in with the central computers. Another seventy were operational but not tied in. Two of the three central computers had been destroyed and the third badly damaged. Pirating a few parts and pulling replacement components from stores, they had managed to renovate the system with one machine in full operation. A half dozen minicomputers were slaved together to provide a backup of sorts for the mainframe. No one knew whether it would be adequate for an emergency, but it was the best they had so they were giving it a try.

A fifth rocket was reported operational but was not fired since there was still too much danger of further collapses in the tunnels. Work shifts were stabilized at sixteen hours, and at any time some two thirds of Claymore's able-bodied survivors were busy mending damage.

A new hazard presented itself. Enough air had been stored in oxygen containers to regenerate the air of Claymore twice over. But every time an airlock door was opened to permit entry into airless space a few more feet of precious air was permanently lost. Some of these gasses would be replaced as the melting rock liberated molecules of aeons-old nitrogen and oxygen trapped within; but it was far from enough.

Strict oxygen-control measures were initiated. Certain locks were designated as exit points, and except in emergencies these locks were to be filled to capacity either with men or with equipment before being opened. Less air would be lost that way and there would be a smaller number of individual openings per lock.

Water had been critical since the initial orbiting about Jove. A further loss during the battle aggravated the situation. Water rationing was instituted and the hydroponics tanks were reduced to a level barely adequate to recycle the air and provide foodstuffs for the remaining population and livestock. Dehumidifiers were set up in the lock areas to dry out the air as much as possible before it was lost to space. Still there was the inevitable escape of the precious liquid. A cup of water spilled on the rock surface of the administration area would lose 25 percent of its volume during recycling. Some would seep into the rock itself. Some would escape as vapor not recovered by the dehumidifiers. And some simply vanished under the carbon arcs of the welders or through the rocket ports or the fissures in the rock. Matters were not yet desperate, but extreme caution was needful.

The destroyers were deployed to the rear as protection from pursuit. A persistent enemy ship had been hanging just at the verge of detector range, presumedly radioing back information for the use of fleets being readied to pursue them. A torpedo from one of the destroyers was released, its detection system limited to thirty thousand miles. Twenty hours later the enemy ship swam into range. The torpedo's sensors located it. The celaenium-boost rockets erupted to life as it accelerated at 35 g's. A few minutes later the enemy ship vanished from the destroyer's screens.

A cautious rotation of the steering gyros on Claymore altered her direction to assist in evading further pursuit.

The first party succeeded in entering the reactor section. Even with heavy radiation armor they could remain only three minutes—just long enough to lay a hasty power line to a repair robot. Outside the reactor room a TV monitor came to life and a physicist, operating the remote circuit, commenced the cleanup, sweeping the debris into a chute where a leaded container received and stored it until other automated machinery could carry it aft to be expelled through the rockets.

Twice the power lines to the robot failed as it twisted over floors and snaked around machinery. Each time a radiation tech, encased in armor, returned to free the vital connections. And each time the tolerance level had increased by a few seconds.

Whole sections of the primary and secondary consoles had been disconnected. There was no sense having a red light indicating the uselessness of a section of Claymore that physically was no longer there. In one spot on her surface there was a gaping crater three quarters of a mile deep and nearly as wide. Fragments of three alien ships were found embedded in the rubble and the radiation level suggested that at least one of them must have rammed with her entire complement of weaponry fused for explosion on impact. The radiated cracks from this one crater extended a full third of the way through Claymore's bulk. A few more shocks and the entire asteroid might break into three separate fragments.

Rubble which had yet to be cast off into space was hastily dumped into the crater and both reserve melters were brought to the surface to be used on the rubble as it was cast in. A few days later the chasm was a quarter filled and Claymore was running out of rubble.

A tunnel was melted across the main axis of the crack. Steel beams, fabricated from the ruins of the alien ships and metal from the demolished torpedoes and machine guns, were anchored into the area to slow further separation. Rock was then melted around them until they were firmly seated and the area was deemed out of immediate danger.

Over three hundred machine guns were now tied into the computer. Possibly a dozen or more might yet be uncovered, but a further substantial increase in Claymore's defensive power was considered unlikely. Most of the eleven thousand guns originally studding the asteroid were long since reduced to their component atoms.

Damage control reported that the ship was probably capable of accepting higher acceleration. Number four rocket was fired and the power settings on the other were eased forward. Acceleration was boosted to 0.35 g before damage control discovered a buildup of new stresses. Leveling down to 0.3 g, work was started shoring up the new danger areas. A month of acceleration at this rate would add some 4700 miles per second to their gross velocity—a respectable increment to their present 9400 miles per second but scarcely a drop in the bucket on the way to 186,000 per second.

The robot cleanup of the reactors had progressed to a point where the first pile was back in operation. The power bypass on the rocket was dismantled and Claymore now had six rockets available for duty, but the overall acceleration was less than that normally provided by two of the units. Nevertheless, for the first time in weeks they had all the power they needed.

With the resumption of full power, communications reestablished total radio monitor over the alien's frequencies and brought their detector equipment back to something approaching normal operating efficiency. "At least," thought Duncan gloomily as he contemplated the status of his ship, "we'll know what hits us now."

The light for the village turned green as the last of the crevasses was sealed and strengthened. Oxygen was released until the pressure stood at five pounds—enough to breathe by but not really comfortable.

Overstressed areas were repaired and shored. Acceleration was successfully boosted to 0.45 g before new danger areas appeared. A further shoring and bracing enabled them to move up to a 0.6 g acceleration. A month at that rate would add 9460 miles per second to their overall speed.

The detector screens picked up signs of pursuit to the rear as a cluster of seven blips hovered at the extreme edge of detector range.

A destroyer was moved to the front of Claymore in a shallow curve, then chopped power to her rockets and drifted silently across her bow, narrowly missing a collision in the process. At the enemy's range even Claymore could only be detected by the distinctive spectrum of her drives. To the pursuing ships it would look as if one of Claymore's rear guard had been moved up to land on her, and with the drive shut down she would remain undetectable until she came into radar range.

With only the velocity of her inertia the destroyer was soon far behind Claymore, directly in the path of the pursuing ships. Turning her stern toward the aliens to present an even smaller target for radar returns, the crew rigged a specially rubberized sheeting and deployed it aft. Held in place by explosive bolts for quick detachment, it effectively absorbed most of the radar impulses. By the time enough of a return was received to alert their pursuers it would be far too late. It was an old trick which had been used as long ago as Earth's Second World War. Presumedly their enemy wouldn't know about it.

They didn't. A pair of 550's destroyed four of their ships before they knew what hit them. Two of the remaining ships didn't have time to fire a shot before the secondary salvos plastered them into oblivion. The seventh ship veered sideways under full acceleration and managed to escape toward Shiva. As the destroyer rejoined Claymore, Duncan again altered course in an effort to confuse pursuit. Dropping the bow 30 degrees and angling some 45 degrees to starboard, the asteroid lost no momentum and at the same time radically altered trajectory.

Another month passed and acceleration was gradually built up to just over 0.8 g. Oxygen rationing was no longer necessary once the cryogenics section returned to operation and they could again synthesize needed elements. All remaining corridors and tunnels were sealed and all possible surface repairs had been completed. Air pressure had been brought up to 7.5 pounds in the village and increased fractionally every time the internal locks were opened to permit entry. A second reactor had been placed back in service and weapons had been successfully decontaminated. Water was still critical, but with the lessened need for hydroponics it was less critical than earlier. Now it was time to take stock.

Using narrow-beam laser, Duncan ordered the destroyers and utility ship back to berth. After their arrival he made his announcement throughout the ship. "Attention all personnel. Tomorrow morn, at ten hundred hours, there will be a general assembly in the village. All persons save maintenance watch and the communications monitors will be present. Personnel on duty will, so far as practical, listen in on the communications system. For all others the day is declared a holiday following the assembly."

The next morning the curious remnants of Claymore convened for the first time since before their assault on Shiva; 2178 men, women and children were the pitifully small fragment there as Duncan mounted a convenient bench.

"Friends and fellow Scots," he began, "this is the first we ha' had time to meet together since our assault. In itself 'twould be cause for a holiday. But there is another reason which calls us together now. And 'tis this I wish to talk over wi' ye.

"We ha' now reached a turning point in our thinking and must commence to plan anew. When we set forth from Styx we had two goals assigned us: to retaliate against Shiva for the destruction o' Earth and to acquire the secret o' the hyperdrive if we could. We ha' achieved both.

"The secret o' the hyperdrive is winging its way back to Styx aboard two torpedoes. And though we were not able to destroy all o' the aliens we were able to ruin their home planet wi' all its industrial capability. Most likely they still ha' important production and research abilities on their other planets. Certainly they will use these in an effort to seek out and destroy whatever remnant o' mankind may still exist. In addition, they ha' at least sixty-five more years afore Styx can hope to receive our information about the hyperdrive. To this extent we ha' not done as well as we might ha' hoped.

"On the other hand, wi' their centre and heart torn out 'twill certainly be some while afore they can enter into any sort o' deliberately organized search for other survivors. So we ha' bought time wi' our blood—time for mankind to recover and gain strength wherever he may be.

"For a while I felt certain the alien would gather all his remaining ships and resources together to smash us. Now I am not so certain. I am inclined to believe we may be safe for the while.

"Consider the matter from the standpoint o' the alien and I feel ye will all agree wi' me. . . . First o' all, Claymore wi' her few destroyers and cruisers challenged a fleet o' more than fourteen hundred ships— and won! The enemy will not soon forget that. Nor will he recklessly launch another attack at us. He will be cautious as he proceeds. He knows we ha' teeth.

"True, if he were to attack wi' as few as a hundred ships and press home his attack we would assuredly be destroyed. Ye all know our condition as well as I. But the point is, the enemy cannot know how weak we are. All he can be certain of is the fact that his shadowing ships— sent to keep us wi'in detector range and engage in no combat—ha' been destroyed by ships o' ours which do not show up on his detectors and trip no alarms. To him this must mean we ha' some gadgetry o' which he has not even dreamt.

"Our very attack on Shiva must further that illusion. The first he detected us we were two billion miles inside his defences. He must perceive us as coming and going like ghosts, striking wi' a strength he cannot match and attacking where he least expects it. He does not and cannot know what we ha' or how weak we are.

"In addition, he cannot be certain but what—at this very minute—we are not preparing a strike at any or all o' his remaining solar systems. He must allocate ships and men for their defence. And further, because o' the way we defeated their fleet here, he cannot feel secure wi' just a few ships to protect each system; he must assign thousands!

"To him, we or others like us may be ready to strike anywhere and at any time. He is placed in exactly the same situation we were back on Earth. Then we were forced to make do wi' slower ships to defend an impossibly large perimeter from an enemy which might approach from anywhere at any time—and from an enemy we couldn't even hit back at. We tried, but it was impossible. Earth was destroyed.

"Now the shoe is on the other foot. The enemy finds himself in the same predicament. He must defend in depth each o' his other planetary systems against an enemy who appears able to strike anywhere at any time wi' weapons strange to his best science.

"O' course we know he faces no such danger. But he cannot know it, and seeing what we ha' done to his home planet he dare not assume 'tis a bluff. He is caught in a bind o' his own making. Even if he were able to destroy every remaining human in this universe he can never be certain he has done it. He must always lurk in fear lest some other Claymore come charging in. This is his dilemma, and 'tis one he can never solve.

"Added together, I ha' come to think we are probably safe for the next years. He must tend to his defences everywhere afore he can come looking for us. And I do not think he can do it.

"All o' which brings us to the heart o' the matter. Presupposing we manage to survive, now we no longer ha' a mission. We ha' done what we set out to do. All our plans stopped once we passed Shiva. So what do we do now?

"There are a number o' factors to consider in this. First o' all, we are now well on the other side o' Shiva, wi' them betwixt us and our sun. To kill our speed and start rebuilding it in the other direction is, in view o' our weakened condition, a time-consuming and near hopeless task.

"Besides, I ask you to consider the possibility that neither Styx nor any o' the asteroids ha' survived. 'Tis at least a chance we are the last o' humanity. Moreover, even if others did make it I would hate to hazard leading so much as a single enemy scout to any o' them.

"As I see it, this rules out any decision to return. I believe we need to set for ourselves new goals. And I do not believe we ha' the right to seek out others o' our own kind again. We must set forth entirely on our own. We must continue in the way we are going and seek out a new home.

" 'Tis obvious the alien controls all star systems wi'in some seventy years about. But the shock o' his defeat will make him cautious about expanding further and I cannot believe he will be able to transform his colony worlds into arsenals o' defence in less than a century or more. 'Tis not likely he will venture into new solar systems till he has.

"For my recommendation, we ha' a good many months yet afore we can build up to a time-compression speed that means much. But still, wi'in a year and a half at most we will be back at speed. Then 'twould be a matter o' from three to five years, subjective time, afore we will be far beyond the enemy's present sphere o' power. We could then pick a likely planet and settle ourselves. There would even be a chance— provided we sent our last torpedo back to Styx telling them where we're going and what we plan to do—that when we finally reach our goal we'll find fellow Earthmen awaiting us in shiny new hyperdrive ships.

"I do not ask that ye decide upon this now. Take your time and discuss it amongst yourselves. Argue all the pros and cons until ye ha' reached your separate decisions. In this matter, as in the matters o' future government, my own voice will speak no louder than the least amongst us.

"Later this week we shall ha' a registry o' the clans represented aboard so new chieftains can be selected to speak for their clans. After a final decision is reached a conference o' the clan heads will assume full control over Claymore and I shall be merely their appointed military chieftain until such time as they choose to replace me.

"I ha' given ye much meat to chew on. Digest it well and gi' me your decision when ye are ready.

"And now let us to the feast and games. . . . Let us rejoice that we ha' survived and can sit amongst friends this day. This shall be our day o' peace."

EPILOGUE

Miles above a fair and handsome planet, five hundred light-years from the swollen sun of Earth and more than four hundred from the ruined planet of Shiva, the pilot of a battered and misshapen hulk of rock and iron made a last delicate adjustment on a throttle and the soundless thunder of the last rocket ebbed and died. Circling in a Lagrangian orbit ahead of the planet's primary moon, Claymore went dead.

An engineer technician in the stern pulled back the lever to commence disassembly of the last celaenium power units. In the reactor room an automatic sweeper picked up the last grams of radioactive material. The lights in the village flickered once, then blackness descended.

A torpedo, filled with unusable fissionable materials, swept back into space toward some unknown destination. The last of the communications equipment was pulled out and loaded onto the utility ship. Screwdrivers and pliers and endless oddments of machinery were piled aboard. The last of the reactor elements, firmly sealed in their leaden containers, were loaded into the cargo space.

The cleanup crew, their work finished, clambered aboard and waited until Duncan, his long task finally done, completed his last inspection. Satisfied, he worked his way to the surface, then turned back for a moment and opened the main bleeder valve on Claymore's surface. Air from below began its slow hiss toward the surface and freedom. The lock from the utility ship snapped shut as Duncan entered and moved into the control room. He had begun as commander of a small utility craft. It was fitting he should end that way. In another moment the ship swept away from Claymore and headed down.

Far below, on a rocky and windswept headland jutting out onto a stormy sea, a small cluster of newly built homes nestled snugly together. As the utility ship descended the flashing brilliance of a hundred differently hued tartans raced up to greet them. Pipes skirled in welcome as the last of the men stepped ashore. On New Skye this remnant of humankind had found its new home.

Far above, in lonely orbit, battery-powered red lights flashed their warning over each opened airlock. "Danger! No air on the other side."

They would soon go out.

Four years later a ship from Styx dropped out of hyperdrive and the reunification began.